BREAKING POINT

Published by Lue Cleveland
Atlanta, GA

Publication Date: February 2019
ISBN 978-0-692-18936-8

Library of Congress Control Cataloging-in-Publication Data
is available upon request.

Printed in the United States of America

Acknowledgements

I am thankful for the good health and well being that enabled me to complete my second novel. I enjoy writing and I'm thankful for the ability and the experience. I thank my family for their belief, love and moral support.

Special thanks to my sons Nathan and Brandon and to Wilbert McBryde for an amazing book cover--a crucial element of the reading experience. I am very grateful for their diligence and impeccable work. Thank you. I truly love the cover.

Words cannot express how much I appreciate Ms. McCartan during this writing journey. I am deeply grateful for her editing advice, encouragement and support. I feel truly blessed for the working relationship we have and to have her accompany me on this journey.

I must offer my profound gratitude and appreciation to all my readers for their encouragement and wonderful comments. I especially acknowledge and thank those who reminded me of my promise to write a sequel. To all of you, your belief and support helped me to stay the course.

Dedications

This book is dedicated to the memory of my dear friend *Alice Arthur* -- minister, comedienne, author, motivational speaker, stress consultant, coach and trainer. She always said, "God is multi-faceted, so am I." I am grateful for Alice's support, her friendship and her willingness to share her knowledge and experience. I thank God she was a part of my life and I hers. I Miss You, My Dear Friend. R.I.P.

I would like to also dedicate this book to my *parents* and *ancestors* upon whose contributions and shoulders I stand.

BREAKING POINT

Chapter 1

A soft ping indicates the elevator has reached the 11th floor of the prestigious Logan Courtyard hotel. A beautiful woman emerges wearing a sleeveless black dress, which perfectly highlights her slim but curvy silhouette. She moves swiftly but gracefully down the hallway until she reaches Suite 1107. She hesitates a moment remembering the telephone call from FBI Agent Dalton asking her to return to the hotel. She takes a deep breath and enters the suite using her passkey.

Brooklin Covington stops abruptly at the sight of the sparsely dressed man lying on the bed in Suite 1107. His face and eyes are swollen and his clothing ripped. There is blood everywhere. His neck and arms are riddled with abrasions and cuts. Furniture, lamps, tables—everything's been tossed around. "Oh my God," she whispers in a trembling voice. Agent Dalton quickly moves to comfort her. Brooklin struggles to compose herself insisting, "I'm fine. I'm all right." Agent Dalton holds her gaze for a moment as if to determine that she is indeed all right and then he returns to Mr. Reed's bedside.

Brooklin runs her hands through her hair, gathering it to the side. She looks over her shoulder and takes in the destruction in the room – chairs and tables overturned and broken, glassware shattered, blood splattered on the floor and walls. However, her face is so poised it's impossible to read. She wonders if nearby guests heard any commotion coming from this suite. Each floor at Logan Courtyard has one suite set apart from the others to provide privacy. On the eleventh floor, it's Suite 1107 located at the end of the hallway and around the corner from the other suites. She is hopeful that the other hotel guests were not disturbed.

Brooklin returns her focus to Mr. Reed. Agent Dalton had called in a doctor to attend to Mr. Reed in the privacy of the suite. Brooklin quietly observes as the doctor cares for him. Levy, Brooklin's attorney and her best friend's husband, enters the suite minutes later. Brooklin talks to Levy in a low tone, "This should have never happened in my hotel. Why did I give the FBI permission to house Mr. Reed here at Logan Courtyard?"

Agent Dalton approaches Levy and shakes his hand.   He informs Brooklin and Levy that the doctor expects Mr. Reed will make a good recovery and that all necessary medical treatments will be provided. He murmurs, "I will not have a witness killed on my watch." Brooklin and Levy glance at each other. After a few restless minutes, the FBI agent continues, "This indeed was a brutal and violent attack, although it seems Mr. Reed put up quite a fight. Ms. Covington, with your permission, I would like to have a couple of our agents check the hotel's surveillance system to see if we can ascertain who entered the suite and committed this attack."

"Yes, that will be fine. Call Erica, my secretary, to make the arrangements. I'll tell her to expect your call." Brooklin looks over at Mr. Reed as he groans in pain and is gently lifted onto a stretcher. The doctor, Agent Dalton and two other FBI agents transport the man out of Logan Courtyard utilizing the private elevator and side entrance.

Brooklin and Levy silently take the elevator down to the first floor and walk to Brooklin's office to discuss the details of what had just transpired. Brooklin tells Levy she received a call from FBI Agent Dalton a couple hours earlier, informing her that Mr. Reed, a young man in the FBI witness protection program, had been beaten and left for dead in Suite 1107.

"Brooklin, this is shocking."

"The FBI believes that an individual who replaced one of the two FBI agents at Logan Courtyard was, in fact, *not* an FBI agent. He replaced one agent and relieved the second agent to get some rest. When the actual FBI agent arrived, the attack had taken place and the impersonator had fled the scene. I immediately telephoned you after my conversation with Agent Dalton and asked you to meet me in Suite 1107."

"Does the FBI have any idea who committed this assault?" Levy asks.

"The FBI thinks Jack Griffin is behind the attack. When Agent Dalton and I spoke on the telephone, he said a couple of agents were going to pick up Jack Griffin for questioning. As you are aware, Mr. Reed is on the witness list to testify against Jack Griffin in a high profile financial fraud and murder case."

"How did Jack Griffin know that Mr. Reed was at Logan Courtyard?"

"We're still uncertain how the whereabouts of Mr. Reed was learned." Brooklin walks over to her desk and orders dinner from the hotel's restaurant for the two of them. "Levy, do you think Mr. Reed will fully recover?"

"I don't know, Brooklin. The man has many injuries but Agent Dalton indicated that the doctor is very positive about a full recovery."

"It's difficult for me to believe that this man was so violently attacked here at my hotel. I asked Agent Dalton to exclude Logan Courtyard's name from any media coverage or discussions in regard to this incident. I explained I do not want any mention or negative publicity for my hotel." Brooklin has worked relentlessly to build the status of and to protect the reputation of Logan Courtyard. She inherited the hotel from her mother, who died suddenly about two years ago.

"What was Agent Dalton's response?"

"He assured me that this is an undercover investigation. He also asked me not to discuss this case or mention this physical attack to anyone. Evidently, the FBI would like the perpetrator to believe that Mr. Reed died from his injuries."

"Brooklin, Griffin is dangerous. And we need to tread carefully as we provide information to the FBI." Levy looks at her with concern, "We have to nail down this case and ensure that Jack Griffin is put away for a long time."

"I know, Levy." She pauses for a moment. "Who would have thought I would be here at this crossroad. I just don't understand how I got to this place. One day, I'm working to build a fine establishment and somehow Griffin slithers into my world and tries to intimidate me into selling my hotel. Now I have this criminal inserting himself into my life through no fault of mine. I have to rid this toxic man from my life and my business."

They are silent as each consumes their dinner and retreats into their own thoughts. Levy breaks the silence, "Brooklin, is that your telephone beeping?" Brooklin hurries to her desk and pulls out her work cell phone. Listening to the voice message, she is visibly upset.

"Levy, listen to this message."

Brooklin replays the message for Levy: "Let me tell you what's going on in your hotel. Blood, determination and very soon victory."

Levy is stunned and proceeds to save the message. He quickly tries to get envelope information regarding the call. "Brooklin, I tried to track the call but, of course, I was not successful. Do you recognize the voice?"

Brooklin thinks for a moment, "No, the voice is unfamiliar but so crude, so ruthless."

"I'm sure the caller probably changed his voice and used some type of caller ID block. I will have my guy place an unmasking service setup on your office and cell phones. I will also have them log on to your cell phone web account to try to obtain the number that appeared as blocked."

"I'm sure that call was about Mr. Reed. Levy, do you think it was from Jack Griffin?"

"Or one of the comrades on his payroll," Levy replied. "He undoubtedly would like you to know he was behind this attack."

"Yes, he probably thinks it might frighten me into selling my hotel."

"Brooklin, this phone call and the attack. This is quickly getting serious." Levy hesitates and then continues, "It's difficult to believe that someone actually stuck a pillowcase in that man's mouth and brutally beat him here in this hotel. It's appalling." Brooklin shakes her head at the thought as Levy continues, "It's just completely insane. Who would ever expect this type of violence to happen here at Logan Courtyard?"

"We have to absolutely make certain that Jack Griffin goes to prison and that no one connects us to his downfall," Brooklin asserts gravely. Levy does not speak but gives a simple nod in Brooklin's direction. "I have worked hard to build a great brand and something beautiful here. I don't know, Levy, sometimes our best is just not good enough."

"Brooklin, you have done a superb job here. Logan Courtyard is a five star hotel. Senators, executives, celebrities, they all love Logan Courtyard and boast about the elegance and impeccable service."

She looks down and repositions the food on her plate, "Either way, what happened here today is *not* a GOOD thing. I just hope Mr. Reed will make a full recovery."

After dinner, Levy walks Brooklin to her Range Rover, a birthday gift from her husband Colin a couple years prior. She drove the SUV today because her car is being serviced. Brooklin and Levy continue to talk as they walk to the staff parking lot. Just as they reach Brooklin's SUV, a black car quickly backs out of the parking space to the left of her Range Rover and drives away. A little startled, Brooklin and Levy look in the direction of the car and then resume their conversation. "Brooklin, I will help you with whatever is needed or required. You are not alone in this. You are like family to Jill and me."

Brooklin smiles and says, "Thanks, Levy. I appreciate your support. You know, I will always be there for you and Jill as well." Brooklin bids Levy a good night and drives out of Logan Courtyard's parking lot. After several miles, Brooklin comes to a complete stop behind a car at the stoplight. She opens the moon roof to allow the fresh night air to rush into her vehicle.

Her gaze falls on a red envelope on the floor of the SUV. As Brooklin reaches down to pick up the envelope, she hits the car in front of her. In all of her years of driving, she has never hit anything. Brooklin sits for a minute overwhelmed. Meanwhile, a black car comes from behind, speeds past her and down the Interstate. She glances at the car, trying to read the license plates but can only see the first two letters, BL or was it BI? Her mind races ahead. "What kind of car was that? Is that the same car that drove past Levy and me at Logan Courtyard?"

Brooklin quickly shifts her attention to the car she hit and exits her vehicle. She walks to the car and a woman gets out. "Are you all right?" Brooklin asks.

The young girl who looks to be around 23 or 24 years old smiles saying, "I'm fine. You just lightly tapped my car. I don't even see any scratches."

"Well, I'm glad you are all right." Brooklin looks at her Range Rover and doesn't see any damage. She introduces herself as Brooklin and the girl replies saying her name is Martina. "Okay, Martina, I'll call so a police report can be filed."

"There's no need to file a police report. There is no damage to either vehicle, Ms. Covington."

Brooklin momentarily remembers Larry, a former Logan Courtyard security personnel and his hit and run case and says, "Yes, we *should* file a police report." She quickly calls 911 and reports the accident. "I'm going to return to my SUV to wait for the police to arrive. Are you sure you are okay?"

"Yes, I'm fine. I'll just wait in my car too."

Brooklin returns to her vehicle and examines the red envelope. There is no return address and no postmark, which adds up to *no* clues. Only her name is written on the front of the envelope. She opens the envelope and reads the card inside: "I know the *Scarlet* secret. Tay."

Brooklin examines the card and envelope again. "The card is signed, Tay. Who is Tay?" Then she remembers, "Could this card be from Taylor, Logan Courtyard's previous assistant manager?" Brooklin is bewildered. "I fired her. If she sent the card, would she sign it Tay?" She reads the card again. "What does it mean? What Scarlet secret?" She tries to analyze the message. "And, how did someone have access to my SUV?" Brooklin looks up, sees the officer at her window and notices the window is slightly down. She realizes she left the window slightly down when she was in the SUV earlier that afternoon. "Okay, that's how the note came to be inside, but who left the note? And what secret?"

"Miss, Miss, are you all right?" Brooklin recognizes the officer is talking to her.

"Oh yes, I'm fine. I'm sorry, Officer, I was lost in thought." Brooklin provides the officer with her driver's license, insurance card and her statement.

Once home, Brooklin calls her insurance company to report the accident. Then she calls hotel security to ask if the staff parking lot surveillance camera has been repaired. "It's been almost a week now. I want that surveillance camera repaired or a new one installed tomorrow. Do you understand? I want surveillance in the hotel parking lot tomorrow," Brooklin tells security.

Brooklin walks into her bedroom and sits in the chair near the window. After a few moments of being unable to relax and feeling some nervous energy, Brooklin changes into her sweats and begins an intense workout in her home gym. Later she returns to her bedroom, undresses and runs bath water. Within minutes, Brooklin is soaking in the bathtub, candles lit with soft music playing in the background. She lays her head back and allows her mind to wonder about everything. Could the card be from Jack Griffin or is it really from Taylor? Brooklin continues to ponder this scenario. Then she abruptly sits up in the tub, "Wait, how did the girl, Martina, know my last name was Covington? After I hit her car, I told her my name was

Brooklin." The expression on her face quickly turns to alarm as she utters, "What is going on? "

Chapter 2

The next morning, Brooklin slowly sits up in bed. She runs her fingers through her hair considering, "Maybe it was all a dream. Could I have dreamt the events of the previous day?" Brooklin shakes her head realizing the events were real. They really happened. She forces herself to get out of bed, shower and go downstairs.

Brooklin sits in her kitchen absorbed in deep thought. She drinks a cup of coffee and eats a croissant, as the television audio plays low in the background. Her son and daughter, Luke 21 and Laila 20, enter through the kitchen door. They both chime in, "Good morning, Mother." Laila works part-time at the Teen Center, a safe venue the family provides to area teens as a way of their giving back to the community. Luke works part-time at Logan Courtyard. Both are full-time college students and share a townhouse.

Brooklin smiles, pushing all thoughts of yesterday from her mind--at least for the moment, "Good morning." She points to the croissants, "Have a croissant."

"Sure," says Laila. "Dad hasn't arrived with our new friend yet?"

Luke grabs a croissant adding, "Mom, I can't believe Dad bought you a Rough Collie. He always told us that we couldn't have pets."

"I was surprised too. He said he didn't want me to be alone in the house."

"Well maybe he should have thought about that before he walked out on you," Luke comments.

Brooklin looks at him and says, "Luke, please don't start that again."

"Mom, you think Dad is giving you a puppy because he wants to return home?" Luke asks.

Laila sits in the chair next to Luke and pokes him in his side. "Stop causing trouble." Luke grabs his side pretending to be hurt.

Laila looks over at her mother and says, "These croissants are delicious."

"Thanks. Have you or Luke thought of a name for the puppy yet?"

"Yes," Laila says, "Blake."

"Blake? I like that name."

"Great! I'm glad we all agree on the name," Laila says as her father walks through the door with a beautiful sable and white puppy.

They rush over to play with the Rough Collie. "Well, I guess he's a keeper," says Colin.

"Yes," replies Brooklin. "He's beautiful. Thank you."

Colin says to Laila and Luke, "We have to help your mother care for the puppy. You know she works 24/7." Brooklin does not comment; however, she didn't miss Colin's last remark.

Luke looks at his mother, winks and says to his father, "Dad, does that mean you will come home to help with dog duties too?"

"Yes, I definitely will. We need a schedule so we all can share in the responsibilities," says Colin. Luke looks at his mother and laughs. Brooklin looks away trying to ignore him.

The family spends the next few hours enjoying Blake and eating leftovers and a large salad. Colin comments, "It feels good having our family together like this again." Brooklin hears Luke chuckle at Colin's remark but doesn't look in his direction.

Later, Brooklin works at the Teen Center while Blake runs and plays with Laila and the teens. Colin and Brooklin take great pride in the Center that provides 13-18 year old teens an afterschool program during the week and opens all day on weekends. Brooklin and her husband Colin--whom she has been separated from for months--purchased a run-down building on a few acres of land about two years ago. The family renovated the building and converted it into a Teen Center. Colin retired about the same time and is currently managing the Teen Center part-time. The site contains a library, computer room, game room, cafeteria, weight room and gym with a basketball court. Also there is an outdoor and indoor swimming pool and a football field with an outdoor track. The Center is supported through fund-raisers and a yearly phonathon. Brooklin volunteers a half-day during the week and a half-day on Saturdays. Parents, individuals from various organizations and community members are part of the volunteer staff sharing their expertise with the kids.

Sunday is normally a family day for Brooklin, Colin, Laila and Luke. However with the arrival of Blake yesterday, Saturday became the family day. Therefore Brooklin arranged to meet Maggie, her

17

part-time housekeeper for a Sunday afternoon dinner at Logan Courtyard while Blake spends time with Laila.

Brooklin arrives at her office early to review a proposal before meeting Maggie for dinner and goes directly to her computer. After a short time, her thoughts drift to Mr. Reed and what occurred here at the hotel. She wonders how he is progressing. Hopefully, Agent Dalton will keep her abreast of his progress and any new developments regarding Jack Griffin. She looks away from her computer, "How am I supposed to get any work done with all these unanswered questions?" She stares at the artwork on the wall and then back at her computer screen, which is now blank. Her thoughts return to the young lady in the black car. "Who is she and how does she know me? She clearly called me Ms. Covington." Brooklin walks over to the black leather couch in her office telling herself, "Don't overreact. Maybe she knows me from some media coverage regarding the hotel." Brooklin sits on the couch, placing one of the accent pillows on her lap. Then she quickly leans forward clutching the pillow she'd been toying with. "Wait, that girl, Martina, what color was her car? Was it dark blue or was it black? The streetlights were dim and I really didn't focus on her car. My thoughts were preoccupied with finding that envelope on the floor of my SUV. Could Martina's car be the car that drove past Levy and me at Logan Courtyard?"

Brooklin returns to her desk and looks through her purse for the paperwork given to her by the police officer. She begins reading the information regarding Martina's vehicle. "It was a black Acura." She hesitates for a moment, "And what about the red envelope that was left in my SUV?" She looks in her purse for the red envelope. Brooklin opens the card and reads it again, "I know the *Scarlet* secret. Tay." She stares at it. "Tay – could Tay be Martina? Could Martina possibly have been driving the black car in the staff parking lot? Could she have driven away suddenly after leaving the envelope in my car?"

Brooklin walks to the window, her mind swirling with negativity and disgust. "Who left that card? Taylor? Griffin? Martina? And why the mystery?" Brooklin turns away from the window. "This is obvious bull," she says rubbing her throat, which is feeling dry and tight. She gets a bottle of water from her office refrigerator and walks back and forth in front of her desk, nausea twisting in her stomach. She needs help. This is becoming far beyond her scope of investigative work. She drinks a few swallows of water and stares at the card. After a few moments, she places the card back in the envelope and tucks both the police paperwork and the red envelope into her purse, "I must have this Martina investigated." She pauses, "And Brooklin, you must concentrate on hotel business ... on this proposal. You cannot allow whoever sent this card to disrupt your life or your work." She takes a seat at her computer again and tries desperately to focus on the proposal. After about fifteen minutes of struggling, she stands, turns off her computer and leaves her office, locking the door behind her. She walks through the double doors and out of the hotel onto the beach.

For a moment, Brooklin stands still and takes in the beauty of the beach and her surroundings. She allows herself to revel in the feel of the afternoon sun on her face. She's dressed in a t-shirt, blue jeans and Nike sneakers. Brooklin removes her sneakers to feel the warm white beach sand beneath her feet. It's a perfect, sunny day and she loves hearing the sounds of the waves. She takes long, deep breaths enjoying the fresh air and the smell of the ocean. With each breath, she feels the tension and anxiety leaving her body. Brooklin walks about a quarter of a mile when she hears someone calling her name. She looks in the direction of the voice and sees Maggie smiling and waving to her. Maggie, who is in her late sixties, full-figured and about 5'5" looks great as usual. She carries herself so well. Today she is wearing a white button down shirt and khaki capris. Brooklin smiles as they walk toward each other. "Hi, Maggie. What do you think of having dinner outside at one of the patio tables?"

Maggie smiles, "That's exactly what I was thinking. It's such a beautiful day." They continue their walk to the hotel, enjoying the extraordinary scenery and the ideal weather.

Later, Brooklin arrives home to find Blake waiting at the door. "Hi, boy." She smiles, reaches down and gives him a big hug.

"Hi, Mom," Laila smiles. "Blake heard you coming. How was your dinner with Maggie?"

"Good. We had dinner at one of the beachside tables. We laughed, talked and came up with a schedule for Blake. It was just the outing I needed."

"That's great." Laila hesitates a moment, "Mom ..."

"Yes."

"Is everything all right?"

"Why do you ask?"

"When you left earlier, you looked a little stressed."

"Laila, please don't worry about me. I'm often thinking about hotel business. Listen, Maggie will email everyone tomorrow. The family, Maggie and a dog walker will all pitch in to take care of Blake. Maggie knows everyone's schedule, so she's the perfect one to prepare the chart every week."

"Sounds good. Okay, Mom, I'm out of here."

"All right, honey, have a nice evening."

"You too, Mom," Laila says.

Brooklin looks down at Blake. "Okay, Blake, it's just you and me. However, I really need to return a few phone calls." She laughs, looking down at him, "Blake, I'm talking to you like you understand what I'm saying." Blake follows her down the hall into her office. Brooklin gives him a ball to play with, then sits at her desk to return phone calls.

After Brooklin's last call, she looks at Blake and says, "Blake, you want to go for a quick walk before dinner?" She runs upstairs, changes clothes and takes Blake for a walk around the neighborhood. "It's such a quiet neighborhood, Blake. I love living on a private street and looking at all the beautiful landscaping, the manicured lawns and shade trees in each of the neighbors' yards. However, I don't remember seeing any neighbors with dogs. We'll have to arrange some

21

play dates for you outside of the neighborhood." Blake continues to walk beside Brooklin, looking up at her as she talks to him. He does seem to understand what she is saying. Brooklin smiles, reaches down and pets him. "I have such a smart puppy," she says happily.

When Brooklin and Blake are in close proximity to the house, Brooklin tells Blake, "Come on, boy" and they begin to run. As they round the corner and the house comes into view, Brooklin observes a black car driving slowly in front of her driveway. As Brooklin gets closer, the car speeds up and disappears around the corner. "Blake," she says disappointedly, "I couldn't tell what kind of car it was or get the license plate number. It drove away too quickly." However, she is certain the driver was looking at her house. Brooklin unlocks her kitchen door, lets Blake in, relocks the door and walks over to the table. She returns to the door, sets the alarm and glances out the window. "The street is clear, Blake, no black or unfamiliar cars." She looks for another moment, "and there's no suspicious activity. Blake, I'm really beginning to think I'm being watched."

Brooklin sits down and says aloud, "What is going on?" Feelings of tension and frustration reemerge, "Is someone actually spying on me or monitoring my house?" The thought makes her angry and uneasy. "Could this be an attempt to make me feel vulnerable? If so, why? Is this the work of Jack Griffin, trying to intimidate me into selling my hotel?" She stands and moves away from the table reviewing all aspects of this dilemma in which she finds herself. "The card and message I found in my SUV, is it a scare tactic or does someone really have some information to share? And if so, how does it pertain to me?   Is this personal or professional?"

Brooklin walks back to the kitchen door and peers out, "I have so many questions. What do they want from me? Is the person who left the card in my SUV and the individual watching my house the same person?" Brooklin turns and look back into her kitchen. She wonders if and how Martina fits into this drama. The car in front of her house looked similar to the Acura Martina was driving. "It would help if I was more familiar with the different makes and models."

Brooklin hears Blake's bark and realizes he is now at her feet. She refocuses her attention on him, prepares his dinner and silently watches him eat.   She, of course, doesn't have an appetite. Afterwards, Blake seems tired and lies in his bed. Brooklin walks to her office. "Okay, Brooklin, who do you trust enough to tell about the red envelope and the mystery car?" She turns on the light in her office, clearly baffled about this situation.   She wrestles with all the thoughts and questions. "Who do I trust enough to tell? Should I phone the police? Do I get the police involved without knowing exactly what the Scarlet Secret is or if someone was actually watching my house?" After some consideration, she decides not to tell anyone tonight.   "I need to spend some time thinking about this before telling anyone. Tomorrow after a good night's rest, I'll decide what action to take." Brooklin settles herself in her chair and begins to reorganize her desk and then her office.   She needs to utilize this nervous energy and walk away from this situation, hopefully returning with greater clarity.

Later she sits on the couch with Blake trying *not* to think of the card, the black car in front of her home, Martina, the attack on Mr. Reed and what it all means to her and to Logan Courtyard. She knows this is the beginning of something. But what? She closes her eyes, trying desperately to block out all the insanity, the panic and unanswered questions. She opens her eyes to find Blake looking up at her. She rubs Blake's beautiful sable and white coat and resolves to let it all go for tonight. No one has tried to physically harm her. All she received was a confusing message. And the black car could just be someone admiring her home. Maybe the card is someone trying to warn her, not threaten her. "But if it's a warning, why not be forthcoming with the information? And what secret?" Brooklin again struggles to let it go. "There's nothing else you can do tonight. However tomorrow, the search for answers must begin." She looks at her little companion, "Blake, how about we just focus on the big screen in front of us?" Blake looks at her with interest. He has quickly become accustomed to her and the family. "So, Blake, what would you like to watch on television? Want to watch a movie?" Blake barks, Brooklin rubs his thick hair again and says, "Okay, a movie it is."

Chapter 3

Monday morning, Brooklin and Blake return from their walk to find Maggie in the kitchen. Brooklin walks in the house thinking, "Great, no red envelopes or unfamiliar cars outside." Then smiles at Maggie, "Morning, Maggie."

"Morning, Brooklin. How did you and Blake spend the evening?"

"We watched a movie and then the Late Show."

"Well that sounds like a good evening."

"Maggie, I would like to make you aware that yesterday, there was a black car driving slowly in front of the driveway when I took Blake for a walk around the neighborhood. It probably was innocent; however, I became a little suspicious when it sped away as Blake and I were returning home from our walk. I just want you to be cautious and please let me know if you notice any unfamiliar cars in the area."

"Oh okay. It probably was someone just admiring your beautiful home."

"Well, I just want you to be cautious--oh one moment, Maggie, my phone is ringing. Good morning, Colin, how are you?" Brooklin motions to Maggie that she is going upstairs.

"I'm fine, Brooklin. How was your evening with Blake?"

Brooklin hesitates, still feeling a little unsettled, "Bizarre, weird and I tossed, turned and was restless most of the night." Then Brooklin stops midway up the stairs, considering Colin's question. "Why did he ask about my evening? Does he have anything to do with the red envelope or the black car in front of the house?" Her thoughts are impulsive and scattered. "Brooklin, no," she scolds herself, "Colin would never do that to me. Don't allow whoever is doing this make you paranoid or arouse suspicion of your loved ones."

"Brooklin, are you there? Is everything okay?"

Brooklin realizes Colin is still on the phone. "Yes, I'm here. Blake and I watched a movie. Colin, I can't talk now. I don't want to be late and I need to get dressed."

"Okay, I'll talk to you later."

Brooklin looks at the phone questioningly, "Talk to me later? Maybe Luke is right. I hope Colin doesn't think Blake is opening any doors for him, because he definitely is not. I have too much on my plate right now to deal with restoring a relationship."

Brooklin walks into Logan Courtyard and as always admires the spectacular spacious lobby with recessed ceiling and chandeliers creating an unforgettable place of grandeur. Sunlight streams through ceiling to floor windows, providing a breath-taking view of the harbor. Brooklin walks past the front desk through the double doors to her office and finds Levy and FBI Agent Dalton waiting for her. Brooklin speaks to both men and then focuses on Agent Dalton. "What information can you share with me this morning about the assault on Mr. Reed?"

"I can only say we are looking into this case."

Brooklin is visibly agitated. "Agent Dalton, you asked me to house Mr. Reed at Logan Courtyard and someone came into my hotel, ambushed two of your

FBI agents and beat your witness almost to death." She pauses a moment then continues, "I know you have questioned Mr. Reed. What has he told you?"

"Ms. Covington, please."

"Agent Dalton, this happened in my hotel. The last thing I need is a crazy person on the loose in Logan Courtyard. I want whoever is responsible taken into custody."

"Ms. Covington, believe me when I tell you, we are working on this case day and night."

"Believe you?" she says in a confrontational tone. "I will not be kept in the dark. Can Mr. Reed identify the person who assaulted him? You're going to have to provide me with some information. I deserve answers!"

Before Brooklin can continue, Agent Dalton begins, "I've spoken to my agents and they believe the man whom our witness was going to testify against is behind this assault. We are convinced that he's the one responsible."

"You mentioned that previously. Do you care to elaborate, Agent Dalton?" Brooklin asks.

Agent Dalton hesitates, "Please keep this information between the three of us. We believe Jack Griffin of Griffin Development whom Mr. Reed will testify against ordered the assault."

"Have you arrested him?" asks Brooklin.

"We have him in custody; however, we are holding him on different charges."

"Different charges?" Brooklin says questioningly, glancing at her lawyer.

Levy interjects. "I understand that we all are on edge. But let's not turn against each other. Let's come together to nail this scum. Now, are we certain that Mr. Reed was the target of this ambush? Beating someone is personal. I think the only way to make certain this Jack Griffin is prosecuted to the fullest extent of the law is for the three of us to work together."

"I will share what I can with the two of you. And yes, we think Mr. Reed was the target. Maybe the two of you can help us with this case. But for right now, I've already said more than I should have. I will give you a call tomorrow." Agent Dalton turns and exits Brooklin's office. Brooklin looks at her cell phone as it vibrates. Detective Greg Ryan is calling. A few months prior, Detective Ryan conducted an investigation into a vehicular hit and run case that injured Larry Carter, one of Logan Courtyard's security personnel. During the course of the investigation, Detective Ryan developed intense feelings for Brooklin.

"Hello, Greg." Brooklin answers her phone as she observes Agent Dalton leaving her office.

"Brooklin, where are you?"

"I'm in my office. Why? Is there some type of problem?"

"I need to talk to you. I'll be at Logan Courtyard in about thirty minutes."

"Greg, what is this about?'

"Just stay in your office, I will tell you when I get there." Brooklin looks at the phone with uncertainty as she hears his call disconnect.

"Brooklin, is there a problem?" asks Levy.

"That was Detective Ryan. He is leaving the precinct for Logan Courtyard now."

"Do you think Detective Ryan knows about the assault?" Levy asks. He perceived an intimacy and familiarity in Brooklin's voice as she spoke to the detective and he noticed she addressed him by his first name.

"No, I don't think he knows." She ponders for a moment and then says, "I'm sure everything is fine."

"How are you holding up, Brooklin?" Levy asks as Walt, the hotel's new assistant general manager, enters Brooklin's office.   He begins to update Brooklin on the events of last evening. He ends by informing her that new surveillance cameras have been installed in the staff parking lot and that Erica, Brooklin's secretary, has not reported to work and has not called.

"I'm a little worried being that Erica arrives everyday by 7am. I don't think she has missed a day since I began to work here," Walt adds.

Brooklin tells Walt to give Erica a call and to report back. Then she walks to the window overlooking the courtyard and says to Levy, "I've been thinking about Kim. Are there any new developments?"

"Brooklin, listen to me, Kim leaving the counseling center is not your fault." Brooklin turns from the window to look at Levy as he reiterates, "Her disappearance is not your fault! When I brought the pictures and other information obtained from Jack Griffin's computer to your attention, you immediately recognized Kim, a 15-year-old from the Teen Center.

You placed Kim and her family in an apartment on the grounds of Jefferson Counseling Center. It is one of the top private counseling centers in the area. Brooklin, you did what you could to help Kim and her mother."

"I just don't understand why Kim and her mother left the counseling center. Do you think she was nervous about testifying?"

"I explained to her when she gave her statement to the FBI that she probably would not have to testify. I think the photos were enough to force Griffin to admit he was with an underage girl."

Brooklin begins to pace in front of the window. "I wonder how this ... this situation with Kim and Griffin came about? She is just a confused teenager. How could that disgusting man be involved with a 15-year-old girl? It's reprehensible. Does he think he can desecrate lives without any repercussions?" Brooklin asks.

"Brooklin, he is a real piece of work. Very few people go up against Jack Griffin. And those who have--have tried and failed. But it will be different this time. He is not without his weaknesses."

"Apparently not, he likes young girls. I really hope these charges will stick," Brooklin says in a low tone of voice. "First, he tried to intimidate me into selling my hotel, he's involved with a fifteen year old girl and he hired someone to beat or perhaps kill an FBI witness in my hotel. So trust me, I know what he is capable of. We are up against pure evil." Brooklin thinks about her decision to hire Walt to replace Taylor, the previous assistant general manager. Among Walt's many talents is his expertise in the computer field. During the investigation Brooklin ordered of Jack Griffin, damaging photos and pertinent incriminating business information were discovered. Brooklin gave Walt instructions to have the photos from Griffin's computer appear in a media blog. All the faces were obscured, except for Jack Griffin.

Walt with his excellent tech background actually had Griffin's blog photos originating from a computer in Griffin's home state of New Jersey, thinking that most likely he had many adversaries there as well. The photos in the media blog provided the FBI with just what they needed to keep Jack Griffin in custody. Good luck, Griffin, explaining to the media, your wife and the FBI about the pictures of you and your associates with prostitutes at one of your parties. Especially, you, Griffin, who appeared to be doing inappropriate things to an underage girl, Kim--whose whereabouts, incidentally, were inconspicuously leaked to Agent Dalton.   "Levy, we have to find Kim before Griffin does. I don't want him to hurt her. I'm sure he wants revenge. He's a corrupt, evil man."

"We will find her, Brooklin. I'm glad she talked and gave a statement to the FBI before she left the counseling center. But don't worry, we will find her." Levy's phone begins to ring, he answers and waves goodbye to Brooklin as Walt re-enters Brooklin's office informing her that Erica didn't answer her phone so he left her a voicemail.

"Walt, please drive to Erica's apartment and make sure she is okay and keep me informed." Walt nods and tells Brooklin he has asked Karla, who provides office support for Logan Courtyard and the

Teen Center, to work in the main office until Erica arrives.

"Walt, would you please ask Luke to come to my office?"

"Brooklin, Luke must be running late. He's not here yet."

"Luke is not here either? What is going on today?"

As Walt exits, he tells Brooklin to take a couple of deep breaths, "The stress is showing."

Brooklin exhales as Karla walks in. She immediately informs Karla that Agent Dalton will telephone her some time today to arrange for two of his agents to check footage from Logan Courtyard's surveillance cameras. Brooklin explains that Karla is to discuss this with no one and reminds her of the non-disclosure agreement she signed when she became an employee of Logan Courtyard. Brooklin further explains that the FBI should have the privacy and discretion they require.

"I understand and I will make the necessary arrangements," Karla replies. "Also, Brooklin, I want to remind you that the 2017 Conference of Mayors will be held in the banquet and meeting rooms this weekend – Friday through Sunday afternoon. The conference organizers actually booked rooms and requested rooms with beautiful views of the beach and harbor."

"Karla, check with Karen regarding the budget for providing complimentary gifts to individuals at the conference. We want to make certain the attendees have a great experience."

"I know we are providing shuttles to and from the airport, use of the spa, beverage services – including a champagne gift card. I can check with Karen if you would like to know all that will be provided to the attendees?"

"No, now that I think about it, there is no need. Karen always does an impeccable job."

"Okay," Karla says and begins to brief Brooklin on the new expansion at Logan Courtyard, a small movie theater and courtyard. The theater, limited to hotel guests only, will have an access door with the capability of opening onto a newly designed courtyard. The multiple outdoor screens with digital projection technology and crystal clear sound will make outdoor viewing the ultimate experience. This addition will allow Logan Courtyard the option of movies or live performances in the courtyard as well as the theater simultaneously.

After about thirty minutes with Karla, Brooklin begins her morning walk through the hotel. She loves this hotel with its twelve floors, luxurious rooms and suites, state of the art spa and fitness center. Logan Courtyard offers a stylish boutique, gift shop, valet parking, hair salon as well as dry cleaning and laundry service. The hotel is one of the city's best venues for gatherings with its impressive banquet rooms, meeting rooms, and 24-hour business center with advanced technology.   Its superb restaurant creates delicious cuisines with patio and fireside tables, stunning beach and harbor views while the bar has a dance floor and private entrance.

Brooklin stops to talk to the contractors about the expansion and to various employees during her walk through the hotel. The expansion is on schedule and proceeding as planned. However, her thoughts return to the red envelope she received and her dispute with Jack Griffin. Their last conversation ended with him speaking in an elevated tone of voice as she walked down a hallway near the restaurant. She recalls him clearly muttering, "Ms. Covington, remember I tried to come to an agreement with you. But no, you want to stand firm. Well, there's no turning back now. Good-bye, Ms. Covington. I'm sure we will meet again."

As Brooklin continues her walk, she recollects her response to him, "I believe one cannot fail unless one quits. And I will not quit on my future. Failure is not an option. So for the last time, Mr. Griffin, I will not sell Logan Courtyard." Brooklin suddenly stops abruptly. She recalls Griffin watching as she walked away from him and Agent Dalton approaching her seconds later. Is that how Griffin learned the whereabouts of the FBI witness? Yes, that is how he knew where Mr. Reed was being housed. He saw her talking to the FBI in the hotel's hallway. It was widely known that federal officers had been investigating and trying to imprison Griffin for years. And Brooklin is sure Griffin knows Dalton as one of the agents who brought charges against him. "But, how did he know which suite? No one except she and Levy knew that the FBI and Mr. Reed was in the hotel. The maids didn't even clean the suite. They didn't realize the suite was occupied." She must call and share this information with Agent Dalton.

As she turns the corner before reaching her office, her mind continues to wander, "Could Griffin have sent the red envelope? Could he have any involvement with the black car in front of my house? I understand keenly that with Griffin's kind of evil, anything is possible and awful things can happen. Nonetheless, I must not get overwhelmed. I have to be ready to handle what is sure to come. Okay, Brooklin, compose yourself and deal with each individual situation logically."

Brooklin returns to her office to find a tall, muscular Detective Greg Ryan pacing back and forth in front of her office. Brooklin admires the detective's wit, intelligence and good looks. He's about 45 years old with closely cut salt-and-pepper hair. He's dressed in his typical pair of jeans, white shirt and sports jacket. Brooklin is definitely attracted to this man.

Chapter 4

Greg smiles as his eyes meet Brooklin's. His gaze travels down the length of her body and he quickly becomes concerned as he notices her uneasiness. "Brooklin, are you okay?"

"Yes," she says trying not to look unsettled. "It's just been a rough morning. So, what is so important that you needed to rush to Logan Courtyard?"

Greg wants to reach out and take her in his arms but instead he just moves a little closer to her. His protective urges toward her intensify. "Brooklin, do you want to talk about whatever is apparently troubling you?"

He is so close to her, right next to her. So close, she can smell the soap on his skin. She takes a step back in order to focus. She shakes her head slightly, "No Greg, I'm fine. Why did you need to see me?"

He observes her for a moment longer and then questions her again, "Are you sure you don't want to talk about it?"

"Greg," Brooklin says placing emphasis on his name as they walk in her office and sit down. "Thank you for your concern but it's not necessary. I'm fine."

He resolves to let it go. Maybe, she is just having a demanding day. "Brooklin, remember I told you, I thought there was something missing in Larry's hit and run case? Even though it looked like the case was solved, I always felt there was more."

"I remember. Was there something else or someone else involved?"

"Yes, I should have followed my instincts."

"Followed your instincts? What is it, Greg? Tell me."

"Erica. Erica was in the car with Ron the night of the hit and run."

"Erica? My secretary, Erica?"

"Yes, Erica."

"No, Greg. You are mistaken. Erica would never be involved in a hit and run. She just wouldn't." Brooklin remembers Erica didn't come to work today. "Where is Erica? Did you arrest her? Greg, you are making a mistake."

"Calm down, Brooklin. Let me update you on what happened. Yesterday, Erica came to visit Ron at the county jail. During the visit, Erica admitted everything, including that she was in the car with Ron when the car slammed into Larry. However, I don't think she realized that the phones are monitored in some way at the jail."

Brooklin is mortified. She recalls that Erica left work early yesterday. "No, Greg, this can't be," Brooklin says exasperated. "This just can't be. Why would she be involved? What could possibly be an explanation for Erica being involved in a hit and run?"

"Apparently Erica and Ron were dating. Erica told Ron that she was pregnant with his baby."

"Pregnant? Erica is pregnant?" Stunned, Brooklin looks at Greg with dismay. "I can't believe this! Erica and Ron were dating? Ron is much younger than Erica."

"Erica asked Ron not to tell anyone about their relationship or that she was in the car with him that night. She said if he told, they both would be in jail and their child would be without a mother and father."

Brooklin is panic-stricken. "Where is Erica now?"

"We don't know. After the officer reviewed the recorded conversation, I was called. We went to Erica's apartment this morning but she wasn't there. She hasn't returned to the apartment today. Is she here?"

"No, she didn't come to work today nor did she call. We were worried because Erica is normally here everyday at 7 am. I actually sent Walt to her apartment to see if she is all right." Brooklin voices her thought aloud, "If she's not at her apartment, where can she be?"

"I don't know if she realized the phones at the jail were tapped and left her apartment or if there is some other reason. If she calls you, Brooklin, you have to let me know."

"I just can't believe this. This day is quickly spiraling downward. Do you think something happened to her? Is her car at home?"

"Yes, her car and her phone are at her apartment. We can't even track her through her phone's GPS. Brooklin, you will call me if she contacts you, right?"

"I just can't believe this. Are you sure about this, Greg? Are you absolutely certain?"

"Yes, I'm sure. I heard the recording myself. I wouldn't tell you unless I was 100% positive. Brooklin, I'm sorry to have to deliver this news to you.

I know that Erica was more than an employee to you. She was like a daughter. "

"Yes, she was. I mean, yes she is."

"Brooklin, have there been any other unusual activities at the hotel today?"

Brooklin reflects for a moment and then answers, "No. It's been a normal day. Greg, I appreciate you coming to Logan Courtyard to personally tell me."

"Of course I came. I wanted you to hear it from me. I care for you, Brooklin. And just so you know, we have decided to keep this quiet for now or rather for the next couple of days." Greg looks down and notices Brooklin's hand trembling on her desk. He places his hand on hers to comfort her, looking at her with concern.

Brooklin recovers and says, "Thanks again, Greg. I just need time to process this. And right now, I have an awful headache."

"I understand, Brooklin," Greg says as he walks to the door.

"Greg," Brooklin says, "What's next?"

"We find Erica."

Brooklin gently sinks in her chair and stares at the door as Greg leaves. She is an emotional wreck – cognizant that destruction and violence exist all around her. She thinks to herself, "Even with this throbbing pain in my head and with all that is happening, Greg can still light a fire within me--just with his touch." Then she remembers Luke. She phones Luke and, of course, the call goes straight to his voicemail.

Luke lies in bed at Taylor's apartment contemplating getting dressed for his morning shift at Logan Courtyard. Taylor walks into the bedroom fully dressed. "You're dressed. Where are you going?" Luke asks.

"I have a job interview?"

"A job interview? Where?"

"Are you surprised, Luke? Did you think I was going to wait for your mother to re-hire me after she fired me from Logan Courtyard?"

"No, Taylor, I didn't. Let's be honest. You stopped working at Logan Courtyard long before my mother fired you."

"Now, you're trying to insult me?"

"No, I'm just telling the truth. I think you lost interest in working for Logan Courtyard."

"Lost interest? I loved working at that hotel. I should have been managing that hotel instead of your mother. And it's not too late, you and I could run Logan Courtyard together."

"Talk like that is what got you fired."

"No, sleeping with you is what got me fired. Luke, you know in your mother's eyes, I am forbidden fruit."

"Well, that is partly true." He turns and takes another look at her in that tight blue dress. His muscles begin to tense as he remembers the feeling of her. "Are you sure you don't want to come back to bed?"

She smiles and says, "Don't you have to work this morning?"

He laughs and says, "I know. I'm getting up," and with much self-restraint he springs out of bed.

Jack Griffin is brought down to a room in the precinct to talk to his lawyer. He is blinded by anger as he enters the room. "I have been in that holding cell for two days. Why the hell haven't you gotten me out of here? I've been treated like a common criminal."

"Jack, there was nothing I could do. You were arrested early Saturday morning charged with a sexual offense and solicitation of prostitutes. Your arrest was plastered on almost every news outlet in the state. "

"What does that have to do with getting me out of here?"

"Jack, today is the first day you could be brought before the judge or that I could go in front of a judge on your behalf. I explained that to you on Saturday."

"I have been here all weekend. When am I getting out of here?"

"The paperwork is being processed now for your release."

"These charges will not stick. I haven't done anything wrong or forced anyone to do anything they didn't want to. And as for the girl, I think she enjoyed our encounter," he brags with a wolfish wink.

"I know you think you have things handled, but they have pictures of you and others with prostitutes and of you, Jack, with an underage girl. We're going to have a tough time with this."

Agent Dalton walks in. "Yes, Jack, this time you are going to spend some time behind bars. And I'm happy to inform you that your arrest made the front page news."

"It's a good story, but that's all it is. It's all circumstantial. A jury will not indict me on the evidence you have."

Agent Dalton smirks, "We have pictures of you having inappropriate relations with a 15-year-old girl. You will not be able to get out of these charges."

"How do you know specifically what girl is in the photo and the age of this girl? What proof do you have? Where is the girl?"

"You will find out in time, Jack. As a matter of fact, I can't wait to expose you and your dirty little secrets."

"What are you doing here anyway? I'm in a private meeting with my lawyer."

"No, Jack, you are in jail. Your lawyer is visiting you. I just want you to know if you make bail, we will obviously be watching your every move. "

"Really? What's the problem? Are you having trouble building a case against me? Need some help?"

"That's enough, Jack," interrupted his lawyer. "Don't say anything else. Agent Dalton, I would like to speak to my client alone before he is released."

Jack Griffin continues, "You just have some bogus charges that you're trying to pin on me. I didn't do anything."

"Sure you didn't," Agent Dalton says sarcastically.

"Jack, don't say anything else."

"And, Jack, don't try to leave town," Agent Dalton adds as he walks toward the door.

"Don't leave town? Who do you think you're talking to? Do you know who I am?" Griffin asks. "The FBI *is* well aware of who I am. Jack Griffin is an outstanding citizen in this state."

Agent Dalton stops and turns toward Griffin, "Right, an outstanding citizen who photographs himself and his associates having sex with prostitutes."

"I will not forget this."

Agent Dalton laughs as he exits, "See you in court. Oh and Jack, thanks for the photos."

"Jack, how many times do I have to tell you *not* to engage in conversation with the FBI? Let me do the talking," his lawyer advised.

"Someone hacked my computer. I want to know who is plotting to take me down. Find out who released those pictures. Joe, you better fix this."

"Fix it? You have already given them an in-road by talking to the FBI before I arrived on Saturday. Jack, you know to exercise your rights and decline to speak until your lawyer is present."

"I know," Griffin says looking down as he rubs his wrist. "I know."

"You know, you just talked to Agent Dalton again."

"You just fix this and find that girl. How could those idiots let her and her mother get away after we finally found her at that counseling center? If they don't have her to testify, they can't charge me. No proof--no case."

"It's my understanding that she has already given her statement to the FBI. I think they have a good case against you. Remember, Jack, the girl is 15 years old."

"Stop making excuses and find her or I will ruin you."

"Jack, I understand your frustration. But don't threaten me. I am all you have right now. Your associates are distancing themselves from you. Why do you think I couldn't get a judge to sign the paperwork for your release this weekend? Because, Jack, they do not want the negative impact of this case or the negative publicity to tarnish them. The FBI was building a case against you before this happened. Now with the new charges," he hesitates and says, "so, don't push me. I've been with you from the start."

"What happened with Ray? You said you were going to check to make certain all went well on Saturday. Did he get on the flight after he got rid of that problem at the hotel?"

"Jack, this is not the place. We'll discuss this after you're released."

"Well, get me out of here."

Walt returns to Logan Courtyard and goes directly to Brooklin's office. "Brooklin, Erica was not home. Her car was there, but she didn't answer her apartment door. I even knocked and looked through her apartment windows. "

"Did everything look in order inside her apartment?"

"Yes. I mean, everything I could see through the window. Why? Do you think something happened to her?"

"No, I'm sure I will hear from her soon. She probably had something she had to take care of."

"Brooklin, you look worried."

"I'm trying not to worry, Walt. I'm hoping Erica had an appointment she forgot to tell me about."

"But, don't you think it's weird that her car is there and she isn't and that she hasn't called?"

"We may have to call her mother if we don't hear from her soon. Walt, I have an awful headache. Can you ask Karla to bring me a couple of aspirins?"

"Sure," he says and quickly leaves Brooklin's office.

Brooklin is lying down on the leather couch in her office when Karla appears with the aspirins. Brooklin thanks Karla, takes the aspirins and considers that aspirins may not rid her of this headache.

"Karla, please close the door and do not let anyone disturb me unless it's Laila, Luke or anything dealing with Blake."

"Sure. I'll hold your calls and clear your calendar until late afternoon."

"Thanks, Karla and I appreciate your help today." Brooklin likes Karla. She is skillful and very competent. Then she thinks of Erica, the best secretary anyone could ask for. "Oh Erica, what have you done?" Brooklin turns and places her head on one of the accent pillows. Her thoughts are of Erica as she drifts off to sleep.

Brooklin is awakened an hour later by her cell phone. She answers the phone not noticing the caller on the display. "Hello," she says, sounding a little dazed.

"Ms. Covington?"

"Yes."

"Ms. Covington, I'm calling to inform you that Mr. Reed will be fine. He is safely situated in his new location at a safe house and is resting peacefully. I will give you a call in a couple of days. Thank you again for your assistance. Oh and you should know, Jack Griffin is no longer in police custody. He has been released on bail." Brooklin quickly sits up hearing Agent Dalton's call disconnect before she can respond.

She didn't have an opportunity to tell him that Jack Griffin probably learned the whereabouts of Mr. Reed from the conversation the two of them had in the hallway at Logan Courtyard. Then her thoughts returned to Agent Dalton's last remark, "Griffin, released on bail." She calls Levy.

"Brooklin. Are you ok?"

"No, Levy, I'm not." She brings Levy up-to-date on the information regarding Erica.

"Brooklin, are you serious? Have you heard from Erica?"

"No, I haven't."

"Do you think she just skipped town?"

"I really have no idea where Erica is. However, Levy, that's not all. Griffin has been released on bail. I'm sure he will waste no time trying to find out who hacked his computer and released the photos."

"Well, Walt did a great job.   He was savvy enough to wipe the computer server clean of any evidence. So if anyone becomes inquisitive, there is a lack of evidence to substantiate that we were involved. Therefore, Brooklin, I don't think you have anything to worry about in that regard. Griffin will not be able to trace it back to us," Levy says.

"Well, not if he is kept busy. The blog helped to bring new charges against Griffin. Let's hope he has to deal with angry associates--like the ones in the photo. We need the FBI and his associates on his back so he won't have time to look into who planted the photos. Levy, remember we have to find Kim."

"I have my private investigator looking for her now. And, Brooklin, my guy was unable to trace that anonymous phone call to your work cell phone. It probably was a burner phone. However, he told me that he placed the unmasking service setup on your phones."

"Thanks, Levy. Yes, your guy was very professional and answered all my questions." She hesitates then says, "Maybe I'll ask Detective Ryan to help with the search for Kim as well."

"Well, it won't hurt to have an investigator and a detective looking for Kim. Hopefully, we'll find her soon. Brooklin, I know the news about Erica must be shocking. But try not to worry. Detective Ryan will uncover the information needed to solve this case. And again, I am sorry you have to deal with this issue regarding Erica's absence along with everything else. Hopefully this situation with Erica is just misconstrued."

Brooklin returns her cell phone to her desk, buzzes Karla for an update on hotel business, and listens to her messages. She focuses on the many tasks before her and works until about 5pm. Realizing she didn't have lunch, she phones the restaurant and orders a light meal. From the small refrigerator in her office she takes a bottle of water and continues to work until Jerry from the restaurant arrives.

"Hi, Ms. Brooklin. How are you today?" Jerry asks.

"Hi, Jerry. I'm fine. How are you?"

"Oh, I'm fine. I see Erica isn't here today. I don't remember the last time Erica took a day off. You would think she owned the place," Jerry says laughing.

Brooklin sighs, "Yes, Jerry, Erica is a great employee."

As Jerry leaves Brooklin's office, he turns and says, "Ms. Brooklin, just call when you are ready for me to return your tray to the kitchen."

"Thank you, Jerry." Brooklin eats her salad while thinking of the many conversations she and Erica had regarding Larry's hit and run case. "Erica, were you really involved?" Karla comes to the door and reminds Brooklin of her appointment. Placing a strawberry in her mouth, she walks down the hall and enters the spacious room. Eleven staff members are in attendance, representing all hotel departments and services. Brooklin opens the meeting and then gives the floor to Karen and her son Luke who provide a presentation regarding preparations for the grand opening of the theater and new courtyard. Karen is head of marketing and Luke is her part-time assistant.

Brooklin has asked them to look into having Ruben Studdard perform during the grand opening. Brooklin loves his voice. Karen informs Brooklin that they have contacted Studdard's agent and will be negotiating when the contractors provide a firm date for the completion of the theater and courtyard. Luke discusses the theater. He explains that movie houses are struggling to switch from traditional 35-millimeter film projectors to digital and that Logan Courtyard has purchased a digital movie projection system. When all department updates are concluded, Brooklin closes the meeting and thanks everyone for attending.

Brooklin returns to her office and notices that Jerry has taken her tray. However, he left fresh fruit and a package of her favorite snack, Fruit' n Nuts. She snacks and, of course, her thoughts return to Erica. She searches for Erica's mother's telephone number. She locates the number, hesitates a moment then phones Erica's mother. "Hello, Ms. Harris?

"Yes, this is Ms. Harris.

"Hi, Ms. Harris. This is Brooklin from Logan Courtyard."

"Brooklin, yes. How are you?"

"I'm fine, Ms. Harris. I'm calling because Erica didn't come to work or call to let us know she wouldn't be here today. We have tried calling her and I even sent a staff member to her apartment. She wasn't there. I'm beginning to get a little worried and wondered if you have spoken to her today."

"Brooklin, you can call me Kelly and no, I haven't spoken to Erica in a couple of weeks. It's a little strange that she hasn't been in contact with you because I know she loves her job."

"Kelly, may I ask when was the last time you saw Erica?"

"Erica was here about a month ago. I went to visit my sisters and when I returned Erica had cleaned my house and painted my car."

"Painted your car?"

"Yes, it was a birthday gift."

"Oh, that was nice. What kind of car do you have?"

"Well now, I have a new car. A Toyota Camry."

"Erica had the Camry painted for your birthday? That was so thoughtful."

"No. Erica had my Mazda painted."

"Your Mazda?" Brooklin is quiet for a moment then says, "Was it a blue Mazda 626?"

"Why yes. How did you know?"

"I think I saw Erica driving it." Brooklin recalls stopping in the maintenance department a few months earlier and noticing a blue car in the parking lot, she thinks a Mazda 626. She remembers the car because it was an odd color blue. Could that have been Erica mother's car?

"Yes, Erica has driven it a few times."

"Was any body work done to the car?"

"No, why do you ask?"

"Well, I thought I noticed there was some front-end damage and that it was missing an outside mirror the last time Erica drove it."

"No, there was no damage. None that I'm aware of."

"Kelly, do you remember the last time Erica drove your car?"

"No and why do you ask?"

"Oh, I'm sorry. Erica is not home but her car is there so I thought maybe she may have your Mazda."

"I don't have the Mazda anymore. I traded it when I bought the Camry."

"Oh, I see. Kelly, if you hear from Erica, would you please call me?"

"If I hear from Erica, I'll tell her to call you."

"Thank you, Kelly. I'm sorry to trouble you but, as I said, I am worried about Erica."

"I'll telephone Erica now and I'll tell her to call you."

"Thank you, Kelly," Brooklin says politely and presses the button to end the call.

"Oh no," Brooklin says as she places the phone on her desk. The missing car," she muses. "The blue Mazda 626 that hit Larry was Erica's mother's car. Erica, you *were* involved. Ron drove your mother's car and the two of you hit Larry and left him lying on the side of the road." She looks in the direction of Erica's office, "But, why Erica? Why would you be involved? Why?" Brooklin walks back to her desk slowly, "NO" she says. "If Erica was in the car, then it must have been an accident. It *had* to be an accident. Erica and Ron left the scene because they were afraid. That has to be the reason. They were afraid." Then Brooklin whispers, "Erica, where are you? Why haven't you called me? I'm so worried about you." After a few moments, Brooklin comes to the realization, "I have to

51

face this head on. Accident or not, we have to find you, Erica."

Brooklin picks up her phone and calls Detective Ryan.

Chapter 5

Greg answers his phone saying, "I miss you too. Want to have dinner tonight?" Brooklin ignores Greg's comment and tells him about her conversation with Erica's mother. "Brooklin, give me Erica's mother's telephone number. And, do you have her home address?"

"Yes," she says and gives him Kelly Harris' telephone number and address. "Greg, what will you do now?"

"I'm going to pay Ms. Harris a visit. Have you heard from Erica yet?"

"No, I haven't. Greg, I just don't know how to feel. I'm worried about Erica and I'm angry with Erica. This situation is unbelievable. I'm just so conflicted."

"Brooklin, hold for a moment."

"What?"

"Just a minute, Brooklin." She hears Greg talking to someone.   "There is still no one at her address? All right, put Nick on it and make certain someone is there watching her apartment at all times. Okay, Brooklin, I'm sorry for the interruption." No response. "Brooklin, are you there?"

"Yes, I'm here."

"Brooklin, I'm not going to Delaware to question Ms. Harris until tomorrow. Do you want to have dinner tonight? I miss the talks we had at the hotel when I was investigating Larry's hit and run case. And Brooklin," he hesitates a moment, "I miss you too."

"Greg, I think I will just go home early. I've had a headache for the majority of the day."

"Okay, I'll give you a call tomorrow when I return from Delaware. Brooklin, go home and get some rest. Work can wait until tomorrow." He remembers her looking rigid and tense when he saw her earlier. "Brooklin, take care of yourself."

"All right, I'll talk to you tomorrow." Brooklin pauses for a moment, "Greg, we have to locate Erica. I need answers. However disturbing or whatever the outcome, we need to find Erica." Frustrated, Brooklin runs her fingers through her hair and places the phone face down on her desk. Her thoughts return to her conversation with Kelly Harris and then to the image of Mr. Reed beaten bloody in her hotel. "No" she says aloud, "Brooklin, you have one last report to do before going home." Brooklin collects her thoughts, turns to her computer and forces herself to begin the report thinking this is pure torture. After she finishes the report, she organizes her desk for tomorrow thinking that so much has transpired that she has not had time to focus on the red envelope. Tomorrow, she will have to decide how to handle that situation.

Kelly Harris walks to the front door with coffee in hand to answer the doorbell. She opens the door and asks, "May I help you?"

Detective Ryan shows his badge and says, "Good morning, Ms. Harris. I'm Detective Ryan. I would like to speak to you for a few minutes about your daughter, Erica Harris."

"Is Erica all right?"

"That's why I am here. I'm trying to locate her. May I come in?"

She glances at him again and then his badge. She unlocks the storm door and invites him into her cozy and nicely decorated living room. "You said you are a detective?"

"Yes, Detective Ryan. I met your daughter at Logan Courtyard when I was investigating a case a few months prior. May I sit down?"

"Yes, please have a seat. Can I get you a cup of coffee?"

"No, thank you. Ms. Harris, when was the last time you spoke to Erica?"

"Detective Ryan, what have you learned about my Erica? Do you have any information about her?"

"Erica didn't report for work yesterday or call her employer. We went by her apartment, her car was there but she hasn't been seen in a couple of days. Have you seen or heard from Erica in the last few days?"

"I called and left a message for her yesterday after Ms. Covington phoned me. Erica didn't answer. But that's not unusual. Erica works so hard that it sometimes takes her a couple of days to return my phone calls. But now, I'm getting worried. You say, no one has seen her in a couple of days?"

"Ms. Harris, I need you to tell me the last time you saw or spoke to Erica."

"I have not spoken to Erica in a couple of weeks. The last time I saw her was about a month ago. I went to visit my sisters and Erica was here when I returned."

"I understand that Erica painted your blue Mazda 626 at that time."

"Why yes, I guess you spoke to Ms. Covington. Erica painted my car as a birthday gift. However, I later traded it for a Toyota Camry."

"Did you ask her to paint your car or was it a surprise?"

"It was a surprise, although I had mentioned that I wanted to have my car painted. Why are you and Ms. Covington so interested in my Mazda 626? Is Erica in some type of trouble?"

"I'm just trying to locate her at this time. Ms. Harris, did Erica have your Mazda on Monday, March 24th?

"Monday, March 24th? I don't remember. That's a strange question. How would I recall if Erica had my car on that date?"

"Can you try to remember, Ms. Harris? From what you told me, that would be about a month before you visited your sisters. Did Erica have your car around the end of March?"

"I don't remember and any way what does the Mazda have to do with your finding my daughter?"

"Ms. Harris, do you have any paperwork here for the Mazda 626?"

"No, I gave all the paperwork to the dealer when I traded the Mazda."

"Ms. Harris, why did you decide to trade the Mazda? Was there any damage to the body of the car?"

"No, there wasn't," she says as she rises from her chair. "Detective Ryan, I'm not answering any more of your questions. I thought you were here regarding my daughter. You seem more concerned with my Mazda than with my daughter. I want to know what has happened to my Erica. Where is she?"

"Ms. Harris, please calm down. We are trying very hard to locate your daughter and I need your help. We need to ask her a few questions. Now, I have spoken to a detective in Precinct 15, Detective Diaz. If you would like, we can go down to the precinct to answer questions. We can certainly do that, if you would feel more comfortable answering questions there. But I need answers in order to find Erica."

"I have a right to know what is going on. Has Erica been arrested for something? Is someone trying to harm her?"

"Ms. Harris, Erica was not arrested. As I told you, we are trying to locate her. Maybe she just needed to take a short vacation because, as you said, she's been working a lot of hours at the hotel lately. Do you have any idea where Erica may have gone?"

"No, I do not. And I want you to leave."

"Ms. Harris, I'm not trying to upset you. I know this must be difficult for you. And I promise you, I will leave in a few minutes, I just have a few more questions."

"What questions?"

"I need the name and address of the dealer that bought the Mazda 626 from you."

"Why?"

"We think your Mazda may have been in a car accident. So Ms. Harris, can you please give me that information?"

"I will give you the information but I know there wasn't any damage to the car when I traded it for the Camry." She walks over to a desk and writes down information and gives it to Detective Ryan.

"Ms. Harris, why did you trade the Mazda? Did Erica talk to you about getting a new car?"

"Yes, we talked about it."

"Did Erica tell you why she wanted you to trade in the Mazda for a new car?"

"No, she just suggested it and I needed a new car."

"Now, I also understand Erica is your only child. Is that correct?"

"Yes."

"Ms. Harris, I can see that you are upset and agitated. Can I call anyone to come and be with you now?"

"No, Detective Ryan. I don't need help from you."

"Ms. Harris, do you have any family members or friends in the area?"

"I said I do not need your help."

"I understand that, Ms. Harris. However, you did not answer my question. Do you have any family members or friends that Erica may have contacted or visited? What about your two sisters?"

"I do not have any family members in the area and Erica would not have contacted any of my friends or my two sisters."

"How do you know that, Ms. Harris?"

"Isn't that the question you just asked me? I'm just answering your question."

"Ms. Harris, how do you know Erica would not have contacted your sisters, family members or friends?"

"My two sisters are my only living family members. Erica doesn't exactly get along with them. Therefore, I doubt she would have contacted them."

"Why does Erica not get along with your sisters?"

"That is personal, Detective Ryan."

"Can you provide me with their names, addresses and phone numbers please?" Ms. Harris provides Detective Ryan with her sisters' information. "Now, what about your friends or friends of Erica?"

"If Erica would have contacted any of my friends, they would have told me. I have no idea where Erica's friends from high school are now. The only friend Erica kept in contact with is Darla and she died a few years ago."

"Do you know anyone she could be visiting?"

"No. I don't."

"Ms. Harris, I need your cooperation in order to help us locate your daughter."

"I don't know of anyone Erica could be visiting."

"I understand her father is deceased. Could she be visiting some of his relatives or friends?"

"I don't know, Detective Ryan."

"Can you provide me with their contact information?"

"Erica and I only know his brother, Erica's uncle. And he is in a nursing home. Therefore, I don't think Erica would be visiting him."

"Okay, Ms. Harris, I'm going to leave my card. If

Erica contacts you, please call me. I know your daughter is a great employee for Logan Courtyard, always courteous and friendly. I will do my best to locate her."

As Detective Ryan stands to leave, Ms. Harris walks behind him. "Ms. Harris, thank you for your time and I apologize if I upset you. We all want to find Erica and make certain she is all right." He leaves saying, "We will contact you when we locate her and please call me if you hear from Erica or remember something that might help us in locating her." Ms. Harris doesn't comment and closes the door behind him.

Brooklin is absorbed in paperwork when there is a knock on her office door. She's thinking it might be Greg with information regarding his visit to Erica's mother. Instead, her brother Jim smiles and says, "Can you take a quick break?"

Brooklin smiles and says, "Sure, come in. I'm surprised to see you here." After Brooklin inherited the hotel from her mother, her brother Jim had difficulties accepting that the hotel was left solely to her. Their mother had supported Jim financially for most of his adult life. Over the years, this financial help created a dependency. When their mother died, Jim turned to Brooklin for the monetary support he'd received from their mother. While Brooklin understood her mother's good intent, she would not be a crutch for Jim. She gave him a job at the hotel and told him he had to work for his salary. Jim felt betrayed by his mother and Brooklin. This had a significant impact on their relationship. After several instances of negative behavior toward Brooklin and hotel staff, Brooklin transferred Jim to the Teen Center to work with her husband Colin.   It was a great match. Jim changed his life style, which led to Brooklin and Jim repairing their relationship.

"So Brooklin, how are you doing?"

"I'm fine, Jim. How are you?"

"I'm good. I found a nice lady friend and I really like her."

"That's great, Jim. Why don't you bring her for dinner on Sunday?"

"Thanks, Brooklin. I will definitely ask her and I'll let you know."

"Good. What's her name?"

"Amber."

"Well, I look forward to meeting Amber."

Jim smiles and asks, "How are things here at the hotel?"

"Things are good. The expansion is going well, so I can't complain. How is everything at the Teen Center?"

"Okay. Colin is a great boss. You think the two of you might get back together? He told me he'd like to return home. What do you think, Sis? Are you going to let him come home?"

"Jim, I just need some time for myself. So much is occurring at the hotel, I don't have time to think about being in a relationship."

"I thought the workload would be lighter now that you hired your new assistant. Walt is his name, right?"

"Yes, Walt is great and I do have more leisure time. However, there is still ..." Brooklin hesitates and says, "Have you seen Kim? Did she return to the Teen Center?"

"No, I haven't seen her. I guess Kim is doing one of her disappearing acts."

"Any of the kids know where she is or how to contact her?"

"You are always trying to help those kids. I will ask and see what information I can find for you."

"Thanks, Jim. The kids like you. Therefore, if anybody can get information from them, it will be you. Please see if you can learn her whereabouts or how I can reach her."

"I will give it my best shot." He stands, balls up a piece of paper and shoots it in the garbage can. "All right, I'll give you a call about Sunday. I better go grab this paperwork and return to the center before they think I'm MIA."

She smiles at him as he leaves her office. She is happy to have her brother back. Brooklin returns to her paperwork and begins to focus on the many tasks before her when her son Luke walks in.

"Mom, I didn't get a chance to talk to you before the meeting. How is everything going?"

"Fine, Luke." How is everything with you?"

"I'm good, Mom. Just a quick heads up. I'm thinking about going to school part-time next semester and putting in more hours here at Logan Courtyard."

Brooklin's full attention is on her son now. "You are going to what? Luke, why do you need to work more hours?"

"Mom, I need more cash."

"Why do you need more cash? You and Laila are living in my old townhouse. You are not paying rent, just cable, electric and your car insurance. So, why do you need more cash?"

"Mom, I'm beginning to date and it is costly. Oh and Mom, we also pay our cell phone bill."

"Luke, you didn't just start dating. Why do you need more money now?"

"Mom," he says putting emphasis on the word.

"Luke, you need to complete your education. Dating is not more important than you completing your schooling. The agreement with you and your sister is that if you attend school full-time, work part-time then you don't have to pay rent. And that agreement stands. You make enough money to cover the few payments you have and date. You don't have a car payment. Who are you dating anyway? Do I know her?"

Luke stands, "Mom, I'm just beginning to date again. And I know what our agreement is. If I don't want to take a full load of college courses next semester, I shouldn't have to. "

"Luke, please sit down. Now no, you do not have to take a full load of college courses if you do not want to. And your father and I do not have to do all that we do for you either. Remember, your father and I are paying for your college to help you to get a good education and a good start in life."

"Mom, why are you so moody? Don't take it out on me because Erica isn't here today."

"What? What are you talking about?"

"Are you moody because you don't have your right hand to help you today?"

"No, of course not. And I'm not moody. This is not the first time that Erica has not been in the office. Karla is filling in for Erica and she's doing a fantastic job." Brooklin hesitates. "And, why am I explaining this to you? Look, Luke, I'm just trying to have a logical conversation with you."

"What does it matter if I go to school full or part-time as long as I graduate?"

"Luke, where is all this coming from? Are you having problems at school? If so, let's talk about it. I know you make enough money. And Luke, you have another option, you can always bring your date here to the restaurant."

"Forget it, Mom. I thought I could come to you and you would be fair-minded and reasonable."

"Fair-minded and reasonable? I am being reasonable. I want you to honor your agreement and realize how fortunate you are. You are living in a nice townhouse and driving a nice car, both at no cost to you. You have a good job with a decent salary and your parents are paying your college tuition. Now who is being unappreciative and unreasonable?"

"Right, Mom. I don't know why I thought this time would be different. It's always your way or no way. What else is new? Now I understand why Dad left."

"What did you say?" Brooklin snaps angrily. "How dare you say that to me. Don't you ever speak to me in that way again."

Luke rises from his chair, "And on that sinister note, goodbye Mother," and he storms out of her office.

Brooklin closes her eyes, lays her head back on the chair and takes a couple of deep breaths. "There are many reasons that result in one having to take deep breaths and this week is certainly one of them."

Chapter 6

Taylor walks up the stairs of Griffin Development. It's her first day of work at one of the largest privately owned real estate development companies. Taylor is proud to have landed a job with Griffin Development. As she is about to enter the building, she hears someone calling her name. She turns to see Jack Griffin, "Good Morning, Mr. Griffin. How are you?"

"I'm fine, Taylor. We're so glad you have joined our family. Come, let me introduce you to my assistant Lara." Jack Griffin continues the conversation as he opens the door for Taylor. "Lara will introduce you to the staff and give you a tour of our facility." As they walk to the front desk, Taylor watches the interaction between Mr. Griffin and the receptionist. The young lady, Carrie, smiles and greets Jack Griffin. She notices that Mr. Griffin doesn't speak to Carrie but nods in her direction. He tells her, "Taylor is a new hire and Lara will provide a tour shortly."

"Yes, Mr. Griffin," the young lady says very professionally. Mr. Griffin continues down the hall and Taylor picks up her pace to remain at his side. Taylor looks in the different offices as they walk through the well-designed building. Griffin looks straight ahead until they reach the office at the end of the hall. They walk into a large elegant office where an attractive dark-haired woman is working on a computer on a beautiful L-shaped desk. Taylor can only imagine the cost with its rich cappuccino wood stain. She looks around the office and admires the décor. Her glance falls on a matching table desk with a chic cappuccino finish and silver accent hardware before Taylor returns her gaze to the woman seated in front of her. Lara having noticed Taylor admiring her office says, "Good Morning, Mr. Griffin."

"Good Morning, Lara." He turns and gestures at Taylor. "I would like you to meet Taylor."

Lara stands and reaches across her desk to greet Taylor. Lara is about 5'10" and looks to be in her mid to late thirties. "Very nice to meet you, Taylor. Welcome to Griffin Development."

As Taylor begins to thank Lara, Mr. Griffin interrupts, "Lara, after you give Taylor a tour of the building, come to my office for a quick briefing."

"Yes, Mr. Griffin," Lara says as Jack Griffin exits the office.

"Taylor, would you like anything to drink--coffee, tea, bottled water?"

"No. I'm fine. Thank you."

"Well first, I will take you to your office and then I will give you a tour and introduce you to our staff."

"That sounds wonderful," Taylor comments.

Lara reaches for her phone and tells someone she will be giving the new hire a tour of the building and then will be in Mr. Griffin's office for a quick meeting. "Come Taylor, let me show you to your office."

Taylor accompanies Lara as they walk to her new office. She notices the respect Lara receives as she stops and talks to different staff members in the hallway. She wonders what the staff members think of

Mr. Griffin's arrest which was plastered all over the news. She, of course, will not mention it. She is grateful to be working again. However, she would prefer returning to Logan Courtyard. She should have played that differently. Oh well, it's too late now. Or is it? She still has Luke in her bed. She gives thought to Brooklin and Luke. What would they think about her working for Jack Griffin? She smiles to herself thinking, "This is part two of the payback."

Michelle, Blake's dog walker, appears at the door to Brooklin's office. Brooklin opens the door and Blake runs to her. "Hi, boy. Did you have a good walk with Michelle?" She pets Blake. "Now Blake, go get some water." Brooklin points to Blake's water bowl. "Jerry put some fresh water out for you." Blake runs over and begins to lap up some water. "Hi, Michelle, how was Blake today?"

"He was his normal self. Looking at everyone and wanting to run in every direction."

"I know. Thank you for walking Blake. And Michelle, stop by the restaurant before you leave. I had Jerry make your favorite lunch. You walked Blake a little longer than usual today and I want to make certain you eat before your class."

"Thank you, Ms. Covington. I love the food here."

"You're welcome. Have a good day and thanks again."

Michelle looks over at Blake, who's now lying on his bed panting. "Bye, Blake. See you tomorrow."

"Okay Blake, I'm going to get some work done. You can play with your toys in the back room or you can watch me work. We have a few hours before we go home." Blake wags his tail again and looks over at the television. Brooklin's tv is on with the sound down.

After about two hours of work, Detective Ryan appears at Brooklin's door. "Hi. Can you tear yourself away from work for a few minutes?"

"Hi, Greg." As he walks into her office, Blake runs out of the back room, pushing a ball.

"Well, who do we have here?"

"Oh, Greg, this is Blake. I forgot you haven't met Blake yet."

"Well hello, Blake." Blake stops and looks at him. He doesn't bark because he is accustomed to people coming in and out of Brooklin's office.

"Blake, you can go play. He's one of the good guys." Blake doesn't move. He just stares at Greg.

Greg sits down in one of the chairs in front of Brooklin's desk. "Brooklin, you didn't tell me you bought yourself a guard puppy."

"I didn't buy him. He was a gift."

"A gift? A gift from whom?"

"Colin."

"Colin? I should have known." He looks back at Blake and says, "So that's why Blake is still staring at me. Colin trained him to keep an eye on me when I'm in your presence."

Brooklin laughs and says, "What can I do for you, Detective Ryan? Any news on Erica?"

"Oh, it's back to Detective Ryan when Blake is in the room?"

Brooklin laughs again. "Thanks, I needed that. I haven't laughed in a couple of days."

"You're welcome. I love to hear the sound of your laughter. You should try it more often."

Brooklin smiles. "Do you have any news about Erica?"

"No, not yet and stop accepting gifts from Colin," he says half jokingly.

Brooklin looks at Greg and then at Blake who is still staring at Greg. Brooklin returns her attention to Greg as he tells her about his visit with Kelly Harris.

"So what do you think? Do you think she knows where Erica is?"

"I'm not sure. But at this point, I'm going to continue to work the case and see where it leads me."

"Do you have any leads?" Brooklin asks.

"I went by the dealership where Ms. Harris traded the Mazda 626 for the Toyota Camry. The Mazda is still on the lot. So, I'll have a couple of our guys go to Delaware to examine the car. Tomorrow, I will go through Erica's apartment again. It's going to take some time to learn if Erica fled on her own or if there is another reason she has gone missing."

"What other reason could there be, Greg?"

"I don't know. All we know is we can't find her. However, we're not going to give up. We will track her down." He's quiet for a moment then says, "Right now, we just try to connect all the dots."

"I wish I knew what is happening here. First, it was the hit and run and now, Erica is missing." And Brooklin secretly thinks to herself, "and of course, a beating in my hotel and an anonymous note. Too much … just too much!"

They talk a few more minutes then Brooklin says, "I think I will visit Ron tomorrow at the Camp. Maybe he knows where Erica could be."

"I talked to him yesterday. We talked about Erica and I told him about his father's arrest. I didn't tell him his father was arrested for illegally bugging your office phone to pay off a gambling debt owed to Jack Griffin and his cronies. I also didn't tell him about Erica's disappearance. He's doing so well and I don't want him to have a setback. I don't think he knows where Erica is. However, maybe you can get him to think about possible locations where Erica could be."

"Greg, do you think Erica is in hiding or that something has happened to her?"

"I don't know and I don't like to speculate. I'm still bothered by the fact that I didn't follow my instinct with Larry's case. I knew something was missing."

"Greg, I'm not going to dignify that with a response."

"I'm serious, Brooklin. If I had followed my instinct, Erica would not be missing."

Brooklin looks directly at Greg and says, "I trust your instincts. You solved Larry's case. No one would have ever thought Larry's son committed that crime. Ron wasn't on anyone's radar. And as for Erica, Greg, you cannot blame yourself for her disappearance. I know it's frustrating. You are working so hard and probably feeling like you are not any closer to finding her."

"Well, finding Erica is my priority. I'm going to examine all the evidence we have so far and if I do not come up with anything solid, we will release a missing person bulletin. Her mother filed a report last evening. We normally wait 48 hours before the release."

"I will let you know what happens during my visit with Ron tomorrow morning," Brooklin exclaims. "Greg, before you leave, I would like to talk to you about another person who seems to have vanished. I wonder if you have time to look for a young girl who is missing from the Teen Center?" Brooklin gives him the information about Kim. She tells him about Griffin's involvement with Kim leaving out the details about how she and Levy provided the leak to the media blog. Kim's face was obscured on the leaked photos. Therefore, Brooklin is assuming Greg didn't know the identity of the underage girl.

"Yes, I heard that the FBI arrested Griffin again and charged him with a sexual offense and solicitation of prostitutes. Sure, I will look into it for you."

"Thanks, Greg."

"All right. I better return to the precinct." He stands and notices that Blake is standing in the back room doorway staring at him. "Colin has trained him well. Okay Blake, you can stand down now. I'm leaving and I didn't lay a hand on her." He looks back at Brooklin and says, "Well, not this time. Tomorrow is another day." He smiles as he leaves the office.

The next morning before leaving home, Brooklin telephones TJ, Inc. Brooklin employs this investigative service to provide background checks on new hires and individuals interested in volunteering at the Teen Center. She provides the service with the information given to her by the police officer regarding Martina and her vehicle. She does not tell them about the car accident, just explains she would like to have a complete investigative report on this young lady as soon as possible, and that she needs a full comprehensive report conducted. As Brooklin exits through the garage door, she quickly checks a second time to make certain that the door is locked and the alarm is set.

Brooklin walks through the door of the boot camp and all eyes are on her. Brooklin is wearing a sheath green shift dress and black heels that flatter her stunning figure perfectly. Her shoulder length black hair falls right at the perfect spot to frame her face and achieve a soft but elegant look.

Brooklin walks to the desk, gives her name and tells the guard she is here to visit Ron Carter. As Brooklin waits for Ron, she remembers her conversation with Greg regarding Ron. "Greg, I know he's guilty, but can you try to get him into a boot camp with a mental health facility? Maybe they can prescribe some type of anti-depression medication. With counseling, hopefully he can begin rebuilding his life. After so many years of abuse and neglect, Ron deserves to get the help he so desperately needs."   She has always felt sorry for Ron being in an abusive home with an alcoholic mother and a father who was too busy gambling and committing adultery rather than taking care of his son.

Now, she has learned that Erica was in the car with Ron. "I wonder if we will ever learn the full story of what really happened that night." Brooklin is a little startled as she hears a loud sound. Her nerves are so unsettled now after seeing the car in front of her home and receiving the anonymous card. She turns and looks in the direction of the noise and sees a woman, man and boy sitting two tables away from her. Brooklin watches as the lady reaches down and picks up her purse from the floor. Brooklin continues to curiously gaze around the room noticing the officers, visitors and the incarcerated young men. They all seem to be relaxed and involved in active conversation.

After about ten minutes, Ron enters the visitor room. His hair is cut shorter but he looks the same. He is dressed in a sweatshirt and sweat pants. He is a nice looking young man. However, his face betrays that he is still a shy 19-year-old. Ron gives Brooklin a hug and sits across from her at the table. "Hi Ron, how are you?"

"I'm okay. How are you, Ms. Covington?"

"I'm good. How are they treating you here?"

"They treat me well."

"Are you getting along with the other guys in the camp?" Brooklin remembers Ron telling her how he didn't fit in with the kids at his high school.

"There are only five other guys in my group and they are okay. My counselor is very nice."

"That's good, Ron. You do look well."

"Thank you."

"What is a typical day like for you here?"

"We get up at 7am. We have breakfast, exercise and either go to work or class. Since I graduated from high school, I go to work. Then I have lunch around 1pm and meet with my counselor. I return to work after counseling and then have dinner. After dinner, we have group and later about two hours of rec time before it's time to return to our room for quiet time or we can go to the library before lights off. I actually work in the library."

"That's great, Ron. Do you like working in the library?"

"I do. It's quiet and I like books."

"Good. I'm happy that you are settling in here. Ron, you mentioned when you were working part-time at Logan Courtyard that you would like to take some business courses at the community college. Do you think you still might want to take some college classes in the future?"

"I have been thinking about that and I would. My counselor said I should continue my therapy after I leave here."

"Yes, she is right. However, I'm glad to hear you are interested in attending college in the future. So, what else do you and your counselor talk about?"

"We talk about my life, my decisions, we talk about lots of things."

"Is the counseling helping?"

"Yes, I'm not so angry anymore. My counselor helped me to understand that I was looking for love from my parents and from a girl and I didn't receive the type of love I was looking for or needed."

Brooklin looks at him sadly as Ron continues, "She told me I can continue to look for lost love or I can choose to find that love within me. Love myself with all my faults, mistakes," he smiles, "and yes a few good traits."

"That's wonderful to hear, Ron. It seems like you are making a lot of progress."

"I'm trying."

"Do you have many visitors?"

"Not really. Just Detective Ryan and Dad."

"Your Mom doesn't come?"

"She came once. But she was drinking. And now I guess my Dad will not be visiting for some time."

"Why not?"

"I guess he got arrested."

"Do you know why he was arrested, Ron?"

"No. He and Detective Ryan didn't tell me. And I'm not going to worry about it. I just need to worry about myself now."

"That's good, Ron. You do have to take care of yourself now. Do you know when you will be released?"

"If I keep doing well, I'm told in about five months."

"How do you feel about that, Ron?"

"I'm okay with it. You know, Ms. Covington, I am sorry about the hit and run. It was like I went through some type of psychotic episode -- having no emotional connection to what was happening. I don't think I was in total control of what I was doing. Like I said, the counseling is helping and I feel I'm getting stronger everyday."

"That's good, Ron." Brooklin remembers what Greg told her of Ron and Erica's conversation at the city jail when they were unaware of being recorded. "Erica, I'm not going to take all the blame for dad's hit and run. You used me. You never loved me. You continually told me how I should hate Dad. You were shouting all those horrible things in the car that night and you said, 'Hit him, hit him, hit him, Ron.' I couldn't think with all the bad things Mom had said and with you shouting at me, I just lost it and then, Erica, you grabbed the wheel. And within an instant, the car hit Dad." Brooklin looks at Ron and asks, "Have you heard from anyone from the hotel?"

"No and I really didn't expect to."

"Not even Erica? I have asked her to deposit money in your account every month."

"No. I haven't heard from her. How is she doing? Is she doing all right?"

"Yes, why do you ask?" Brooklin knows that Erica also told Ron she was pregnant during their conversation at the city jail.

"I was just wondering."

"Why, Ron, do you have a crush on Erica?"

Ron looks startled, "No. No, I just asked because you mentioned her name. Oh and thank you for the money each month. You have always been so nice to me."

"You're welcome, Ron. After you're released, I would like to pay for a room for you at the Jefferson Counseling Center so you can continue with counseling. Would that be okay?"

"Yes, thank you so much. I heard some talk here about the Jefferson Center. I heard it was very nice."

"Good and when you and your counselor feel you are ready, I can help you with the cost of college tuition." Brooklin stands, "Okay, Ron, I'm going to leave now. But I will come back to visit you soon."

"Thank you for coming and for everything, Ms. Covington. I really appreciate your support."

"You are welcome. You take care of yourself now."

"I will," Ron says as Brooklin smiles at him.

After Brooklin exits the building, she thinks about her visit with Ron. She realizes Ron is not as shy and timid anymore. There was eye contact and real conversation. He looked at her as he talked to her. That, in itself, is an improvement. Well, it looks like the counseling is working.

Brooklin arrives at the hotel after her visit with Ron and enters her office. She will support Ron and hopes the Jefferson Counseling Center can help him turn his life around. He has had such a sad and troubled childhood. And now, we're looking at the results. This is what happens when kids don't receive what they need in childhood.

After only a few minutes, Karla comes in and tells her that John, the head contractor, called. There are apparently problems with the theater and courtyard renovations and the construction has come to a complete halt. "What? Did he say what type of problems?"

"No, he didn't say."

Brooklin takes a deep breath. "Okay, if you need me, I will be meeting with the contractor." Brooklin walks down to the theater and looks around as she enters the dusty area.

The contractor sees her and calls out, "Ms. Covington, we have a problem."

Chapter 7

Brooklin looks at the contractor, "Okay, what type of problem?"

John explains that the Bureau of Permits and Inspections reviewed Logan Courtyard's application and construction documents for the planned renovations and improvements. The permits were issued and the work began. The bureau returns periodically to inspect the work at specific stages throughout the construction. They returned today and after their investigation identified some work violations determined to be serious hazards. "We were given a list of deficiencies, Ms. Covington," said John gravely. "I've been in this business for over twenty years and I have to tell you there's something more going on here. I am skilled in my craft and I have good people working for me. I inspect the structure before I leave and I'm the last person to leave the site daily. These violations we have just found happened after I left last night. Does anyone else know the code to enter this area of the hotel?"

"Just you, Erica and myself. Oh and my attorney, Levy."

John thinks for a moment, "I'm sure they all can be trusted. What about maintenance?"

"No, I didn't give maintenance the code because they do not need to maintain this area during construction."

"Only my maintenance supervisor and I know the code," says John. "I will talk to him. But as I mentioned, I am the last person to leave the site daily. Now, Ms. Covington, we will go back and repair the deficiencies but this changes our timeline substantially and will increase the total project cost."

"John, I know and trust your work. We have contracted with you for a number of years at Logan Courtyard. However, I would like to have more information regarding the financial costs for completing the work involved in these violations. And I would also like to have the new timeline for the completion of this project."

"Yes, I'll have the new numbers for you tomorrow." He hesitates a moment then says, "I hate to think or even say this. However, I think someone deliberately created the code violations knowing that the inspector would come today. I think someone is trying to slow down or even stop the development of this project."

"I will take that into consideration, John. I will have the local engineering company that we work with do some investigative work and reevaluate the plans. I am also thinking about another addition to this project. After I see your numbers and the proposal from the engineer, we will talk again. Now is this area safe? I don't have to worry about this side of the building collapsing?"

"No, it is safe in that respect, although I will post signs that no one should enter this space."

"John, tomorrow can you schedule a meeting with James, the head of our maintenance department? I would like the two of you to check the entire building, electrical panels, security systems, alarms, sprinklers, everything. Make sure that the hotel is safe and secure. Then once the two of you talk about this problem with the engineering company, hopefully we can come to an agreement about what should be our next step for the construction to continue. I will have security cameras installed in this area and have one of our security personnel stationed here around the clock until this project is completed."

"All right that sounds good. I will schedule a time with Erica to meet with you after I've met with James and your engineer."

"John, I want to thank you for the work you have done so far." Brooklin shakes his hand, "We will talk again tomorrow or in the next couple of days."

Brooklin decides to take her morning walk through the hotel before returning to her office. Brooklin walks to her favorite quiet place of escape, the terrace garden. She begins to sort through how the construction had been coming along beautifully and the great progress they were making. Now this! "However, this bump in the road gives me an idea for possibly adding a rooftop VIP room overlooking the city," she thinks to herself. "I believe in paying it forward and it's my responsibility to provide this area with one of the finest hotels in the region."

Brooklin breathes in peacefully as she takes in the terrace garden's stunning scenery and gorgeous flowers. The background music is calming and soothing as she relaxes in the swing at the back of the terrace. Thinking she is alone, she's startled to hear a man's voice. "Hi, Ms. Brooklin." She looks in the direction of the voice and sees Andy from maintenance.

"Hi, Andy. How are you?"

"I'm good, Ms. Brooklin." Andy studies her carefully and says, "I hope you are taking care of yourself. Are you worried about Erica?"

"Why, what do you mean?"

"I've heard that Erica didn't come in yesterday or today and she didn't call either," he says looking at Brooklin.

"Andy, tell me more. Have you heard any other information about Erica?"

"Ms. Brooklin, you know working in maintenance, you see and hear a lot."

"Andy, what have you heard?"

"I just heard that Erica is missing. That she hasn't been to work or home. Is that true?"

"Well, Andy, Erica has not been to work. I do not know if she has been home and yes, I am worried about her. Because this is unlike her."

"It definitely is. That Erica is a responsible one and she loves her job. Ms. Brooklin, something must have happened to her or Erica would have been at work or contacted you."

"I think you are right, Andy."

"Are the police looking for her?"

"I do think they are investigating. We have to pray that all is well with Erica and that she just needed some time for herself."

"Yes, we certainly will pray for her." Andy says as he walks toward the door. "Have a good day, Ms. Brooklin."

"You too," Brooklin says. After Andy leaves, Brooklin repeats Andy's comment, "Have a good day." She sighs, "Right, that may be easier said than done. I can't get away from drama and problems. It's all around me." She sits for a few more minutes and then leaves the garden, continuing her walk around the hotel.

Taylor opens the door to Griffin's office. He is seated in his chair facing the wall. "Well you tell him, he better start taking my phone calls. Tell him not to forget, we are in this together and if I go down, so will he."

Realizing Griffin is talking on the phone, she closes the door quietly and knocks softly. Taylor then opens the door as Griffin is ending his call. "Mr. Griffin, you wanted to see me?" She says thinking to herself, "Wow, that was quick thinking on my part."

"Yes, Taylor, close the door behind you and have a seat."

Taylor closes the door and sits in the chair directly in front of Jack Griffin. She's a little nervous and unsure of what to say. "Mr. Griffin, I would like to thank you again for this job opportunity."

"Taylor, we're glad that you are a member of our organization. Lara gave you the tour?"

"Yes. It's a beautiful building."

"Thank you, my dear. Taylor, I want you to know that I appreciate the information you gave me regarding the expansion on Logan Courtyard." He smiles, "I think they're going to have a little delay in their plans."

Taylor looks a little awkward.

"Now, your office is to your satisfaction?"

"Yes, it's very impressive. Thank you."

"Good, the staff is treating you well?"

"Yes, everything is great."

"Very good. Now, I'd like you to tell me everything you know about Logan Courtyard and start with their computer system."

"Mr. Griffin, Brooklin changed all the passwords. And Luke told me that Brooklin installed extra firewalls into the system that are tough to get through. And I can vouch for that because I tried."

"Interesting. Now before we continue, can I get you anything? Coffee, water, tea?"

"No, I'm fine."

"Well, I will not accept *no* for an answer." He leaves the room and returns with a cup of tea. "I understand you like tea?"

"Yes," she says.

"Well, go ahead, try it." Taylor drinks some of the tea. It's a little bitter. "Is it to your satisfaction?" he asks.

"Yes, it's delicious," she says.

"Good now, sit back, relax and tell me everything you know about Logan Courtyard."

Taylor looks a little anxious, "I don't know where to start."

"The beginning, of course."

When Brooklin returns to her office, she phones Greg to tell him about her visit with Ron. "Brooklin, perfect timing. Just about to grab some lunch. You wanna talk or you wanna see me?"

"Greg, I saw Ron and I agree with you."

"You do? You want to see me?"

"Greg, please. I agree with you about Ron. I don't think he knows where Erica is." Greg listens as Brooklin tells him about her visit with Ron. They talk for a couple more minutes then Brooklin tells Greg she will talk to him later in the week.

"Brooklin, will you have lunch with me? I could use some relief from a taxing day."

"Greg, I just can't. My schedule is full today."

"Brooklin, that's exactly the reason you need to take a break from everything. Have lunch with me."

"Greg, I can't. Too much is happening at Logan Courtyard now."

"Or is it just that you don't want to have lunch with me?"

"Greg, don't."

"You are going to treat a stressed, hungry law enforcement man like this?" He hesitates and when she doesn't respond, he continues, "Fine, I'll have lunch alone. I will eat at a large table in a restaurant, all by myself," he emphasizes every word. "You know why I'm having lunch all alone, Brooklin?"

"Because no one else wants to have lunch with you?"

"No, because I'm starving and there is this beautiful, amazing woman that has an intoxicating smile and I only want to be in her presence. So I must eat alone or not at all until she graces me with her presence."

Brooklin could not contain her amusement. She throws her head back laughing heartily. "Greg, maybe you should have been a comedian rather than a detective." She laughs again as she places the phone on her desk.

Minutes later, Meghan from accounting appears in Brooklin's office for a quick meeting. Brooklin smiles to herself, "Laughing break is over – time to return to work." Brooklin oversees all accounting matters and signs all checks for the hotel and Teen Center. Colin and Brooklin have given strict instructions that the Teen Center and Logan Courtyard accounts must be kept separate and Meghan does a great job maintaining each account. "Meghan, I would like you to hold Erica's paycheck here. Do not deposit it into her bank account. If she calls you regarding her check, please let me know. I would like to talk to her."

"Sure, Brooklin," Meghan says as she exits the office.

Around 5:30pm, Brooklin calls Jill, her best friend and her attorney Levy's wife. "Hello, Jill. Want to come to the house for dinner tonight? I've had a rough day and need some friendly conversation."

"Hi, Brooklin. Sure, why don't we go to Talb, our favorite meeting spot?" Talb, a popular gathering place for locals and visitors, offers great food, friendly and efficient service and is just down the street from the Teen Center and Logan Courtyard.

"Can't, I have Blake tonight."

"Okay well, I'll grab dinner from Talb and be at your house around 7pm. Then you can relax and not have to prepare any food."

"Sounds good--see you at 7." Brooklin places some paperwork in her desk drawer, grabs her purse and calls Jamie at the front desk to inform her that she's leaving for the day.

Brooklin's doorbell rings at 6:50pm. She opens the door with Blake at her feet. Brooklin smiles as Jill enters with a large box. Jill is a petite woman with a beautiful smile and a beautiful heart to match. She reminds Brooklin of the girl next door. Brooklin looks forward to their talks. "Here, let me help you with that," Brooklin says as she takes the box from Jill. Brooklin is surprised at how heavy it is, "How much food do you have in here?"

Jill removes her shoes at the front door and reaches down to pet Blake. "Hi, Blake. I brought dinner for you too." Blake rolls on his back looking for more attention. Jill smiles and rubs his stomach. "Do you realize you have Blake spoiled already?"

Brooklin laughs and says, "I know. He's my new baby. So, what did you bring to eat?"

Removing the food from the box, Jill says, "I brought spinach salads, grilled salmon fillets, rice and, of course, red wine." She looks down at Blake and says, "Blake, I brought a chicken breast for you. I know how you love chicken breast."

"Okay, Jill, now what did you bring for dessert? I know you never leave a restaurant without ordering dessert."

Jill says shyly, "Cheesecake with berries on top. I know how you love berries and I love cheesecake."

Brooklin laughs, "There is no way we are going to eat all of this food."

"Well, put the leftovers in the frig and have it tomorrow."

Brooklin laughs again, "Jill, you are taking all the leftovers home."

They cut up the chicken breast and place it on Blake's plate. He immediately starts to eat. "Okay, Brooklin, let's eat before the food gets cold." Jill's favorite pastime is eating. One would never guess because she only weighs about 110 pounds. Brooklin and Jill wash their hands, return to the kitchen and begin to eat their salads. "So, what happened that made you have a rough day?"

"Jill, let's eat first and talk about my day later. Otherwise, I won't be able to enjoy this wonderful dinner."

"That bad?" Jill asks.

"That bad. Let's change the subject. Now, when are we going to look for that new house for you?"

Jill smiles and says, "What days are you available?"

"Weekends are better. I will be at the Teen Center until around 1:30 on Saturday. Maybe we can schedule appointments starting around 2pm?"

"Great. I'll call my realtor to schedule appointments for Saturday. I really can't wait for Levy and me to buy a new house. I moved into Levy's home when we married ten years ago. Well, now I want my own house." She looks up from her salad and says, "Thanks, Brooklin for going with me. I love your house and would appreciate your input as I begin my search for a new home."

"I'm looking forward to it. I need some time away from the hotel and all the drama surrounding me now."

"Okay, tell me about it."

"I guess I will start with Erica." Brooklin tells Jill just what Greg told her including that Erica has not been to work in two days nor called.

"What? Erica? This is like a bad dream."

"Well, Jill, you are wide awake."

"Brooklin, do you think someone is setting up Erica? I just don't believe she would be involved in a hit and run. And Erica being pregnant by Ron?"

"Jill, I think it is true." She tells Jill about her conversation with Erica's mother.

"Brooklin, this is just too much. Do they have any leads as to where Erica is?"

"No and I don't know what to think. Is she in hiding? Is she hurt? I just don't know."

"Oh, Brooklin, I'm so sorry."

"I am too. I need to know what has happened to Erica." Then Brooklin tells Jill about the violations regarding the hotel renovations.

"That is ridiculous. John is a great contractor. He does exceptional work. Everyone in this city and the surrounding areas speak highly of his work. I agree with John, there must be something fishy going on," Jill insists.

"Yes, I trust John completely. Hopefully, John and James in maintenance can work through this and find a solution. But that's not all. Listen to this." Brooklin tells Jill about the card, the accident with Martina and the mystery car.

"Now, Brooklin, this is scary. Have you told Levy about all of this?"

"No. Right now Levy is working on another big project for me."

"You tell Levy or I will. Maybe you need to hire some security for your house too, Brooklin."

"I am thinking about doing just that."

"Brooklin, I'm sorry you have to deal with all this."

Brooklin thinks to herself, "I didn't even tell her about Jack Griffin, the FBI and Mr. Reed being beaten in Logan Courtyard."

"Have you told Colin? He and the mayor are good friends. Maybe he can talk to Mayor Jenkins about the violations."

"No. I do not want Colin's help. I don't want him getting mixed signals from me." Brooklin looks over at Blake lying on his bed. "I probably shouldn't have taken Blake from him. However Colin knew how much I wanted a puppy."

"Yeah, Brooklin, it's a little late now. You love that puppy."

"I know. I do."

"Brooklin, I know what you are going through is frustrating and overwhelming. However, I'm sure it's all going to be all right. You are a strong, resilient woman. You'll get through this and come out of it okay," Jill says as she gives Brooklin's hand a gentle squeeze.

"I have had my battles. But this time, I don't know."

"Trust your friend. You will come through this just fine. Just don't lose yourself in all of this. You have always been smart, caring and sensible. Just remember to be true to who you are and everything else will work itself out."

"I'm just really worried about Erica. I hope she will be all right. I just don't understand how she allowed herself to be involved in this chaotic situation. Jill, if Erica really was involved, how could this end well for her? I mean a crime was committed."

"Brooklin, I was thinking, since Ron and Erica were dating, do you think Ron may know where Erica is?"

"No. Detective Ryan and I visited Ron on separate occasions and we both came to the conclusion that Ron does not know Erica's whereabouts or even that she is missing."

"How is Ron doing?"

"He's doing well. He's actually doing better at the Camp than he was at home."

"Really?"

"Yes, it seems the counseling is helping. He credits his counseling with helping him become stronger and more self-aware."

"Ron said that?"

"He seems to be making some real progress and says he's not as angry anymore."

"Well, I'm impressed with that facility."

"I am too. However, I'm concerned about the pregnancy. I don't think either Erica or Ron is ready to be parents."

"It's so strange that those two would hook up. Isn't he too young for her? Erica has that cougar thing going on?"

"I have no idea how the two of them became a couple. Ron seems so fragile. I just don't see the two of them together." Brooklin is quiet for a moment then continues, "After dealing with my separation and then with this dilemma with Erica, I've really had to adjust my thinking and perspective on life. People are not who I thought they were. It's like you are doing everything you can, day in and day out, just to have the rug pulled out from under you."

"It's just your time to go through these tribulations. Brooklin, you know that even the most positive among us go through trials and hardships. Sometimes it seems like the road is so long and bumpy and the pressures and struggles insurmountable, but you survive and get through it."

"I'm trying." Brooklin hesitates, "No, I *will* get through it. I have no choice. I have to." Just as Brooklin completes her sentence, the doorbell rings. Brooklin looks at Jill, "I don't know who that can be." Blake runs to the door, barking.

"Well, Brooklin, you said you had a rough day. Therefore, I thought you could use some pampering. So I booked an in-home massage for us."

"A massage?"

"Yes, I arranged for Joli and Mae to give us massages. Now get the door."

Brooklin opens the door to find two of the massage therapists from Logan Courtyard. They smile,

"Hi, Ms. Covington. Jill booked a massage for the two of you."

Brooklin tells Blake to quiet down as Jill comes to the door and greets the two ladies. Brooklin invites them in and gives Jill a hug. "Thank you. You have no idea how much I needed this tonight."

Joli and Mae begin transforming the space into a massage therapy treatment room. As they set up the massage tables and equipment, Jill walks over to Brooklin and says, "Girlfriend, don't worry, Levy and I got you." Brooklin smiles at her friend as they walk to separate bedrooms to ready themselves for their massages. A few minutes later they emerge in beautiful plush, white robes to find the lights off, music playing, candles lit, oils, fragrant lotions waiting. Jill smiles, "Brooklin, after the information you shared with me tonight, a massage is just what I needed too. Girl, let's get pampered!"

Chapter 8

Thursday morning, Detective Ryan is on the telephone when Kelly Harris walks into the precinct and requests to see him. He completes his telephone call and tells the receptionist to send Ms. Harris in. Kelly Harris walks to Detective Ryan's desk and looks at him impatiently. "Good Morning, Ms. Harris. Please have a seat." Detective Ryan points to the chair in front of his desk. " Now, what brings you here today?"

"What brings me here today? My daughter, of course. What have you learned about Erica?"

"I actually just left your daughter's apartment about an hour ago and there is still no sign of Erica. Do you have any new information or do you remember anything that may help us to locate her?"

"Do I have information? That's an interesting strategy. You want me to find my daughter? Maybe you should try doing some basic police work."

"Now, Ms. Harris, I understand you are upset. And of course, you have a right to be. However, there is no need to be offensive."

"I would like to know what new information you have about my Erica's disappearance."

"We have talked to some of Erica's colleagues, her landlord, neighbors, family members and we went through her apartment a few times. And I would like to thank you again for providing the contact information for those family members. We are trying to retrace her steps. This investigation is a priority for us and we are slowly making progress."

"Priority? I don't believe that. And I don't see where you have made any progress."

"Ms. Harris, we did find a few pin drops of blood on the living room floor of Erica's apartment. Do you know her blood type?"

"Oh my God! My daughter is hurt?"

"I don't think it's anything serious, Ms. Harris. It was only a few pin drops. We would just like to know if it is Erica's blood. Do you know her blood type?"

She thinks for a second, "No, I don't remember. Nevertheless, Detective, I need you all to find my daughter."

"I have to say, it would be a lot easier if you would be more cooperative."

"What?" Ms. Harris says with a distasteful look on her face.

"You see, Ms. Harris, I think you know more than you are telling me. Do you know or have any idea where Erica could be?"

"You said you went to Erica's house this morning. Do you have a warrant to search Erica's apartment?"

"You didn't answer my question, Ms. Harris. Do you know where Erica is?"

"No, I do not. Now, do you have a warrant to search my daughter's apartment?

"Why ask that question, Ms. Harris? Do you *not* want me to search Erica's home? You want us to locate her, right? Or do you or someone else have something to hide?"

"What? That's insane."

"Really, is it? Maybe, you are just here to learn what the police know so you can report back to someone. Is that what's happening here, Ms. Harris?"

"Erica is gone. She is missing. I don't know where she is. I came here hoping you would have some information for me regarding my daughter."

"If you know where Erica is or what happened to her, Ms. Harris, you need to tell me."

"I do not. Can you tell me what you learned when you went to Erica's apartment? What did you find?"

"Ms. Harris, you are quite hostile."

"Hostile? This is me trying to be nice."

"Really?" Detective Ryan laughs. "Well, this is me being suspicious. Would you be willing to submit to a polygraph test?"

"What? A lie detector test?"

"Yes, that would remove any suspicion or doubt about your involvement or your knowing Erica's whereabouts. Because like I said earlier, I think you know more than you are saying."

"Know more than I'm saying? Erica has disappeared and it doesn't seem as if the police are doing anything to find her. Have you put out a missing person report? It's been over 48 hours."

"We will release a missing person's bulletin tomorrow morning. And I will do everything in my power to learn Erica's whereabouts. Now, Ms. Harris, what about that polygraph test?"

"Why don't you try doing something creative like – police work? I want to talk to your boss. Who is your boss?"

"You can return to the front desk and the receptionist will direct you to whomever you would like to see."

Kelly Harris stands to leave and says, "Maybe I should get a lawyer."

Detective Ryan responds, "Ms. Harris, maybe you should."

Officer Randy Baker who sits a few desks away from Greg says, "You think you were a little tough on her being her daughter is missing?"

"No, I think she knows more than she is telling me. I can't quite put my finger on it but there is more than meets the eye here."

"You think she knows where Erica is?"

"I don't know. I just have to investigate everyone including Erica's mother. I think I will have an officer tail Ms. Harris. My investigation needs to be extremely thorough. We don't know the full truth yet but my gut is telling me that we might stumble onto something quite unexpected. Something that can throw everything into a tailspin."

"She was coming off as pretty aggressive."

"Yes, rarely have I've seen a mother of a missing person come into a police station with that type of attitude. It was a little strange. However, I'm not going to speculate. Like I told Ms. Harris, I will continue to work this case until there is a breakthrough and we solve it. Now, I'm going to get a cup of coffee and run out to see an informant of mine. Then when I return, I'll start on my next case, which is a missing 15-year-old girl."

Detective Ryan leaves the precinct and drives down Waters Avenue on the south side. He sees Corey walking near a vacated building. Detective Ryan parks his unmarked vehicle and leisurely walks behind him. Corey looks over his shoulder and sees Detective Ryan and begins to walk faster. "Corey, we need to talk."

"I have nothing to say to you or, should I say, report to you."

The detective takes hold of Corey's arm and pushes him into the abandoned building saying, "We need to talk."

"What's wrong with you? You gonna jump me because I don't want to talk to you? Why don't you show some restraint?"

"I didn't jump you and that *was* restraint. You should be glad I didn't drop kick you."

Detective Ryan reaches into his pocket and pulls out two photos. He holds up Kim's picture and asks, "Have you seen this girl?"

Corey looks at the picture and says, "No."

"Have you heard anyone talking about a teenager named Kim?"

"No."

Detective Ryan shows Corey Erica's picture, "What about this woman. Have you seen her?"

Corey looks at Erica and says, "Umm, I saw that one in my dreams."

"Corey, I'm not going to play with you today."

"Look, I was on my way home. I don't know anything about those two."

"Corey, you know everything about what goes on in these streets." He begins checking Corey's pockets.

"What are you doing, man? Leave me alone."

"Oh look, look what I found in your pocket. Are these drugs?"

"No, it's not drugs. Just a little marijuana."

"Last I heard, Corey, marijuana is classified as a drug."

"Give me my stuff back," Corey says trying to grab the plastic bag from Detective Ryan.

"Now, Corey, you are looking a little nervous. You might want to start talking."

"Give me my stuff. I spent my last dollar on that stuff."

"Is that why you are trying to rush home? You going home to get high?" Detective examines the plastic bag. "Now, let's see what else is in this bag. Corey, do you have some other drugs in here? I see a couple of pills."

Corey tries to snatch the bag. "I don't know anything. I swear."

"Corey, I don't think you are being completely honest with me."

"You think I'm lying? I'm on the level."

"Corey, you are walking around with illegal drugs in a plastic bag. Either you talk or go to jail. What do you think of those odds?"

"My bad. It's like that huh? I'm telling you, I don't know. It's the truth. I have no secrets."

"Corey, I'm getting impatient. What is the story and maybe, I'll let you go."

Corey shrugs his shoulders as if he is giving up, "All right, I'm going to tell you. But this is it. No more favors."

"Favors? I'm doing you a favor by not hauling you in. Now talk!"

"The other night, I heard there is going to be this sex party Saturday night downtown. I heard they were rounding up local girls to take to the party. I don't know if those two girls are going to be there. But some are going to be there. Can I have my bag back? I've told you everything I know."

"Where is the party?"

"At some place on Oak Street."

"Who is giving this party?"

"I don't know. They just said that it was some big shots. That's all I know."

"Corey, I thought you were doing better. But you are using again. You need to get off that stuff." The detective begins walking Corey to his unmarked car. "Get in the car."

"Get in the car? Can't I go now? I gave you the information you wanted."

"Get in the car, Corey."

Corey gets in the back seat. "Where are we going?"

Detective Ryan places Corey's plastic bag of drugs under some papers in his car. "We are going for a ride," he says as he starts the car and begins driving.

"Hey, Detective, you got some coins?"

Detective Ryan doesn't answer Corey. Within minutes they pull up in front of a brick building. "Come on, Corey, let's go."

Corey looks out the car window and gets anxious. "No, man, I'm not going back to rehab. I told you everything I knew about the parties. Now, give me my stuff and let me go home. I'm not going in there. I'm not going back to rehab."

Detective Ryan grabs Corey's plastic bag of drugs and gets out of the car. He opens the back door and pulls Corey out of the back seat. "Corey, this favor is for you. Now, let's go."

Brooklin buzzes Karla and asks her to come to her office. Karla enters and realizes Walt is seated in front of Brooklin's desk. "Karla, come in and have a seat."

"Sure," Karla says and sits in the empty chair beside Walt as she wonders what this impromptu meeting is about.

Just as Brooklin begins to speak, her cell phone rings. She sees that it's Levy. "Excuse me a minute," Brooklin says.

"Do you want us to leave?" Walt asks.

"No, this should only take a minute." Brooklin returns to the phone call. "Levy?"

"Hi, Brooklin. I'm going into a meeting but I wanted to let you know that I have placed 24-hour security at your house. This is the security firm I have been working with for years. They are superb."

"Levy, I ..."

Levy continues speaking. "Brooklin, I'm not going to argue with you about this. You are living alone and Jack Griffin fights dirty. Now I would also like to assign a security guard to accompany you at all times at least until Griffin goes to prison."

"I guess Jill told you about our conversation."

"Yes, she did."

"Okay, Levy but just for the house."

"All right but if you feel unsafe at any time, let me know immediately. Remember, where Griffin is concerned, you have to be careful."

"Thanks, Levy. I will be fine."

"I know you have security at Logan Courtyard. But I want you to be protected at all times."

"I appreciate that. Anything else?"

"Yes, I'm sending my assistant Abby over to pick up the card and red envelope tomorrow morning. I will have it dusted for prints. Has anyone touched the envelope other than you?"

"No, just me and whomever sent them."

"Okay, don't allow anyone else to touch them. I'll have Abby pick them up by 9:30am tomorrow morning."

"Okay, Levy, thanks again. And thank Jill for me as well."

Levy sounding a little rushed says, "All right, we will talk soon."

Brooklin places the phone on her desk, hesitates for a moment and then returns her attention to Karla and Walt. "Okay, my apologies for that interruption. Karla, I wanted to tell you, I am very pleased with how you have managed Erica's workload in the last few days. You have been extremely helpful and handled whatever I have asked of you with ease."

"Thanks, Brooklin. I really enjoy working with you, Walt and the staff here at Logan Courtyard."

"Well you have been great, accomplishing all tasks efficiently. We are happy with the service you have provided in Erica's absence," Walt adds.

"My job is very hands on and sometimes my workload can be very difficult and overwhelming. You have been a tremendous help and I have to say this process has been seamless," Brooklin adds.

"Well, I'm happy to help. I was trained by the best. Erica is very passionate about her work here. She's a wonderful office manager and is committed to Logan Courtyard."

"Well, I never really thought of it that way. But you are absolutely right. She is an office manager."

"Do you know when she will be returning?"

"At this time, we are a little uncertain of Erica's return date. Therefore, I would like to offer you the secretarial position in the main office. This, of course, comes with a salary increase and some special benefits. Walt will walk you down to accounting and make the necessary arrangements."

"Thank you, Brooklin. But may I ask, what happens when Erica returns?"

Brooklin knows that will not happen due to Erica's participation in Larry's hit and run. Nevertheless she says, "When Erica returns, you will continue to work in the main office and Erica will be, as you said, the office manager. Now, I would like you to call my friend Jill and arrange for you and Walt to interview a few candidates for your previous position." Brooklin had hired Karla from Jill's employment agency. "Thank you again, Karla. You have worked hard for us and we appreciate the work you have done thus far."

Walt shakes Karla hand and says, "Congratulations. Thank you for all the assistance you have provided. You came through for us."

"It's my pleasure."

"Karla also, I would like you to schedule lunch for you and me Monday at Talb. If you are going to be my new secretary, I think we should get to know each other better. And, thanks again for going above and beyond the call of duty."

"Thank you. I am very happy to be working one-on-one with you. I have so much respect for you."

"Thanks, Karla. Now if the two of you will excuse me, there is some paperwork I must complete before lunch."

Brooklin decides to have a late lunch on her balcony. She calls to order lunch and asks Jerry to bring the tray to her private balcony. It's a beautiful day and Brooklin sits at the table and enjoys the fantastic view of the courtyard and beach. Brooklin has a telephone conversation with John, the contractor, about the next step regarding the expansion. They briefly discuss that the surveillance cameras were installed and around-the-clock security personnel is stationed in this area until the project is completed. In spite of the setback, she agreed with John, James and the engineer's suggestions. They will complete the work involved on the inspector's deficiency list and move forward with the project without further delay. And it looks like they will be able to include the rooftop

VIP room. John and the engineer are working together to make this a reality for Brooklin. She is aware that she will face challenges but realizes that the hospitality market will continue to flourish as the economy improves and business and leisure travel continue. "I have worked tirelessly to create a brand and an image regionally and nationally. Our new additions should boost business and attract national conventions and leisure travelers." Brooklin's goal is for there to always be something to take pleasure in at Logan Courtyard from the style and beauty of the hotel, the stunning scenery, the entertainment, and the unparalleled accommodations. She would like Logan Courtyard to be an incredible experience.

Jerry walks out on the balcony and places Brooklin's lunch tray in front of her. "How you doing today, Ms. Brooklin?"

"I'm fine, Jerry. How are you?"

"I'm okay. It must be a little weird without Erica?"

"I miss her but Karla is doing a great job."

"That Karla is a nice lady. But Erica was our girl. She used to write me little notes if she needed something or to remind me of some job she wanted me to do. She made sure things in this hotel ran smoothly."

Brooklin looks a little sad. She adored Erica. "Yes, Erica is devoted to Logan Courtyard."

"And to you, Ms. Brooklin. Erica wanted to make sure things were right for you. I hope nothing happened to her."

"Why would you say that, Jerry?"

"Some people were saying that Erica is missing and that the police found blood in her apartment."

"Really? Who said that?"

"Well, I was just in the kitchen listening. Have you heard that, Ms. Brooklin?"

"No, Jerry, I haven't. Maybe it's just gossip and there is no truth to the rumors circulating."

"Well they say Erica was speed dating and met some crazy guy and he took her."

Brooklin stops eating and looks up at Jerry. She remembered that Erica does like going to speed dating. "He *took* her? You mean kidnapped her?"

"Yes, ma'am. That's what they said."

"That's what *who* said?"

"Well, I don't rightly know. Like I said, I was just in the kitchen and I heard some people out in the restaurant talking."

"You don't know who was talking in the restaurant? Was it employees? Hotel guests?"

"I, I, I'm not sure, Ms. Brooklin, "Jerry says stuttering a little. "Someone else was talking in the kitchen at the same time. I do know, it was two women though." He hesitates for a moment, "Ms. Brooklin, you think that detective that was working on Larry's case can find Erica?"

"Erica may not need to be found. Maybe she is taking some needed time off."

"Maybe you're right, Ms. Brooklin."

Brooklin returns to her lunch, "Okay, Jerry, thanks for bringing my lunch."

"You're welcome, Ms. Brooklin. Enjoy!"

Brooklin puts her fork down after Jerry leaves and phones Detective Ryan. "Hello, Greg."

"Hi, Brooklin."

"Greg, I just heard from one of the kitchen workers that he heard that Erica was kidnapped by someone she met at speed dating. He also mentioned that some blood was found in her apartment. Is this true?"

"Yes, there was a very small amount of blood found on her living room floor. Which kitchen worker mentioned this to you?"

"Jerry and why didn't you tell me that? Why am I hearing this from one of my workers and not from you? Erica could be hurt."

"Brooklin, it was a few pin drops of blood. Our CSI unit collected the blood sample, packaged and delivered it to the crime lab. There was only a small amount of blood, hair and fibers collected along with some fingerprints. The crime lab processed the evidence. We know the fingerprints are Erica's from our previous investigation of Larry Carter's hit and run case. However, we don't know whose blood."

"Did you tell her mother?"

"Yes and that's probably how individuals at Logan Courtyard learned about the blood, although Ms. Harris informed me that she does not remember Erica's blood type. And yes, we are looking into the rumors about speed dating as well."

Brooklin turns to see Colin standing in the doorway. "Greg, I have to call you back."

"Okay, Brooklin, that will work. I'm actually driving. I have a couple of people I have to talk to before I return to the precinct."

"Okay, I'll talk to you later." Brooklin turns and says questioningly, "Colin? I'm surprised to see you here."

Chapter 9

"Brooklin, was that Detective Greg Ryan you were talking to?" Colin asks abruptly.

"Yes, why?"

"Brooklin, exactly what is your relationship with that Detective?"

"We are friends. Not that it's any of your concern. Remember, you walked out on me."

"Are you certain the two of you are just friends?"

"Yes, Colin. I am not ready to get involved with anyone at this point in my life. And it's really none of your business."

Colin ignores Brooklin's last statement and continues, "Does the detective understand that you are not interested in being in a relationship?"

"Colin, why are you here? And why are you probing into my private life? Your questions are insulting and presumptuous."

"Brooklin, I need to talk to you. I'm just miserable without you. I'm just not functioning well without you in my life."

"Colin, we are separated because of your actions ... you left me."

"Brooklin, I left home because you were always here at Logan Courtyard."

"Colin, I'm not in the mood to discuss this today."

"Brooklin, you never want to discuss *us* anymore. You inherited this hotel and it's your only priority."

"Colin, there is no need for a discussion. We don't have young children anymore. Luke is 21 and Laila is 20. My family was always my priority and the reason I did everything. Now, my children are adults and my husband walked out on me. I have decided to devote my energy to Logan Courtyard and to my children when they need me. End of story."

"That may be the end of the story for you. But it's not for me. We were a close family and I miss that. I'm sorry I lost sight of that."

"Colin, please stop. We have both moved on. I'm glad I have other interests in my life to focus on. My family is one of the reasons I've worked so hard and turned this hotel around."

"You are only concerned about this hotel. It is what you are committed to," Colin says angrily.

"Really, Colin? You know that is not true. I am very concerned and committed to my family. If you or the kids needed me even though they were older and out of the house, I was there and still will be. My family has always come first and you know that. If you want to talk about the past, remember me, the wife that never complained about you working long hours or your time away from home before you retired. How convenient for you to forget that I managed everything--the children, the household, my career and making sure your needs were met. So if now the hotel is one of my priorities, so be it!"

"Brooklin, please don't let the mistakes I made cost us our marriage and our family. We had a great life and now, right now, I'm here for you and the kids 100 percent."

"Mistakes, what mistakes? I only know of one – your leaving me. Is there another mistake that I'm not aware of or should I say others?"

"Brooklin, please. We had a great life and now, right now, I'm here for you and the kids 100 percent."

"You are here right now? So, let's just forget you walked out on me. Right, Colin? And I noticed you didn't answer my question. However, this is not the first time there was no communication between the two of us. Colin, after my mother died and I inherited this hotel, I worked hard to generate success for the hotel. You and I agreed on the time it would take to turn Logan Courtyard into one of the best hotels in the northeast. You, Colin, walked out instead of supporting me."

"I understand I agreed to give you the time but..."

"No buts, Colin. I didn't leave you when you worked long hours, week after week, month after month."

"I know you were a great wife. But this hotel became so important to you."

"I'm proud of this hotel and what has been accomplished here. Logan Courtyard has been named one of Fortune 100 best companies and I'm aiming at Logan Courtyard becoming one of the best hotels in the world. I worked hard to achieve what I have here and I'm not about to apologize for it. I'm going to walk away from this conversation, Colin." Brooklin turns to re-enter her office.

"Oh, you are going to walk away from me, Brooklin? You can't talk to me for a few minutes?"

Brooklin turns to him with resentment in her voice, "You walked out on me, Colin, after agreeing to give me at least a year and half to transform Logan Courtyard. You broke your promise and left without even sitting down and having a conversation with me. I came home one day and you were gone." Brooklin looks at him in dismay. "Colin, why are we discussing this again? I do not wish to continue to talk about this. Why are you here? A simple straight forward answer is preferable."

"I'm meeting Michelle, the dog walker here."

"What? Why here? I have meetings." Brooklin is annoyed with him now.

"That's why I scheduled an appointment with your secretary to make certain we have time to talk. And, of course, I walk in and you're on the phone with that detective."

"You scheduled an appointment?"

"Yes, I wanted to talk to you and you seem to never have time."

"I had time for you before you left me. Besides, I'm at the Teen Center twice a week and we have our Sunday dinners every week."

"Yes but we are never alone."

"Colin, there is no need for us to be alone."

"Brooklin, can you just listen to me for a few minutes?"

Brooklin looks agitated. It's obvious, she is still angry with him for leaving her. "I *have* been listening to you."

"Okay, Brooklin, I made a mistake. I shouldn't have left and definitely shouldn't have left without discussing it with you first. You were working long hours and I missed you.

"In the beginning, I worked long hours. I cut back my hours and you still left."

"I know. I was angry and probably jealous of your work. But, Brooklin, listen, it's not always easy taking an honest look at oneself. That's what I've been doing. And I've come to realize, I don't like the person I've become. I deeply regret being so selfish and hurting you. I miss you—I miss us."

Brooklin turns her head and looks down at the rippling of the beach water.

"Brooklin, I think this is where you say, Colin, I miss you too."

"Colin, you miss me adhering to your needs."

"Don't say that, Brooklin. I know I've been selfish. But ..."

Brooklin interrupts him, "Colin, I really don't want to have this discussion—it's all too late."

"Too late? Brooklin, we had some good years together. We can get back what we had. I will do everything I can to earn your trust again. I want you back, Brooklin. Give me the opportunity to prove myself. "

"Colin, it's not about what you want anymore. It's finally about what I want. What's right for me. I need time to decide what that is." Brooklin looks down into the courtyard and sees Michelle and Blake. The dreary lines around her mouth turn into a smile. Colin follows Brooklin's gaze and observes Michelle and Blake as they begin the walk up the stairs from the courtyard. Blake is so excited. Brooklin reaches down and places Blake in her arms as they reach the top of the stairs. "Hi, boy. Did you have a good outing?"

"Hi, Michelle. How are you today?" Brooklin asks.

"I'm great. Blake and I went to the park."

"Oh, I know he enjoyed that," says Colin.

"He did. We had a great time, didn't we, boy?" Michelle says as she pets Blake.

Brooklin walks back into her office, "Come in, Michelle, it's getting a little hot on the balcony," Brooklin says glancing at Colin. As they enter Brooklin's office, Blake runs to his bowl, drinks some water and lies on his bed panting. Michelle smiles at Blake and says her goodbyes leaving the office. Colin begins to speak and Brooklin quickly interrupts him, "Colin, did Luke talk to you about attending school part-time instead of full-time next semester?"

"No, he did not. Why would he attend school part-time?"

"He says he doesn't have enough money for dating. Therefore, he wants to work more hours at the hotel."

"What? That is ridiculous. I'll talk to him tomorrow. He will remain a full-time student."

Then Brooklin tells him about Erica. Colin is shocked by the news. "What, Brooklin? Erica? I don't believe it. Who told you this? Or do I really have to ask."

"It is true, Colin." She tells him about her conversation with Erica's mother.

Colin is visibly stunned. "You talked to Kelly?"

"Yes. You know Kelly?"

"I've met her a few times."

"You have? I didn't realize you knew Erica's mother."

"Brooklin, I'm not going to believe this until I hear it from Erica's mouth. Now, no one has seen Erica in a few days?" Colin asks, looking very concerned.

"No, no one has seen or heard from her and she has not been to work or called."

"Brooklin, if I can help in any way, let me know. And, please keep me informed."

"Thanks, Colin."

"Now if I can change the subject for a minute. Brooklin, I arrived a few minutes early for my scheduled appointment with you," he says a little sarcastically. "And, I took a quick walk around the hotel. You've done a great job. You have really transformed Logan Courtyard into a grand hotel, the architecture, technology ... everything is sophisticated, luxurious and very appealing. I have to say, it's beyond impressive."

Brooklin is surprised and a little confused at how the conversation changed so rapidly. "Thank you, Colin. Coming from you that means a lot. And Colin, in the future, you never have to make an appointment to see me."

"I know, but I wanted some quality time."

"Quality time? How long is this appointment you scheduled?"

He laughs. "Two hours."

"Two hours, Colin?"

"Yes," he laughs again.

"Colin," Brooklin shakes her head. She is beginning to remember how much she really did love this man before everything turned so wrong.

"How is the occupancy here? I'm sure the hotel is always booked to capacity."

"Yes, normally we are booked solid. There are a few suites and rooms that we do not book in case of emergencies."

"Yes, I remember that."

"However, right now I am happy to say our reports show two consecutive years of record-setting revenues. We are projecting at least five percent growth this year alone."

"Brooklin, I am proud of you and I believe in you. I'm sorry I let you down. If you allow me to come home, I will stand by you and never leave your side."

"Colin, before I forget, let me just tell you that Levy has placed 24-hour security at the house. It's a security firm he has used for years."

"That is good thinking considering the uncertainty surrounding Erica's whereabouts. I'm glad security will be at the house."

At that moment, Karla buzzes Brooklin to tell her that her next appointment is early and is waiting in conference room three.

"Brooklin, can you give me an answer?" asks Colin.

"Colin, I really can't tell you what you want to hear. I just want time for myself now."

"Brooklin, will you at least give it some thought? I would like us to be a family again."

"Colin, I enjoyed our talk today. Thanks for stopping by. Will you be at our family dinner on Sunday?"

"I will," Colin says as he picks up Blake from his bed.

"Okay, I'll see you then," Brooklin says as Colin and Blake exit. Brooklin grabs her IPad and hurries down the hall to the conference room.

Her meeting now over, Brooklin relaxes on the couch in her office and removes her shoes. She thinks about going home, taking a long bath and getting in bed with a tray of snacks--some fruit, chocolates, a glass of wine when she hears a familiar voice. "Hi, Brooklin, your secretary wasn't at her desk, so I hope it's okay that I'm a few minutes early for our appointment."

Brooklin turns to see Agent Dalton. "It's fine. Come in. Can I get you something to eat or drink from the restaurant? Coffee, tea, wine?"

"No thanks, Brooklin, I'm fine," he says and sits on the couch eyeing her beautiful well-shaped legs and bare feet.

"Oh I guess I should *not* have offered you wine. You are still on the clock, so no wine for you," Brooklin says smiling.

Agent Dalton laughs and says, "I would much rather have a beer anyway. But, you are right, not until after work."

Brooklin begins their conversation by telling him that the day of Mr. Reed's attack, Jack Griffin was in the hotel and probably learned the whereabouts of

Mr. Reed when she and Agent Dalton spoke in the hallway. She explained that she had only walked away from Jack Griffin moments before Agent Dalton approached her.

"That's interesting. Our agents viewed the tapes from the surveillance cameras and realized Jack Griffin did see you and me talking in the hallway. We also saw Ray Marino in disguise entering then leaving Suite 1107 on the day that Mr. Reed was assaulted. This corroborates Mr. Reed's story. He knew his attacker."

"Ray Marino? I don't think I know a Ray Marino."

"You probably do not. He works for Jack Griffin and is wanted on a number of charges. However, the FBI has not been able to locate him." He provides Brooklin with a photo of Ray Marino and a few other photos of individuals on Jack Griffin's payroll.

"I will provide a copy of these photos to security, our front desk personnel and a few other staff members. Of course, this information will be securely maintained and kept strictly confidential. Agent Dalton, the one thing I do not understand is how this Ray Marino knew which suite Mr. Reed was in."

"We were unable to ascertain that information. Marino entered the hotel and went straight to the elevator. Marino and Griffin did not talk to any of Logan Courtyard's staff when they were in the hotel. Therefore, we don't know how they learned which suite Mr. Reed was in." They talk a few more minutes before Brooklin asks about Mr. Reed.

"Mr. Reed is doing fine and is ready to testify against Jack Griffin."

"When will he testify?" asks Brooklin.

"Mr. Reed is scheduled to testify on Thursday. I am certain we have enough evidence to indict Jack Griffin for fraud and to prosecute him for having Mr. Reed's father killed."

"I wonder why Griffin was so desperate to obtain that property that he would have Mr. Reed's father killed?"

"Well, they couldn't get Mr. Reed, Sr. to sell the property. And apparently, Mr. Reed, Jr., our witness, has a gambling addiction and had borrowed money from Big Mel which he could not repay."

Brooklin thinks, "Big Mel again - another person on Jack Griffin's payroll." She remembers that Big Mel beat a young man that was in Memorial Hospital. Luke had injured his ankle playing basketball and they overheard the conversation about the beating while waiting in the emergency room. Also, Big Mel coerced Larry, Ron's father--a previous security guard at Logan Courtyard--to bug Brooklin's office phone. Brooklin looks at Agent Dalton and realizes he is still talking.

"Big Mel forced our witness, Mr. Reed, Jr. to sign papers that gave ownership of the parcel of land to Jack Griffin if and when he inherited the property from his father. Thereafter, we have it on good authority that Jack Griffin paid Ray Marino to kill Mr. Reed, Sr."

"That is absolutely demented." Brooklin's thoughts return to Jack Griffin wanting to acquire Logan Courtyard. Levy was correct in hiring security for the house. Her thoughts then shift to Kim. "What about the charges against Griffin regarding Kim?"

"He will have to return to court on a different date for that offense."

"Good, he will stay in court and be very busy fighting the pending charges."

"Yes, the charges facing Jack Griffin will require much preparation by Jack and his lawyer. However, the fraud charges." He shakes his head. "The case against him would be much stronger if we had more detailed information on Jack's real estate deals."

"Real estate deals?"

"Griffin is responsible for hundreds of bad real estate deals. If we had more information regarding those deals, we could be certain of a guilty verdict. And we could propose to the judge that reparations be paid to the alleged victims. This man has made millions of dollars off the backs of working people. We would like to return some of their money to them."

Brooklin realizes that she *does* have that information. During the investigation Brooklin ordered about Jack Griffin, damaging photos and pertinent incriminating business information had been discovered. She must talk to Levy and have that information transferred discreetly to the FBI before Griffin's trial date. Hopefully with this data, other corrupt executives will be prosecuted and the FBI will be able to access and break-up Jack's inner circle. And maybe she can learn if Jack Griffin is working for or with someone. She reflects for a moment. She could finally learn who really wants to acquire Logan Courtyard and why.

"Brooklin, I want to thank you for your assistance in this case. I am sorry that Mr. Reed was attacked in your hotel. I hope you are not harboring any resentment because of this."

"You are welcome," Brooklin says as she stands up. "Now, can we finally clean, sanitize and exterminate Suite 1107?"

Agent Dalton laughs, "Yes, we have collected all the evidence we need from that suite. It can be," as you said, "exterminated."

"Did you find any evidence in the suite linking Griffin or his associates?"

"No, the evidence from that suite did not match Griffin or any of his associates' fingerprints we have on file. I'm sure Marino wore gloves." Agent Dalton walks to the door and says, "I will keep you informed."

Luke is completing some computer work for Logan Courtyard at his and Laila's apartment when his telephone rings. "What's up, Pops?"

"Luke, want to meet at Waters Avenue Park and play a little one- on-one?"

"Pops, you want play some ball?"

Colin laughs. "I wouldn't mind playing a little ball."

"When was the last time you played some ball, Dad? I don't want you to get hurt now."

"I'm not going to get hurt. I don't know about you but I'll be fine. Wasn't it just a few months ago, you got hurt in the gym playing ball with your friend Lamar?"

Luke grins, "Dad, you know that was just a freak accident. But I really don't remember the last time I have seen you balling."

"Remember, you just beat me for the first time last year."

"No, Dad, I think it was about three years ago."

"I don't know about that. Luke, you want to play or not?"

"Yeah, I'll be there. When you wanna play?"

"I'm at the park now."

"All right, sounds good. I'll be there in about twenty minutes. It'll give you time to practice."

"Practice? I don't need any practice. Maybe *you* need some practice."

"I'll be there in twenty minutes, Dad, and we're going to see who needs some practice."

"All right," Colin says, "We will see. What do you young guys say? You better bring your game." They both laugh.

Colin begins to shoot around until he sees Luke walking onto the court. Luke grabs the ball from his Dad, shoots it and makes a basket. "Dad, you ready for this whipping?"

"Just take the ball out," Colin says to Luke.

"Okay, first one to 11," Luke says.

Luke drives to the basket and scores on Colin. "Okay, you got that one," Colin says and takes the ball out. Colin takes one dribble and shoots a jump shot straight into the net.

"Dad, what are you trying to do?" You trying to win?"

"Don't worry about what I'm trying to do. Just play ball."

"Watch out now, Dad, I'm going to shoot this jumper in your face." Luke pulls up, takes a jumper and scores again. "Nothing but net, Dad."

"Okay, good shot."

Colin takes a step and in the process of shooting a jumper, Luke grabs his arm so Colin can't get the shot off. Colin calls a foul.

"We calling a touch foul now, Dad?"

"A foul is a foul."

"Okay, take the ball out, Dad. It's on now."

Colin shoots and misses, Luke gets the rebound. "Dad, you all right? You're moving a little slow. You tired?

"No, I'm not. All I need is two more baskets. Maybe you are tired."

"All I need is one more basket." Luke goes for a lay up, scores and wins the game.

"Dad, that was a good game. You still have it."

As they sit on the bench, Colin passes Luke a gatorade. "So, Luke, where are you off to when you leave here?"

"I'm on the schedule for babysitting Blake."

"What do you have planned for Blake?"

"We're going to hang out at Lamar's apartment. Watch some college basketball."

"That's for you, Luke. What are you doing with Blake?"

"Blake loves basketball. He sits on the floor by the couch, plays with the soft cloth ball I bought him and watches the game with us."

Colin laughs. "Son, you got Blake hooked on basketball?"

"Yea, he loves watching the game and the commercials."

"Now, Lamar is a junior too, right?"

"Yes, we both are juniors."

"What's this I hear about you talking about going part-time next semester?"

"Oh, Mom told you?"

"Yes, what is that all about?"

"I changed my mind. I'm going to take a full load so I can graduate on time."

"That's good, son," Colin says as he pats Luke on the back a couple of times.

"Luke, are you having any problems? I don't understand why you were thinking of going part-time."

"I was thinking of putting in more hours at Logan Courtyard. I can't really splurge when I go on a date."

"Splurge how? What do you want to do?"

"I want to ... Dad, it doesn't matter. I'm good now."

"Who are you dating? Anyone I know?"

"Dad, I'm just dating. I want to show my dates a good time."

"Well, your dates know you are a college student working part-time right?"

"Yes."

"Luke, don't try to show off or impress the young lady – just be yourself. Let her see who you are. If you don't gel, then you move on."

"I'm good, Dad. How about you and Mom?"

"I'm trying, Son. Your Mom is very focused on Logan Courtyard."

"Dad, you shouldn't have left. You should have stayed home and worked it out. You never should have left home."

"I know, Son. I made a mistake. I'm trying to make it up to your mother." Colin pauses a moment, "I'm not going to lose my family. I'm not going to let it happen."

"Well, I hope not. I want our family to stay together."

"We will, Son." Colin stands up. "All right, I have to return to the Teen Center and shower before I meet with the staff."

"Dad, how do you like staying in the apartment above the Teen Center?"

"It's comfortable, but it's not home. Hopefully, your Mom will let me return home soon. Listen, Luke, I don't want you and Laila worrying about your mother and me. We will work it out. Your mom and I will work through this." Colin turns back to Luke as he reaches his car, "See you at home on Sunday for dinner?"

"I'll be there," Luke says as he revs his car motor loudly. Colin turns and gazes at Luke. Luke laughs and drives away.

Brooklin walks to her desk to finally get some work done. She has been in meetings all day. She works for a few hours and then decides to takes a momentary breather. She turns and looks out the window behind her. She watches the sailboats as they slowly drift by when she hears someone calling her name. "Ms. Covington!" She turns and sees Jack Griffin standing in her office doorway.

"Hi, I knocked, but you didn't hear me. Sorry to interrupt, but is it possible to talk to you for a few minutes? Your secretary isn't at her desk and your door was open."

Brooklin thinks, "Jack Griffin. This can't be good. How did he get back here? I will have to speak to the front desk personnel and security."

Brooklin looks up at this revulsion of a figure. "My secretary hasn't returned yet? No, I do not have a few minutes.   I'm actually running behind schedule."

Jack Griffin enters Brooklin's office and closes the door saying, "Ms. Covington, I only need a few minutes of your valuable time."

"Mr. Griffin, we really have nothing to discuss. If you are on another mission to coerce me into selling Logan Courtyard, I'm tiring of your crusade. I have explained to you I am not interested in selling my hotel," Brooklin says decisively however feeling a little uncomfortable.

"Ms. Covington, I don't think I realized until today, just how beautiful you are. Let's not be so formal."

"What?" Brooklin looks at him with absolute repugnance.

"Can we be done with the formalities? Please, just call me Jack."

Brooklin looks at him, loathing him, "Mr. Griffin, please leave my office and my hotel."

"Okay if you insist on formalities, Mrs. Covington."

Brooklin impatiently says, "Mr. Griffin, I have deadlines. I do not have time to entertain any drama. I just don't have that kind of time."

"Ms. Covington, I do not want to intrude on your time any more than necessary. Therefore, I will be direct. I have thought better of the matter we previously discussed and concluded I would like to offer you more for Logan Courtyard. Here is my new offer." He writes a number on a piece of paper and passes the paper to Brooklin who returns the paper to him without looking at the offer.

Brooklin's work cell phone rings. "I need to take this call," she says. "Hello."

Jack Griffin interrupts. "Ms. Covington, I don't mean to be a nuisance but can I use your facility?"

Brooklin looks at Jack Griffin with disgust. "You want to use ..." Brooklin shakes her head, "No, no, you cannot use my facility."

Brooklin returns to her phone call and hesitates a moment, trying to focus on what the caller is saying.

"Brooklin, it's Karla. Just wanted to let you know that Meghan asked me to come down to accounting to complete some paperwork. It took longer than I expected. I just stopped at the restaurant for a cup of coffee and want to know if you'd like anything while I'm here."

"No, Karla, just return to the office as soon as possible. And for future reference, I need to know your whereabouts at all times during the workday. The uninvited are walking into my office without appointments."

"Oh, I'm sorry. I'm on my way." Karla says.

Brooklin places her cell phone on her desk and looks across at Jack Griffin with distaste.

"It's hard to find good help, isn't it?"

"Mr. Griffin, I am not interested in selling Logan Courtyard. Now I have work to finish."

"Ms. Covington, I had thought we could have a discussion about this. A serious conversation about strategies we can ..."

Brooklin interrupts sharply, "Mr. Griffin, for the last time, I will not sell Logan Courtyard to you or anyone else. Now, I don't have time for this."

"I would advise you to take the time," he says with contempt. "I don't think you know who you are dealing with. Perhaps a small reminder of who holds the key to this city is in line. By the way, how is your expansion going?"

"The expansion? Did you have anything to do with creating those code violations in the theater?"

"Why, Ms. Covington, I have no reason to want to hurt you or Logan Courtyard. I intend to own this hotel. Therefore, if Logan Courtyard does well, it's good for everyone, including me."

"You know the first mistake people make who think they hold all the power? Overestimating their importance and power."

"Overestimating?" he laughs. "I think fearful would be a more appropriate term to use when speaking of me."

"Fear is a choice and I will not allow you to use fear to control me. You may get your way with frightened little girls but you will not get your way with me."

"Ms. Covington, you have been watching too much television. You mustn't believe everything you hear."

"Believe everything I hear? In the photos on the blog, you had your hand all over that young girl. Not to mention the other x-rated photos."

"Which brings me to another reason for my visit today. Someone hacked into my computer. You wouldn't know anything about this would you, Ms. Covington?"

She rolls her eyes intolerantly, "Are you actually accusing me of hacking your computer? Really? I have bigger issues to deal with than your computer. Now, Mr. Griffin, we have had an intriguing conversation. However, it's late and I don't have time to engage in your outlandish accusations or your pretense of computer hacking."

"Ms. Covington, this is no pretense. Did you have someone hack into my computer? Whatever happened to being above board and honest and respectful?"

"Honest and respectful? Are those words really coming out of *your* mouth? Mr. Griffin, I do not know what you are expecting me to say or do here. Let's say your computer was possibly hacked. Do you expect me to plead with you to accept that I had nothing to do with it? Possibly be fearful of the likes of you? Or perhaps say, 'Of course, I didn't hack into your computer? I would never do that!'"

"Perhaps, Ms. Covington, a small demonstration will convince you that I'm serious and that it would be unwise for you to challenge me."

"I don't know what you are accustomed to or how others deal with you but if you are waiting for me to say, 'I thank you for your interest or it's an honor for you to allow me to be in your presence.' Well, it will be a cold day in hell before that will be said here. You should know I didn't get where I am by being stupid and timid."

The gleam in his eyes turns cold, "I don't make empty gestures."

Brooklin looks directly at him. "Do not threaten me. I have been patient but you continually cross the line. I will not give in to your tactics. Now, leave my office and the next time wait for an invitation. Some people can't be bought or intimidated. Now, take your presumptions and threats and leave."

Karla walks in with Walt and Max, one of Logan Courtyard's security officers. Mr. Griffin stands and murmurs in a low tone to Brooklin, "You're beginning to piss me off – not a good idea. Everyone has their price. I am warning you, you may not like yours."

"Leave, Mr. Griffin," Walt says sternly.

The security officer walks up to Jack Griffin and says, "Ms. Covington has asked you to leave. So, let's go."

Jack Griffin looks back and says, "Good day, Ms. Covington."

"Max, inform security that in the future, this man should *not* be allowed in Logan Courtyard or on the grounds," Brooklin says forcefully.

"Yes, Brooklin, I will see to it. And I will escort him out of Logan Courtyard and off the premises."

"Thank you, Max," Brooklin says as she turns to work on her computer.

After they exit her office, Walt says, "Brooklin, I'm sorry about this. Are you all right?"

"Yes, Walt. Thank you and I'm fine. You can return to work," Brooklin says as she walks to her refrigerator for a bottle of water. Walt glances at her again as he leaves the office. "That piece of filth. I'm sure he had something to do with creating those code violations in the theater. He will not destroy what I have built here nor will I surrender my hotel to him and his associates." She paces back and forth thinking about the arrogance, the outrageousness, the brazenness of that man. Then she remembers the comment he made about finding good help. "Was he speaking about Karla or does he have something to do with Erica's disappearance? If he has harmed Erica in any way," Brooklin says with fury. "Okay, Brooklin *don't* get angry, *don't* get frustrated. Greg will find Erica and as for, Griffin--get even. Execute your plan." She pauses, "*Take* control!"

Brooklin returns to her desk and places a call to Levy. She tells him about her visits with Agent Dalton and Jack Griffin. She calmly advises Levy to discreetly transfer the incriminating business information pertaining to Jack Griffin and his associates to the FBI tomorrow.

"Brooklin, would you like me to transfer all the information or just the information pertaining to the real estate deals?"

"Yes," Brooklin says, "I do recall there were details about other parties, right? Names, locations and dates?"

"Do you want to hold that information for another time? You never know when you will need dirt on Griffin."

"No, print *all* the information and transfer the material to the FBI. However, Levy, let's maintain a copy for our records on a flash drive. Be certain to wipe the server clean and place the flash drive in your private safe. Oh and Levy, don't forget to clean the printer history after you print the copy for the FBI. You are right, we may need to secure this data for a later time."

"Okay, will do. Talk to you soon."

Brooklin stands and stares out the window behind her, "Jack Griffin, you will not win. I simply will not allow you to. It's time for you to pay for the crimes you have committed and for the stress you have caused. Jack Griffin, your pay day is coming sooner than you think."

Chapter 10

Brooklin enters her office Friday morning thinking of what needs to be accomplished before the weekend. She looks up to see Walt standing at her door. "Brooklin, you have a few minutes?"

"Certainly, Walt. Come in."

"I was thinking about the visit from Jack Griffin yesterday. Brooklin, there is a man, Brent, who worked for my previous employer. He is a decorated veteran and will handle whatever job you request. He is on call 24/7. He can stay in the background if you would like. He owns a number of cars and therefore he can really be invisible. I'm thinking you might want to employ him. I know his work. He is well worth every dollar you pay him. He only takes on one client. And my previous employer retired and relocated."

Brooklin is visible shocked. "He's a hit man?"

"Well, I wouldn't call him that. I think if you were to give him a title, it would be more like *bodyguard*. But he will certainly handle whatever job his employer requests. I was thinking with the disappearance of Erica and with Jack Griffin barging into your office uninvited, you might want to employ him."

Brooklin looks at her phone and notices that she has an incoming call. It's Levy. She quickly changes her phone from silence and then says, "Hi, Levy. Can you hold for a minute?" Then she returns her attention to Walt, "I'm not sure about employing someone of this nature, Walt."

"I understand. However, just give it some thought," Walt says as he walks out of the office.

Brooklin is slightly unnerved by the conversation with Walt but returns to her telephone conversation. "Levy, thanks for holding."

"Hi, Brooklin. Just wanted you to know everything is in motion. I made the transfer last night. And from what I hear from one of my sources, the FBI began acting on the information last night."

"Really?" She ponders for a moment thinking this could go very wrong but resolves not to agonize over it. What's done is done! She recalls the smug look Griffin had on his face when he was in her office. It's imperative that the FBI has the information to put Jack Griffin behind bars for a long time. "Great, Levy. Thanks for getting this done quickly."

"Not a problem. You said you wanted this to happen before Thursday. And Brooklin, you don't have to worry, our tracks are covered. Nothing can be traced back to us."

"Wonderful. And Levy, thanks for the security at the house. It's good to know there are qualified personnel safeguarding our home."

"That's why you pay me the big bucks, right?"

Brooklin laughs. "I guess you are right about that."

"Also, I was thinking about the conversation we had yesterday. Brooklin, I can file a temporary restraining order against Jack Griffin. He would have to remain at least 100 yards away from you at all times including the workplace. If he violates the order, he will go back to jail."

"Thanks, Levy. I think I don't want to go to that extreme at this point. I don't want to bring any more attention to us than necessary. Griffin mentioned his computer was hacked. However, I do not think he believes I had anything to do with it. I think he is desperate and grasping at straws or just trying to get a rise out of me."

"If you change your mind, give me a call."

Brooklin places her personal cell phone on her desk and uses her work phone to call Jerry and asks him to bring her a large cup of coffee. "However, with the conversations I've had this morning, do I really need caffeine? Yes," she tells herself. Brooklin turns on the television and then quickly checks her messages. Normally, she mutes the television. However today, she would like some background noise. As she begins to work at the computer, she hears the announcement for a breaking news report. Brooklin looks up at the large television screen mounted on the wall as a photo of Erica appears. "Police have issued a missing person bulletin for Erica Harris who lives on Clay Drive in Fort Washington. She is 28 years old, 5'5, weighs approximately 140 pounds. Ms. Harris was last seen wearing a gray dress. If you have any information regarding Ms. Harris, please call the South End Precinct at (877) 628-2527.

Brooklin is absorbed in the news report and Jerry's entrance is unnoticed. "Oh my God," Jerry says. "They are talking about Erica being missing on the news." Brooklin turns to see Jerry with her coffee and the look of horror on his face as he watches the developing news.

"Yes, they released a missing person bulletin," Brooklin says as she takes the cup of coffee from Jerry's hands. "Erica's disappearance is on television," Brooklin says in disbelief as Karla walks into Brooklin's office.

"You saw it?" Karla asks.

"Yes, I saw it," Brooklin says in a low tone. "Jerry, please have a seat. I'm holding a staff meeting shortly." Brooklin understands she must keep Jerry close otherwise there will be an enormous amount of gossip floating around the building before she is able to talk to the staff.

"Karla, please call two staff meetings. Follow the emergency guidelines. After the first meeting, the employees in attendance should resume their duties and thereafter, I will meet with the second group of staffers. Make certain there is adequate coverage for all positions in each department. The day-to-day operation of Logan Courtyard should continue to run smoothly and not be disrupted. And please call Detective Ryan and tell him I will stop by the precinct in a couple of hours."

Brooklin asks Jerry to accompany her to the Banquet Room and to sit in the front as staffers begin to file in. Brooklin brings the meeting to order and informs her staff of the missing person bulletin just released by the news media and provides them with the information she has. Brooklin ends the meeting by stating, "If you have any information regarding Erica and/or her whereabouts, please contact the South End Precinct or Detective Ryan."

The staff begins to question her. "Are there any new details that the news reporters haven't mention?"

"None that I'm aware of. I know the police are following every lead and exploring every avenue," Brooklin comments.

"Have the police looked into a connection with Speed Dating? I heard there could be a possible connection."

"I have given you all the information I have. However, I'm sure the detectives are examining that theory. As I mentioned, they are following all leads. After I leave the staff meetings this morning, I plan to go to the South End Precinct to learn as much as possible about this case. I will have Walt inform staff members of any new developments. Regardless, I'm certain Detective Ryan will appreciate any information or theories you have that may help him in locating Erica. All right, let's return to work now."

After the second staff meeting, Brooklin leaves Logan Courtyard feeling a little unsteady. It seems everything is unraveling. Her mind is reeling. While driving, she finds herself continually glancing in her rear view mirror. "Brooklin, get a grip. You have to continue to move forward against these adversities. And you mustn't drive with your eyes peeled to the rear view mirror. You haven't received any new red envelopes in the last few days." She recalls again finding the red envelope on the floor of her SUV. "Don't I have enough to deal with? Who sent that card? Griffin, Taylor, Martina, Kim? Or was it Erica? Who?"

Brooklin's cell phone rings. It's her brother Jim.

"Hi, Brooklin. How are you?"

"I'm good, Jim. What about you?"

"Good. Good. Just wanted to let you know if the invitation still stands, Amber and I would love to join the family for dinner on Sunday."

"Great. I'm looking forward to seeing the two of you."

"What time is dinner?"

"Three pm. We normally have dinner and then watch a movie or two. The two of you can stay as long as you like."

"Okay, we will see you around 3 on Sunday."

"Take care, Jim, and thanks for calling."

"Thank you for the invite."

Brooklin thinks about her conversation with Jim. "There are good things happening and I need to grab every good moment I can."

Brooklin walks into the South End Precinct and asks for Detective Ryan. She notices press people waiting for some sort of statement or interview. The receptionist phones Detective Ryan telling him that Ms. Covington is here to see him. He tells the receptionist to send her back. Brooklin walks into the crowded squad room filled with desks. She doesn't see Detective Ryan but hears his voice. She follows the sound of his voice until she comes to a cubicle where he and another man are in an intense conversation in front of a display board. Erica's and Kim's photos are pinned to the board along with photos of Jack Griffin, Big Mel and Ray Marino. There are also a few names that she doesn't recognize pinned to the board.

Brooklin speaks to both men and asks Detective Ryan if she can talk to him for a few minutes.

"Certainly. Ms. Covington, this is Detective Baker. Detective Baker, this is Ms. Covington from Logan Courtyard."

"Ms. Covington, it is so nice to finally meet you. Logan Courtyard is one of the positive draws of our city and of our state. It is truly a place of grandeur – much like you."

Brooklin looks at him questioningly and murmurs, "Thank you. Thank you very much." Detective Baker looks a little awkward and walks away.

"Greg, I just wanted to come by to see if you have any new information regarding Erica's case. It's really becoming increasingly frustrating that I don't know where Erica is or if she is all right."

He leads her to a chair in the cubicle. "Brooklin, I know how much you care about Erica and that you are concerned about her. I want you to know that this case is personal for me. I will do everything in my power to find her."

"I know you will, Greg. But, I'm really getting nervous about Erica and her safety." She wonders if she should tell Greg about the red envelope and the black car in front of her house. She doesn't know if they have anything to do with Erica's disappearance or even Kim's disappearance.

He can see the look of stress in her face and eyes. "I can see that this is weighing on you." He looks at her reiterating, "I'm going to find Erica. You hear me? I will find her."

"I know. I believe you will find her. I know if anyone can find her, it will be you."

He squeezes her hand. "Now, I am surprised to see you here. However, it is a wonderful surprise." He gives her a warm smile. "Can I get you anything? Coffee?"

"No, I'm fine. I just held two staff meetings at the hotel in regards to the missing person alert for Erica. My staff have questions and I really don't have any answers."

"Yes, speaking of the hotel. I would like you to retrace Erica's steps for me for the last couple of weeks. Who came to see her at the hotel and any errands she may have made during work hours."

"Errands?"

"Yes like, did you send her to the Teen Center in the last couple of weeks."

"Sure, I can do that."

"We have received a number of tips and we follow-up and take each one seriously. However so far, the leads we have received have not led us to anything significant. Then again, we must take into account the missing person alert was only aired a few hours earlier."

"Erica didn't just vanish from the face of the earth. We have to find her. Did you find any type of evidence in her home? What about fingerprints?"

"You are getting pretty good at this detective work," he says smiling. "There were fingerprints. We were able to identify Erica's prints. We are still searching to learn whom the other prints belong to. However overall, we really didn't find anything that provided any new leads for us. We found something that tested positive for blood."

"Yes, we talked about that the other day."

"It was some dried blood that blended in with the wood grain so we didn't see it initially. It wasn't that much. It could have been planted."

"Greg, was it Erica's blood? Do you think it may have been a self-inflicted wound or staged? Maybe Erica set up an elaborate deception?"

"We don't know. The amount of blood was like from paper cuts. The blood found in Erica's apartment belonged to Erica. We have spoken to her family, neighbors, landlord and some of Logan Courtyard's staff. We checked for neighborhood surveillance cameras and found there weren't any in her neighborhood. And no one fitting Erica or Kim's description got on a plane, train, bus or rented a car."

"The truth is you have nothing," she says solemnly. "There have been no calls for ransom?"

"No, no ransom calls. Brooklin, just know I am going to track down and find Erica and Kim. Remember, Erica is now a suspect in Larry's hit and run case."

"Yes, how can I forget that?"

"And, I'm not sure that it's a coincidence that Erica and Kim are both missing at the same time."

Brooklin is shocked. "What? Greg, do you think there is a connection? I noticed Erica and Kim's photos on the corkboard when I walked in."

"As to any obvious connections between these two ladies?" He points at their pictures on the corkboard and shrugs. "There are none except there were strands of Kim's hair on a jacket left on a chair in Erica's kitchen."

"What? You just said you didn't find anything in Erica's apartment. You think Kim was at Erica's apartment?" Brooklin continues before Detective Ryan can answer. "How do you know the strands of hair were Kim's?"

"Okay, to answer your first question, we are not sure if the hair holds any meaning. It really is just evidence of contact between the two. We know that Erica knew Kim from the Teen Center. Therefore, the hair could have gotten on Erica's jacket when she came in contact with Kim at the Center. There is nothing else that links the two. And to answer your last question, Kim left her comb in her locker at the Teen Center and we were able to test the hair from the comb against the strands of hair at Erica's apartment."

"Were Kim's fingerprints found in Erica's apartment as well? I'm sure you tested the prints from Kim's comb, right?"

"Yes, Kim's prints were found in Erica's apartment. But, that only tells us that Kim has been in Erica's apartment. It doesn't tell us when."

"Greg, tell me what you are thinking. Is that why you asked me to trace Erica's steps? You want to know if Erica came in contact with Kim in the last few weeks?"

"Brooklin," Greg laughs, "I am fascinated with your theories and your trying to put together the puzzle pieces. But I just want to know whom Erica interacted with during the workday. I'm trying to retrace her steps."

"Greg, I know you. Come on, talk to me."

"Brooklin."

"Okay, I will just do some investigating on my own."

"Brooklin, please. This could become dangerous."

"Well, if you want me to stay out of it, Greg, you need to talk to me."

He gives in to her in a temporary defeat. Looking at her with some frustration, he says, "Yes, Brooklin. I *do* want to know if there was any contact between Erica and Kim in the last few weeks. Do you remember if the two may have had any communication?"

Brooklin reflects then answers, "None that I'm aware of. Erica didn't go to the Teen Center on my behalf in the last couple of months. However, Erica provided a monthly cooking class for the kids at the Center. Therefore, she is frequently there. You will probably need to talk to Colin, my brother Jim or Lorna, the Teen Center's receptionist."

"I plan to visit the Teen Center tomorrow."

"Greg, do you think Jack Griffin is in some way connected to Erica and Kim's disappearance?"

"Although Griffin may have motive to kidnap Kim, there's nothing to suggest he was involved with Erica's disappearance."

"But you are not ignoring a possible involvement?" Not waiting for Greg to respond, she declares, "That's the reason you have pictures of Jack Griffin, Big Mel and Ray Marino on the board."

"Brooklin, I am a detective. I look at everything and everyone."

"Greg, you have a picture of Ray Marino on the board. He's like Jack Griffin's hit man. Greg, you don't think Marino has hurt them, do you?"

Greg replies, "Brooklin, calm down. How do you know Ray Marino?"

"What?" she asks.

"Brooklin, how were you able to recognize Marino from his photo? And how could you possibly know that Ray Marino may have a connection to Jack Griffin? Whom have you been talking to?"

"I've done my homework when it comes to Jack Griffin."

"You are getting too involved in this investigation. And I'm not comfortable with it, Brooklin. Let me do my job and let's see where it leads. Maybe I should have turned that board to the wall when you walked in."

Brooklin is oblivious to his comments. "Greg, who are the other people listed on the board? What are their connections?"

"Brooklin," Greg says in a cautioning manner.

Brooklin glances at the board, "The ring is also on the board. What is that about?"

Detective Ryan's telephone buzzes. He looks at Brooklin and says, "Let me just answer this." He stands and turns the board away from her view. She walks over to the window, peers out and tries to listen to Greg's phone conversation. She notices that Greg is speaking in a low tone of voice. "What do you have? You received this information last night? And you have checked out this evidence? Well, I was hoping you could tell me. Do you have an address? The chip you mentioned that can be used as a tracker--is it on their person? Hopefully, we can trace their location as well. So, what do you need from us? Can you repeat that ... according to your Criminal Division, the circumstances of their disappearance was what? Listen, I'm in." He looks at Brooklin and says, "I'm working a case where there are two people missing and the trail maybe getting cold. We need answers fast. So, you can count me in on this one."

Brooklin turns from the window and looks at Greg questioningly.

"A Joint Task Force seems the appropriate next step. All right, sounds like a plan. I'll see you here tomorrow."

Brooklin walks over to Greg. "Was that call about Erica and Kim?"

"Brooklin, I'm not going to discuss my cases with you."

"Is it a human trafficking ring, Greg?"

"Brooklin, why would you say that?"

"Because you mentioned the tracker."

"Brooklin, I do not want you to visit me here at the station. In the future, I will come to Logan Courtyard. Apparently, you cannot control that imagination of yours. And I do not want any harm to come to you."

"What?"

"You are too emotionally involved in these two cases and you have a vivid imagination. "

"I do not have a vivid imagination. You have 'the ring' on the board. Then you mentioned the tracker during your telephone conversation."

Greg doesn't comment.

"Fine, Greg. I'll just hire a private investigator."

"You will do no such thing. Stay out of it, Brooklin."

"I will not. I want to know what happened to Erica. And if you will not give me any information, I will hire my own investigator."

He grabs a chair and sits in it backwards. He faces her with his legs spread wide and his muscular forearms resting on the back of the chair. He is aware that he is losing this battle. He sighs, "If I tell you about one of the leads I'm following, will you stay out of the investigation and allow me to do my job?"

"I will."

Greg shakes his head and tells Brooklin, "You can be extremely frustrating at times." He pauses for a moment. "All right, have a seat, I'm going to explain this as accurately as possible. First, I want you to know I'm going out on a limb here talking to you about this investigation."

Brooklin nods. "You know, I will not divulge anything you tell me."

"We are following up on an anonymous tip. I'm not sure if Erica or Kim is involved in this case. However if not, we can still help other victims who may have been lured or kidnapped. Along with the FBI, I am looking into a sex trafficking ring. It's high level corruption."

"High level? Are they public servants?"

147

"We are going inside to find out. That's why this investigation is critical. I can tell you that girls are being abducted and some are held for sex parties and other are micro-chipped and are sold to the highest bidder in other countries."

Brooklin is horrified, "And you think Erica and Kim maybe victims?"

"Brooklin, again, I don't know if Erica or Kim was taken. Erica may have just skipped town. Our plan is to follow the tips we have been given and the money trails and see where they lead. We are hoping they will lead us straight to the offenders.

"Yes, probably following the money is definitely the way to go. Anything I can do to help?"

"Yes, stay out of it. I don't need you to get mixed up in this and complicate things."

"Greg."

"No, Brooklin, I mean it. This is dangerous business. These girls can be shipped off at anytime. They can move these girls, go to a different location and start over. If I have to worry about you or if you get involved in *any* way, I can't work effectively and do what is needed to help retrieve these girls."

"Okay, I will stay out of it. Just please keep me posted and Greg," she hesitates, "please be careful."

"Hey, don't worry about me. I will be fine. Now tomorrow evening, I will not be available. You promise you are going to behave while I'm gone?"

"Yes, will you contact me Sunday morning?"

"I will contact you when I return. If I need to get word to you or you need to contact me, we will go through Detective Baker. You can trust him. All right?"

"All right, please be careful, Greg, and arrest those pathetic excuses for human beings."

Before Greg can answer, Detective Baker appears. "Ryan, can I talk to you for a minute?" Without waiting for a response, Detective Baker quickly walks away.

Brooklin tells Greg to give her a call when he returns and she walks toward the door. Detective Ryan watches Brooklin as she leaves the squad room. He quickly realizes he's in love with this woman. He walks over to his desk, makes a brief phone call and then goes to the break room and finds Baker getting a cup of coffee. "What's up, Baker?"

Baker turns to Detective Ryan, takes a sip of his coffee and says, "Ryan, man, I …" Baker stops in mid-sentence, looking a little sheepish and then continues, "Man, I can't believe what I said to Ms. Covington. She must think I'm pretty weird."

"Oh you mean, 'It's truly a place of grandeur – much like you,'" Detective Ryan laughs.

Baker shakes his head, "Why did I say that? She probably thinks I'm such a dope."

Detective Ryan continues laughing. Noticing Baker is looking a little embarrassed and uncomfortable, he adds, "She has that effect on the opposite sex. Don't worry about it, man."

"She is truly a woman of beauty and grace. And I just wanted to make a good impression."

Detective Ryan looks at him, "Hey, earth to Randy Baker." Baker pre-occupied with his thoughts returns his attention to Detective Ryan. "Why do you care about making a good impression on Ms. Covington?"

Baker realizes he has probably said too much. "Hey what can I say? I guess I can be a moron when I'm in the company of a beautiful woman."

"No, just a meathead," Ryan says.

"Can we just leave this subject?"

"Baker, I'm just joking. Listen, tomorrow night I'm going on this undercover assignment. There is a good chance I may need you to be the contact person between a few people and myself including Ms. Covington. Do you think you are going to be able to handle it?"

"Of course."

"Well, I want to be certain. You are looking a little lovesick."

"Lovesick? No, it's nothing like that. She just intrigues me." He notices that Ryan is amused. "But hey, I'm over it."

"Great, now why did you need to talk to me?"

"Oh, Sarg wants to see us in his office."

"Is it about the reporters in the lobby?"

"I'm not sure. He didn't tell me. He just told me, he wanted you and me to report to his office.

"Okay then, let's go," Ryan says.

Chapter 11

Walking to her SLK Mercedes convertible, Brooklin is grateful that she was able to find parking close to the precinct. She lets the rooftop down on her car and welcomes the sun and the gentle breeze. Brooklin sits for a few minutes thinking about her conversation with Greg. She considers that Greg said Erica and Kim might *not* be among the women kidnapped for this human trafficking. She must not allow herself to think the worst. Brooklin starts her car and pulls out into traffic. As the soft smooth jazz plays, she blocks out the noise in her head and observes the men and women hurrying along the streets. She drives slowly looking at the different buildings, thinking how she loves the metropolitan areas of Maryland, Washington and Virginia. As Brooklin drives on the Interstate, a call comes through her car's bluetooth phone system. It's her brother Jim.

"Hi, Brooklin."

"Jim? Wow, two calls in one day? I must really rate."

He laughs. "I forgot to mention something when I was talking to you earlier. Where are you?"

"I'm on the Interstate right now. Is everything okay?"

"Everything is fine. Are you coming to the Center later?"

"No, I probably will work a little late at the hotel today. However, I will be at the Center tomorrow morning. Is there a problem?"

"No, nothing urgent. I spoke to a few of the kids about Kim and I wanted to bring you up-to-date. I'll be at the Center tomorrow around 11 am, so we'll talk then."

"Great Jim, I will see you then." After the call ends, Brooklin mulls over the thought, "I should have asked Jim what information he has regarding Kim." She looks in her rearview mirror and notices a car coming up behind her very fast. She remembers her car accident a few days ago and quickly re-focuses her attention on driving. The car passes and she exits off the Interstate as a second call comes through her car's bluetooth. It's Greg.

"Brooklin, where are you?"

"Exiting off the Interstate, I should arrive at Logan Courtyard in about ten minutes."

"Brooklin, meet me at LaTorra."

"LaTorra. The resort?"

"Yes, the restaurant at the resort. Brooklin, it's just a few minutes from where you are now."

"Why, Greg? What's going on?"

"Just meet me there. I'll tell you when you get there."

"All right, I'll meet you there." Brooklin drives to LaTorra wondering if Greg has information about Erica or Kim. Brooklin enters the resort grounds, admiring the surroundings. She decides to take the scenic route and drives past the golf course entrance to the restaurant. She gives her key to the valet and walks into the restaurant.

Before she can give her name, the host says, "Good afternoon, Ms. Covington, please follow me."

She follows him to a private outside dining area draped with curtains.

A waiter hands her a glass of wine and announces, "Welcome, Ms. Covington to LaTorra's waterfront dining. Detective Ryan will be joining you shortly."

Brooklin smiles, "Thank you." She loves the atmosphere at the waterfront tables, casual and just perfect. Brooklin sits on one of the overstuffed pillows on the floor as the waiter places a bottle of wine on the low table in front of her. She soaks up the beautiful views as she awaits the detective's arrival.

"Well, hello gorgeous, you made it." Brooklin turns to see Greg.

"I certainly did. This is heavenly."

"I thought you would enjoy a quick get-a-way. You are too wound up. You need to relax a little."

"Greg, you don't have any information on Erica or Kim?"

"No and I don't want you to think about them for a couple of hours. Let's leave the rest of the world behind just for a short time."

"I'm surprised you have enough time with your pending cases."

"Let's just enjoy this time together, our waterfront get-a-way. Tomorrow, I'm going on this mission and you have so much on your plate. Let's just leave it all behind for a couple of hours."

Brooklin smiles and says, "You've got a deal." The waiter interrupts their conversation with a buffet of various Italian creations. "Greg, be careful, I can get use to this."

"I hope so," he says with that devilish smile. Then his look changes as his gaze becomes serious, "Brooklin, you can count on me. I will always put you first." He looks at her with so much passion in his eyes, "I want you more than I have ever wanted anyone. However," he pauses, "I'm going to give you the time you need."

She looks at him with tenderness and admiration. She has come to care for this man deeply, "Greg, you have been the constant and solid one in my life for a while now. And I want you to know that I do appreciate you. I just want to be ..."

He interrupts her. "Brooklin, you never have to defend yourself with me. Just trust me. I'm here for you."

She looks at him getting lost in his eyes, "Thank you, Greg. I hope you know, you mean a lot to me."

"Great, just what I wanted to hear. And may I say, you look absolutely beautiful today."

"Thank you and you look pretty nice yourself. What did you do? Go home and change?" He looked handsome in his casual shirt and khaki pants.

"No, I took a quick shower at the precinct and changed into clothes I had in my locker."

"Well, Detective Ryan, you do clean up well," she says admiringly.

"Here I thought you were only interested in me for my police work, now I know it was for my body." He gives her that sultry smile that only he can deliver. She feels a tingle that makes her shiver. She is so attracted to this man. "Come on. Let's eat some of this delicious food," he says, "before I change my mind and

show you just how much I really do care about you."
Brooklin stands up quickly and they walk to the buffet
table. Greg chuckles to himself.

"Just as I thought," Brooklin says. "This is
delicious."

"It is, isn't it?" He looks at her admiringly.
Brooklin quickly looks down, so as to not meet his gaze
again, and continues to eat.

"Greg, I love this resort. Someone mentioned
that the owner is thinking of selling it. What do you
think about my buying LaTorra?"

"I think it could be a great investment and it's
just minutes from Logan Courtyard. However as you
know, real estate can provide great success and
challenges. Therefore, I would gather as much
information as possible on LaTorra and learn why the
owner wants to sell."

They return their plates to the banquet table
and Greg refills their glasses. "You have been very
successful with Logan Courtyard. And I think once you
have acquired all the necessary data, you will make the
right decision. You are quite brilliant," he looks at her
with respect, "and you have a lot of knowledgeable
people working for you. That's a powerful and
noteworthy combination."

"Well, thank you, Greg. I happen to think you
are quite distinguished and brilliant yourself, Mr.
Detective." She smiles at him. "And I think I just may
have to look into this resort."

"It does seem perfect. Just like my time with you
today."

Greg opens the curtains to the view of the ocean and returns to sit close to Brooklin. They sit back on the pillows and look out onto the water, the cloudless skies--not having to say anything.

After some time Brooklin says, "Greg, this luncheon and the time with you is just wonderful."

"See, and you didn't even want to come. So, what does that tell you?"

"I don't know. What?"

"That I know exactly what you need so next time, don't ask questions, just do it."

"Not a chance. Not a chance." They both laugh. "Greg, this is so nice – so thoughtful. I am loving every minute. I've been so busy lately."

"I just wanted to, or I should say, I wanted you to relax, have a delicious lunch, a nice bottle of wine, a great view of the waterfront. I just wanted to return the smile to your face. I wanted to make you happy."

"Well, you did and I appreciate it. I've been putting in a lot of hours lately and this gave me time away from all of the drama."

Greg stands, takes her hand and gently helps her up. He leans down and kisses her hand tenderly and leads her to her car. "I will call you when I return."

"Yes, please," Brooklin says as she drives away thinking, "How am I ever going to concentrate on work after this glorious luncheon with Greg?"

Brooklin drives to her personal parking space near the front of the hotel. As she walks to the entrance, she takes time to once again admire the elegant exterior design, the luxurious landscaping and the magnificent central fountain. Entering the spacious lobby, she notices a large group of individuals near the suspended fireplace, the "Jewel of the Lobby," which dominates the rear of the reception area.

Brooklin walks to the front desk with a quick questioning glance at the large group. Jamie, one of the desk clerks, provides her with yesterday's minutes from departmental meetings. Jamie explains, "These guests are attending the 2017 Mayor Conference & Exhibition, which runs from today through Sunday. Two of the individuals who booked the conference have said they would love to meet you. Walt probably will talk to you about saying a quick hello to them. He met with them when they arrived earlier."

Brooklin recalls that the mayors' conference was scheduled here this weekend. She thanks Jamie for reminding her. Brooklin is mindful that there is too much confusion in her life these days. She cannot allow the pressure to mount and consume her thoughts. She must refocus her attention on her priorities. She has invested too much and come too far to fail now on any fronts.

Brooklin walks into the hotel restaurant and orders a cup of coffee. Jerry sees her and says, "Ms. Brooklin, I can bring the coffee to your office."

"Thanks, Jerry. But, I'm fine."

"Okay, Ms. Brooklin. Let me know if you need anything."

Brooklin takes her coffee and walks down to her office. As she reads yesterday's minutes from each of the hotel's departments, there is a knock on her door and Walt enters.

"Hi," Walt says as he sits in a chair in front of Brooklin's desk. "Did you learn any new information regarding Erica at the police station?"

Brooklin is quickly thrust back into the reality of all the chaos around her. "Just pretty much the same information."

"Brooklin, what do you think happened to Erica?"

"I'm not sure anything happened to Erica."

"You think she willingly disappeared?"

"Walt, I really don't know. I'm just hoping she is all right."

"I'm praying for the same. It was weird seeing her picture on television as a missing person."

"I know."

"Anyhow, Brooklin, I came in to tell you two gentlemen who booked the mayors' conference would like to meet you."

"Sure. I have a few minutes now."

"Great. They are actually sitting in the lobby."

"All right, I'll go and meet them in a couple of minutes."

"I'll leave their business cards with you. I wrote a few details about each individual on the back of their card, so you'll have some information before you meet them. Also, Jill is sending three young ladies to be interviewed for Karla's previous position. The first is waiting in the lobby now. Karla will provide a brief tour of the hotel before we interview the candidates in my office."

"Good, hopefully Karla's old position can be filled quickly. And thanks, Walt. I appreciate all that you do."

"You are welcome. I will have Karla schedule a final interview with you and the young lady that we feel is the best candidate."

"I look forward to meeting the young lady the two of you select." Brooklin says as she finishes her coffee.

"Brooklin, may I ask, how you are doing?"

"I'm fine."

"The other day, you were looking quite stressed. However today, you do have a little glow about you."

Brooklin blushes a little, "All right, I'm going to brush my teeth quickly, reapply my lipstick and I will meet the two gentlemen in the lobby." Brooklin enters her private bathroom thinking, "a glow ... I have a glow about me today?" She laughs to herself.

A few minutes later, Brooklin walks to the back of the lobby where the two men are talking with Mayor Jenkins. As she approaches, the two men stand to greet her. The mayor who had been standing in front of the men turns and gives Brooklin a hug whispering in her ear, "I'm so sorry to hear that Erica is missing. We will talk soon."

Brooklin nods saying, "Thank you." Mayor Jenkins introduces her to the two men. They talk for a few minutes about the conference before the mayor boasts about the hotel and asks if she would provide them with a grand tour. "Yes, certainly," she says.

"The conference is going well. Ms. Covington, I would like to express how much we are enjoying our stay at Logan Courtyard. Our suites, banquet and meeting rooms are so spacious and fully equipped with everything one could possibly need. Everything is above our expectations," exclaims David, the Mayor of Albany, New York.

"Thank you. We are glad you and your colleagues are enjoying your stay," replies Brooklin.

"Yes," says Sean, Mayor of Atlanta, Georgia, "We can't tell you how much we appreciate the exceptional services and all the breathtaking views. Just exquisite. And your staff is wonderful - always available."

"Thank you and we hope you will return again in the near future." Brooklin, the mayor and the two men talk as they cross the lobby to begin their tour of the hotel. The mayor continues to speak very highly of Logan Courtyard as Brooklin provides them with new information regarding the hotel and the planned addition. As they leave the lobby, Brooklin notices Karla walking with a young lady who looks very familiar. But Brooklin cannot recall who she is. "Where do I know her from?" she asks herself.

Chapter 12

Saturday morning, Brooklin is getting ready to go to the Teen Center when Laila enters Brooklin's bedroom. "Hi, Mom, I wanted to talk to you privately about something," Laila says as she walks over and gives her mother a hug. "And you know, one can never have any privacy at the Teen Center."

"Morning, Honey. Sure, what do you want to talk about?" Brooklin looks at Laila dressed in torn jeans and a t-shirt. Laila is 5'6 and looks like Brooklin's twin except for the tattoos and trendy style. Laila also definitely has her father's eyes and personality. "Would you like a cup of coffee? We can have coffee while we talk."

The two of them walk down to the kitchen. Brooklin is wearing a casual blouse, capris and sandals and is absolutely looking forward to just sitting and having a conversation with Laila. She realizes she will be late to the Teen Center. However, this is more important. It will be nice to spend some quality time with her daughter. She will focus on business at the Center when she arrives.

"So, Laila, how are you?"

"I'm okay. I just wanted to have some personal time to talk to you."

"Are you sure everything is okay?"

"Yes. Everything is fine. Oh, I brought us brunch."

Brooklin laughs. "Brunch? It's a little early but okay. This is beginning to be a special morning ... personal time and brunch with my daughter."

"Well, I'm not sure if you will think so after you see what I brought."

"Well, I'm sure I will enjoy whatever you brought." Brooklin calls the Teen Center to inform them she will be late while Laila looks in the refrigerator. "Hi, Lorna, I'll be a little late coming to the Center this morning."

"Okay, I'll let the front desk volunteer know. I'm not scheduled to work today. I just stopped in for a few minutes," Lorna says.

"Lorna, while I have you on the phone, do you have any information regarding Kim's whereabouts?"

"No, why do you ask?"

"Because I'm concerned about her disappearance. None of the kids have discussed Kim?"

"Not that I am aware of."

"Lorna, you don't have any thoughts of where Kim could be?"

"No. I'm sorry, I don't."

"Okay, thanks, Lorna. Have a good weekend."

"You too."

Brooklin places the phone on the island in the kitchen and sees the box of food. "The food smells delicious. What did you bring?"

"Burgers."

Brooklin looks at the box and eyes her daughter. Laila laughs, "Mom, at least I didn't bring you greasy fries."

"You brought burgers for breakfast, I mean brunch?"

"Yes, Mom. Don't be so stuffy. Live a little."

"Okay! I don't eat burgers often but I will have a burger today for brunch with my daughter," Brooklin adds casually.

Laila hands Brooklin a burger and takes a burger for herself. She takes a bite while eyeing her mother.

Brooklin unwraps the burger and says, "At least it's on a whole wheat bun."

Laila chuckles and continues to eat her burger. "I have no empathy for you, Mother. Just eat the burger."

Brooklin glares at Laila. Laila smiles pointing to the bottled water, "And Mom, see, I got us bottled water from the frig. No sugary drinks for us."

Brooklin is about to comment when the doorbell rings. "Excuse me, Laila." Levy's assistant is at the door. She reaches for the package with the red envelope and card from the table in the entryway and opens the door, "Hi, Abby. Here is the package for Levy." Abby takes the package, thanks Brooklin and tells her to have a good day.

Brooklin returns to the kitchen, "Before I forget, you and your brother should know, Levy ordered security personnel for the house."

"Security guards? Yes, I did notice the men when I arrived. However I forgot to ask you about them. Why do we need security for the house?"

"Well for safety reasons and certainly until we learn what happened to Erica."

"Oh okay. Is there any news on Erica?" Laila asks between bites of her burger.

"No, no news yet."

"What do you think happened, Mom? It's like Erica just disappeared."

Brooklin looks sad, "I don't know what happened, Laila. I just know it's very disturbing. And I pray for Erica's safe return."

"It's weird and a little creepy, don't you think, Mom? I think we probably should have security. You are here most of the time alone."

Brooklin finally takes a bite of her burger. "This burger is good. I didn't realize how much I have missed eating a good burger."

Laila smiles, "Sometimes a daughter knows just what her mother needs."

Brooklin smiles again. "Maybe. Listen, I don't want you to worry about me being at home alone. We have security now. However, I am thinking about some protection for you and Luke as well."

"No, Mom. We are fine. Don't even go there."

"Talk to Luke and let me know what the two of you decide."

"Okay, Mom but I'm sure Luke will agree … no security."

"Speaking of Luke, I only see him briefly at the hotel and Sunday's dinner. How is he doing?"

"Fine. Luke is great. He's going to school and he's dating again."

"Do you know who he is dating?"

"No, Mom, I do not. Maybe you should ask him."

"Okay, all right. What about you? What is going on with you?"

Laila beams, "I met this guy at school. He's really nice and I like him a lot."

"Do I know him?"

"No, I doubt it. He is originally from New York."

"New York? You are dating a guy from NYC?"

"No, Mom. He's from upstate New York. But let me reiterate, he is a nice guy and he's been living in this area about four years."

"Yes, I heard you say he was *nice* earlier."

"I met him last semester. He attends college part-time."

"How long have the two of you been dating?"

"We really have only been dating about a month. We met in the snack bar at school."

"About a month … why haven't you introduced him to me or your father?"

"Well, I am taking it slow. "

"Does this guy have a name?"

"His name is Randy."

"Now you said, he's been in the area about four years and he attends college part-time. How old is this young man?"

"He's 25 years old."

"Laila, he's five years older than you?"

"Yes, Mom. But, he's really a good person."

"What does this good person do other than attend college part-time?"

"He is taking classes in the human service field at school and that's the field he is currently employed in and that's all I'm going to say right now. As I said, I'm taking it slow. We are just dating."

"Okay, but what is troubling you? Is there a problem with Randy?"

"No, nothing about him, Mom. I met this girl, Tina, around the same time I met him. She is looking for work and I was wondering if you would be willing to hire her at Logan Courtyard?"

"Hire her at the hotel? Laila, with her being a college student, what about the Teen Center instead?" replies Brooklin.

"She's not a college student yet. Tina is looking for new employment so she can take some college classes. And Dad said no. There isn't money in the budget."

"You have talked to your father about this?"

"Yes."

"I don't think it's a good idea, Laila."

"Mom, why not? She's nice and she only needs part-time work."

"Part-time work? What is she doing now?"

"She's works part-time at a hair salon and is planning to start college in the fall."

"Laila, this is very sudden. What's her employment history? Laila, I don't hire individuals without a good employment background."

"You hired Ron."

Brooklin is flabbergasted. "Ron was hired on a temporary basis and Laila, I do not owe you any explanations regarding individuals I employ."

"Mom, can you just meet her and give her an interview?"

"Has she held a job other than her employment at the hair salon? If so, what type of work?"

"As I said, she is working minimal hours as a secretary at a hair salon now and she worked as a receptionist at the YMCA for almost two years."

"Well, it seems the Teen Center would be a better fit for this young lady."

"Mom, can I invite her to dinner on Sunday? The two of you can talk after dinner about possible employment?"

"Laila, how about next Sunday. Your Uncle Jim is bringing his new girlfriend Amber this Sunday. I would just like the family to be at the house to meet Uncle Jim's friend this week. However, I will commit to having dinner with your friend Tina and your guy friend Randy next Sunday. But, dinner only! I would like to meet these two people you have developed new friendships with. And if your friend impresses me, maybe I will tell Jill about her. Then she can apply at Jill's employment agency."

"Oh, Mom, give me some credit for being able to read people and develop good relationships."

"Sure, Honey," Brooklin says.

"Thanks, Mom. So, are you ready to go to the Teen Center?" Laila asks.

"Sure, I'll see you there." Brooklin sets the alarm and locks the door thinking, "Great ... another distraction. With all the current distractions, I hope this new boyfriend of Laila's will not create more conflict for the family."

Detective Ryan walks into the Teen Center and tells the receptionist he is there to see Colin Covington.

"Do you have an appointment?" Lorna asks thinking what does he want now. He was just here going through Kim's locker.

"No, but if you would let him know that Detective Ryan is here to see him."

"Please have a seat. I'll see if Colin is available," Lorna says reluctantly. Detective Ryan smiles at Lorna despite her cold tone. He watches as she disappears into the back office. Detective Ryan had questioned Lorna at Logan Courtyard when he was investigating Larry Carter's hit and run case. She wasn't very truthful or forthcoming with information until he threatened to take her downtown for obstruction of justice. Then, common sense prevailed. Apparently she hasn't forgotten their conversation.

Lorna returns after a few minutes and tells Detective Ryan that Colin will be with him shortly. Detective Ryan sits on the couch and looks around the reception area at the colorful flyers and posters. "Detective Ryan, Colin will see you now," Lorna announces after about five minutes. "His office is down the hall. The last office on the right." The detective follows Lorna's directions to Colin's office.

Colin is sitting in a large espresso leather chair at his desk. It is a sizeable office, conservatively decorated with neutral comfortable furniture. "Good morning, Mr. Covington."

"Detective Ryan, what can I do for you?" Colin and Detective Ryan had a heated exchange a couple of month's prior when Colin asked Detective Ryan to stay away from his wife. Detective Ryan explained to Colin that he had no intention of staying away from Brooklin. And furthermore, if he had been fortunate enough to have a beautiful and captivating woman like Brooklin, he would have never let her go. He ended the conversation by thanking Colin for providing him this opportunity because, otherwise, he wouldn't have even gotten a second glance from Brooklin.

"I'm investigating the disappearance of Erica Harris and want to ask you a few questions."

Colin doesn't comment. Detective Ryan sits in one of the chairs in front of Colin's desk. "Mr. Covington, when was the last time you saw Ms. Harris?"

"It's been a while, maybe a couple of months. As you are aware, she was my wife's secretary. Other than a few days ago, I had not been at Logan Courtyard in a couple of months."

"It's my understanding that she did some volunteer work here at the Center. Do you recall the last time she was here?"

"Still no word about Erica? So, you guys have no idea where Erica is?"

"As I stated, I am currently investigating Ms. Harris' disappearance. Now, do you recall the last time you saw her?"

"Well, I haven't seen Erica here in a few months. However, I can check with Lorna in regards to the last cooking class Erica provided to the teens. Erica informed Lorna she was going to take a few months off from volunteering. Lorna schedules the volunteers and the classes at the Center."

"Did Ms. Harris give a reason why she wouldn't be volunteering for a few months?"

"No, Lorna said she didn't give a reason. Just said she had to take care of some personal issues."

"Would you mind if I ask Lorna a few questions after I talk to you?"

"No, but you are going to have to call her to schedule a time. She left for the day."

"She already left for the day?"

"Yes."

"Will she be here on Monday?"

"Yes, she is scheduled to be here on Monday."

"Was Lorna scheduled to leave early today?"

"Lorna wasn't scheduled to work today at all. However, one of our staff members called in sick. Therefore, Lorna volunteered to come in for a few hours. However, she wasn't feeling well, so I told her to go home."

"Really? She just told you she wasn't feeling well a few minutes ago?" Detective Ryan is quiet for a moment thinking, "Why did Lorna leave so suddenly? Does she have information regarding Erica or Kim? She is pretty good at hiding information."

"Yes, she just told me she didn't feel well a few minutes ago. Now do you have any other questions for me, Detective Ryan?"

"Yes, a few more. How close were Lorna and Erica? Were they close friends?"

"Yes, I think they were good friends. Why do you ask?"

"How close were Lorna and Kim?"

"I don't know. Lorna is nice to all the kids in the program. What are you getting at? Are you trying to pin something on Lorna, Detective Ryan?"

"No, but you are always so protective of Lorna. Why is that, Mr. Covington?"

"That's it. Get out of my office. Get out of my office right now."

"Or what Mr. Covington? Why are you getting so angry? So agitated? How close are you and Lorna?"

"She is my receptionist. That's all."

"Really? That's all?"

"That's all. Now are you finished with these insane questions?"

"Insane questions? I don't think they are insane at all. But maybe we will have to revisit this line of questions at a later time. Now Mr. Covington, do you know if Ms. Harris was mentoring Kim or if they were friendly?"

"No, but that would be a question for Lorna or Brooklin's brother, Jim. They know more about the relationships between the staff and the kids who attend the Center."

"What about your daughter, Laila?"

"What about her?"

"Did she and Kim have a close relationship?"

"No. Laila works with the older kids. So she would not have been involved in any capacity with Kim or that age group."

"Is Jim here today?"

"Yes, but I rescheduled Jim's shift. He will not be here until late this afternoon."

"Okay, well I'll have to return to talk to both Lorna and Jim. And I may have a few more questions for you at that time." Colin glares at Detective Ryan. "Do you know who Kim's friends were here at the Center or anything about her personal life?"

"I know Kim's mother and that the two of them did not have a really good relationship. And I've heard Kim was not really friendly with the other kids."

"Can you tell me any more about Kim and her mother's relationship and why Kim was not very friendly with the other kids?"

"I don't think Kim was particularly friendly with kids her own age. However again, I think Lorna and Jim can provide you with the information you are trying to acquire. I only received this information in passing. Now, is there anything else, Detective?"

"Did you have a relationship with either Ms. Harris or Kim?"

"What? A relationship? What type of relationship would you be referring to?"

"Any type of relationship?"

"You are absolutely deranged."

"Why am I deranged? Because I'm doing my job? Can you please answer my question, Mr. Covington?"

"NO, I haven't cheated on my wife with Lorna, Erica and of course not with Kim, a fifteen-year-old. This line of questioning is absurd. I only spoke to Erica in passing here at the Center or at my *wife's* hotel. As for Kim, I only knew her as one of the kids attending our program. Again to answer your question, I did not have as 'you call it' a relationship with either or these females."

"Well thank you for your time, Mr. Covington." Detective Ryan stands to leave Colin's office.

"Before you leave, Detective Ryan, I'm going to ask you once again to respect that Brooklin is still my wife. I would appreciate if you would stop pursuing *my* wife and allow us the time to rebuild our life together."

"I'm not rehashing any of this with you. You are frustrated and I understand why. Any man would be lucky and overjoyed to be with Brooklin. You didn't appreciate her and she deserves to be appreciated." He turns to leave Colin's office.

"I know you want to be in a relationship with *my* wife. You have stated that you would like to have her for yourself. But it's not going to happen."

Detective Ryan turns around sharply to face Colin. "You are right, Colin. I do want to be the only man in Brooklin's life and I'm not going to apologize for that. Remember, Colin, you left Brooklin."

"I made a mistake. But I want to be clear about this. I'm not going to lose Brooklin to you or anyone."

"What are you saying, Colin? That sounds to me like a threat. You want to come at me? Fine, but I will make certain you don't hurt Brooklin again."

"Hurt her? Brooklin is my wife. I will keep her safe."

"But, Colin, who will keep her safe from you?"

"Keep her safe from me? That's ridiculous. Listen, I'm asking you nicely - don't try to move in on my wife. I'm very serious about this or one day you just might find yourself reassigned to foot patrol."

Detective Ryan laughs. "I just lost what little respect I had for you. Brooklin deserves way better than you. Did you really think you would leave her and she would be alone? You pulled the rug from under her and threw away something that you can't replace. Believe me, if I have the opportunity to be with her, I will not make the same mistake you made."

"Well, you will *never* have that opportunity. Brooklin and I were happily married and we will be again."

"Yes, happy as long as it is on your terms. And, Colin, I would be careful about using the word *never*. Never is a long time. You see, I believe in Brooklin and her abilities. You don't want her to succeed. You want to hold her back. You want her to settle and just focus her life on you. I intend to give her the *time* and the space to make her own decisions and support her in her endeavors."

"Don't tell me what I want. You don't know what I want. However, *you*, detective, have been warned," Colin says with malice. "And as for Brooklin, we will work through this."

"Maybe. But maybe you have lost her and it doesn't matter how hard you try to hold on to her, it could just be too late. How many times does she have to reject you before you realize it's over between the two of you?"

"It's not over. It will never be over between Brooklin and me," Colin raises his voice.

"Colin, Brooklin may have just moved on. Sometimes, you have to lose something good to realize what you had. And the ultimate word here is 'had.' However, give it your best shot. Because I know I will and that is not a threat or warning. It's a fact. Goodbye, Colin, I'm done talking about this with you." Detective Ryan walks out of Colin's office and the Teen Center.

Brooklin and Laila arrive at the Teen Center and enter the building minutes after Detective Ryan exits. Brooklin walks to her office and begins checking her messages. She removes her laptop and places it on her desk when she notices Colin standing in the doorway. "Morning, Colin. How are you?"

"You just missed your boyfriend. Or did you talk to him in the parking lot?"

Brooklin looks confused. "Colin, what are you talking about? What boyfriend?"

"Detective Ryan was here asking questions about Erica and Kim."

"I do not have a boyfriend, Colin, and I do not wish to argue with you. So, if you will excuse me, I would like to get some work done before I meet Jill."

"Sure by all means, get some work done." Colin turns to leave Brooklin's office mumbling, "You perfect and unblemished people who have never made any mistakes." He turns back to Brooklin, "Maybe, I haven't made all the right choices but remember you are still *my* wife." He raises his voice and points to himself, "*my* wife. Remember, we took vows." Colin walks out of Brooklin's office and out of the Teen Center.

Brooklin stares at Colin and then at the door thinking, "Wow, what was that? And he used the word, 'mistakes' again. Colin, what are you not telling me? What other mistakes have you made that I'm not aware of?" Brooklin thinks for a minute, "Does it really matter at this point? We are separated. But what does concern me is that Colin and I cannot co-exist in the same area anymore. We cannot have an entirely civil conversation." Brooklin shakes her head in disbelief. "It's becoming increasingly sad how Colin has changed but not for the better as he previously stated. I am a little uncertain about what he expects of me regarding our separation. Does he not recollect that he left me? I can no longer ignore all of this and must address Colin's tone with me. I'll ask him to stay after dinner tomorrow so we can talk." Brooklin refocuses her attention remembering she has to meet Jill for house hunting. Brooklin returns phone calls and then begins working on a new grant application for the Center.

Brooklin works until about 1:20pm and then closes her computer. As she begins to pack her bag, her cell phone rings. She looks at the incoming call, "Hi, Jill."

"Hi, Brooklin. I made an appointment for you and me at Allure. Meet you there in thirty minutes."

"Allure? Okay, I'll meet you there! I'll get my hair trimmed." Brooklin finishes packing her bag and asks the volunteer at Lorna's desk to tell her brother Jim when he arrives that she will see him tomorrow. She stops in the gym to say good-bye to Laila and then walks out of the building to her car. She is still a little distressed by the conversation with Colin and his departure. Hopefully, they can agree tomorrow to start fresh and leave the past in the past. Maybe they can finally move forward and be civil with one another. "These constant disagreements are emotionally exhausting and not good for either of us."

Brooklin parks her car and enters Allure's spa and hair salon. Beth, the receptionist, greets Brooklin and offers her a drink from the complimentary beverage bar. Beth tells her that Jill and her stylist are expecting her. Beth escorts Brooklin to Leah's station making conversation along the way. She informs Brooklin that Allure has a new owner. They haven't met her but know she is an older woman. Brooklin smiles as she sees Jill. Each station is private and has floor-to-ceiling mirrors, sleek surfaces and bright red leather styling chairs. Called by its patrons the 'glam salon,' Allure is one of the most upscale beauty salons in the area.

After about an hour and a half, Brooklin and Jill leave the salon. "Brooklin, leave your car here and ride with me. We'll return for your car after we look at the two houses."

"Okay, that's fine. I really don't feel like driving anyway." Brooklin is still a little nervous about her new haircut. Her stylist Leah and Jill had talked Brooklin into getting a blunt bob haircut. Leah explained the haircut is classy but with a touch of attitude. It can be worn sophisticated and sleek or in a wavy bob.

Jill notices Brooklin's apprehension, "Brooklin, stop looking uneasy and own it. Your hair looks great.

You didn't go too short so you have plenty of gorgeous movement. Own it girl, you champion that look."

"Why is it, Jill, that I have a haircut and you only got your ends clipped?"

Jill laughs. "I already have short hair. Besides, you needed a change to go along with your newfound evolution. Now let's go house hunting."

Jill drives out of the parking lot and into traffic. Brooklin relaxes as Jill begins to talk. "There is something psychological about cutting your hair. It's empowering. Makes you feel your best and most powerful self."

Brooklin considers Jill's words and begins to become less tense. She has to admit that she does like the hairstyle. It's just that her hair is cut shorter than she normally wears it. They have only traveled a few miles when they stop at a traffic light. Brooklin looks across the street and notices Taylor walking from her car to meet a man. She kisses him briefly on the lips. Totally shocked, Brooklin shudders, "Oh my God, it's Luke. Taylor kissed Luke on the lips." Brooklin watches as they walk hand-in-hand down the sidewalk. Stunned, she turns to watch them enter a restaurant as Jill drives past. Brooklin says nothing to Jill. She sits back in her seat thinking, "So, *that* is who Luke is dating! Luke, how could you be so gullible? Now, I will definitely need to decide how best to handle this situation."

Chapter 13

Brooklin and Jill are seated and order dinner at their favorite meeting spot, Talb. "So Brooklin, are you feeling better about your haircut?"

"I am," Brooklin smiles, "I have to admit, I really like it. Sometimes, change is good."

"Yes, I noticed the men looking at you when we walked into Talb and did you notice how my real estate agent was flirting with you?"

"Oh, Jill, stop."

"All work and no play makes Brooklin a dull girl. Outside Logan Courtyard walls, there are a lot of men who would love to spend time with you. You need a break from the hotel. You need to start dating."

Brooklin has a flashback moment when Erica discussed dating with her. She even suggested that Brooklin come with her to speed dating. Of course, Brooklin declined. Her attention returns to the conversation with Jill, "I have a date with my couch, television and a rough collie."

"Brooklin, please. Are you really not ready to start dating? Aren't you getting lonely for a man's attention?"

"Nope and I'm going to keep it that way for a while. Don't worry about me. I'm okay."

"Do you think you may need to talk to a therapist to help you get through this separation from Colin?"

"Nope, I have Blake, my official therapy puppy."

179

"I'm serious, Brooklin. You seem to always be on edge lately. I know there is a lot of turmoil in your life right now but personal conflicts are also primary causes of anxiety." The waitress interrupts their conversation as she delivers their dinner.

"Jill, I'm fine really."

Jill studies the plate in front of her. "I love the food here. This chicken dish looks and smells delicious."

Brooklin smiles and says, "It does." As they eat, they discuss the two houses they saw today. "I liked both houses we saw today."

"I liked them too but, neither one is 'the house,'" Jill says.

"I understand. We'll just keep looking. Your house is definitely out there."

Changing the subject, Jill asks, "You haven't received any more red envelopes or cards, have you?"

"No, I haven't. Levy said there were no fingerprints except mine on the envelope and card. Whoever this culprit is, he or she knows exactly what they are doing. Levy's man is now concentrating on having a handwriting specialist look at both the card and the envelope to try to analyze if the handwriting belongs to a man or a woman. Levy said he will contact me with the outcome."

"Well, this entire situation is a little scary, but Levy's detectives will solve the mystery. Have you told Colin or the kids?"

"No and I don't want them to know."

"I hear you. Levy and I will not say anything. I'm just glad you have security at home and the hotel."

They eat in silence for a few minutes. "So, how is Ron doing at the boot camp? Have you heard anymore about his progress?"

Brooklin stops eating and looks at Jill, "I think being removed from the pressure of the outside world is really helping Ron. Surprisingly, he likes his counselor and is open to treatment. And his counselor says he is doing well. Therefore, I'm happy he is getting the help he needs."

"That's good to hear. Any news about Erica's whereabouts?"

"No, and it's very frustrating. Detective Ryan and, of course, work are helping me through this."

"The detective and not Colin? So Brooklin, have you made any decisions? Are you going to give up on you and Colin?"

"Colin gave up on our marriage when he walked out. I deserve to be with a man I can count on."

"You are right. So maybe, you *are* dating now. Are you dating Detective Ryan, Brooklin?"

"No, Jill. I'm not dating anyone. I'm still really confused. Therefore, dating just isn't a possibility for me now."

"Brooklin, are you in love with Colin and Detective Ryan?"

"I don't know, Jill. Can you be in love with two people at the same time? I have feelings for both men."

"Yes, I think you can love two people. You love different things about each one. However Brooklin, you have to make a decision." Brooklin begins playing with her food, moving the food around in her plate. "Brooklin, are you stringing them both along?"

"No. I wouldn't do that."

"Unconsciously?"

"Jill, the last thing I want to do is hurt Colin or Greg. It's complicated."

"Complicated?" Jill asks. "Complicated for you, but think how they must feel."

"I know I'm not being fair," responds Brooklin. "But when you love someone it's hard for the heart to let go. I don't know if I'm still in love with Colin or love Colin because of the years we spent together and, of course, because we have a family together."

"It sounds like you might be thinking of letting Colin go?"

Brooklin stares straight ahead, "You go into marriage with all these hopes and dreams. Build a family, then life can take a different path. It all can go very wrong. You start off so bright, in love and preparing for a future. Then things just go down hill. Life pulls the rug from beneath you." Brooklin pauses.

Jill is silent. She just listens to Brooklin, letting her get it all out.

Brooklin continues, "For so long, my identity was wrapped into being a mother and a wife. I don't remember who I was *before* Colin. I don't know if I ever really knew myself. I allowed parts of myself and my needs to be neglected. I'm not complaining, I loved my family and I gave them my all. Then I inherited the hotel. I felt free. My children were adults and had moved out of the house. Colin was retired. It was finally time for me." Jill listens to the tone and the expressions in Brooklin's voice. "I had entered a totally new space in my life, a transitioning and it required things of me that I didn't know I had. Now I can't turn back. I can't return to the old Brooklin and that's what Colin wants. I just can't do it."

"Well, I think you have to make a decision, Brooklin. You cannot have them both."

"I'm not trying to. I'm just living my life and fate keeps bringing the two of them into my path."

"Fate? It's not fate. Colin will not let go. What about you, Brooklin? Are you really letting Colin know that it's truly over?"

"Yes, I've told him many times. However, Jill you're right. Colin will not let go. I've always made excuses for him. I don't know anymore. He's my husband, the father of my children. Should I give up on the life we built together? How will it affect Laila and Luke?"

"I think you need to focus on what *you* want, not on what Laila and Luke want. Think about what a life without Colin looks like for you. Is that a life you can live with?" Brooklin doesn't answer. She just stares at her plate. Her thoughts center on how a divorce would affect her children.

"What about that sexy Detective Ryan? Are you allowing him to think he has a chance of being the man in your life? How do you feel about a life without Detective Ryan?" Jill asks.

"A life without Detective Ryan?" Brooklin shakes her head. She doesn't want to even think about a life without him. However, she questions whether this indeed must become her reality in order to keep her family together.

Luke and Taylor are sitting at the bar with their drinks. "Taylor, are you feeling better?"

"Yes, I'm fine. I've just been feeling a little tired," she says as she takes Luke's hand. "Come, let's move to a table in the back." Luke follows Taylor to a small, candlelit table in the rear of the restaurant. "Now this is better. I want to have a private conversation with you."

Luke looks at her questioningly, "Okay, what's up?"

"What do you say, we work together and take over Logan Courtyard?"

"Taylor, please don't start this again. Is this what you wanted to have a private conversation about?"

"Yes. I know you don't want to, but we must talk about this. Your overbearing mother is no match for the two of us. Luke, you will never get the respect you need or deserve."

"Taylor, I'm fine. I get plenty of respect."

"We should work together and take what is rightfully ours."

"Rightfully ours?"

"Yes, ours. I have worked for Logan Courtyard for five years. Your grandmother practically left me in charge of the hotel. Come on, Luke, let's come up with a plan of attack."

"Taylor, you really want to do this?"

"Yes, no matter what it takes. This is the time to breakaway from your mother, from your family."

Luke raises his voice, "Are you just straight up crazy?"

"I know it sounds irrational. But what if I had a plan where you can take over Logan Courtyard?"

Luke questions, "A plan? How long have you been thinking about this?"

"Luke, this is our chance, a chance to make things right. We can make this work."

"No, Taylor, and stop talking like this."

"Come on, Luke, let's dethrone her. Let's agree. I'll let you know when I have enough information to move forward."

"Information? No, Taylor. My mother and I are getting along. We've come to a new understanding. And I would never as you said, *dethrone* my mother."

"Luke, we can have the power and control. Let's take it. We can work together and force her out." Taylor has a look of hatred in her eyes. "Your mother owes me. I ran Logan Courtyard before her, when your grandmother was alive. And did she appreciate it? No, she fired me. She needs to step down. If she doesn't agree to step down, we'll just take control of the hotel."

"And how would we do that, Taylor?"

"We could expose your family's business. Or we could blackmail her into stepping down by threatening to expose what we know. Come on, Luke, we can do this."

Luke looks at Taylor questioningly, "Taylor, is this why you wanted us to give our relationship a second chance?"

Taylor grabs Luke's hands, "No, Luke, of course not. I love you."

"Have you exposed any information or my family's business dealings to anyone?"

"No, Luke. I can't believe you would think that of me."

"What family business dealings were you talking about earlier?"

"I just want to be back in the game, Luke. That's all. Don't you want us to work together again?" Taylor rubs his leg under the table.

"Your ego is clouding your judgment. My mother made Logan Courtyard into the Five Star Hotel it is today," Luke insists.

"Fine, Luke, I see this is not the time to have this conversation. We can discuss it another time." She sees that he's annoyed with her and her tone quickly changes. "I'm sorry. I didn't mean to upset you. I shouldn't have pressured you. I apologize if I upset you. Now, let's not allow this to ruin our evening. I have something special planned for you when we get home."

Brooklin and Jill laugh as they return to the salon to pick up Brooklin's car. Jill exits the car with Brooklin. "Okay, Brooklin, I'll call you. I just need to run in to purchase some spa products for Levy's massage tonight." She winks at Brooklin.

Brooklin smiles, "Okay, have fun tonight."

"I definitely will try," Jill says.

Brooklin walks to her car. As she gets closer, she sees a red envelope on the car's windshield. "Jill, Jill, come here." Brooklin's voice is a little elevated but composed.

Jill comes to her friend's side quickly hearing the wariness in her tone. They both stare at the red envelope and then at each other. "Well, Jill, I guess I spoke too soon when you asked me if I had received another red envelope." They both turn suspiciously and look across and down the street and then toward the brick building that houses Allure. Seeing no one or nothing suspicious, Brooklin walks closer and reaches for the envelope, while thinking, "No, not another special delivery."

"Wait, Brooklin, maybe you shouldn't touch it."

"Why not? My name is written on the front of the envelope." Brooklin hesitates and then grabs the envelope and opens it. A key falls out of the card onto the ground. They look down at the key curiously. Brooklin reaches down, picks up the key and examines it. The key has what looks like a red heart on the front and back. The card reads: "This key will *unlock* the Scarlet secret. The time is drawing near for the secret to be revealed. Nice haircut! *Tay*"

"Give me the card, Brooklin. I will give it to Levy tonight. I don't know who is playing these games. Are you okay?"

"Sure, I'm just living in an absolute nightmare."

"You're strong, you can survive what comes your way."

"Well, I guess I don't have a choice."

"Brooklin, I'm so sorry this is happening. I don't know. I guess in life we can expect the unexpected. But these cards are downright creepy. I hope this is some type of joke or prank and no harm will come to you." Jill hugs Brooklin.

"I know. I'm sure I will be fine." Brooklin places the card and key back into the envelope.

"It's just that so much is happening with you right now. I just wish you could catch a break. You are a wonderful person and you deserve more positivity in your life."

"Jill, it seems that for me, things never slow down. I'm always dodging whatever the universe throws at me. Hopefully, I'll come through this relatively unscathed."

"Well, we cannot ignore these cards." Jill takes the red envelope from Brooklin's hand, "I will give the card, envelope and key to Levy to pass along to his investigators. These investigators need to find who is doing this ASAP."

Brooklin hugs Jill. "I'll be fine. Now go in and get your products and have a good night." She looks at the envelope in Jill's hand. "Now your prints are on the envelope too."

"I'm going to follow you home to make certain all is well."

"No, Jill, go home. I'll be fine."

"I know you will. No arguments. I'm going to follow you home."

Jill walks in the direction of her car. "Jill, what about your massage products?"

"They can wait."

Knowing that Jill will follow her home regardless of what she says, Brooklin exclaims, "I'll wait here for you. Go get your products. I don't want Levy to be angry with me because I spoiled the night."

Jill laughs. "Never, we both love you too much. Now don't leave, I'll be right back."

"Okay," Brooklin says as she walks over and takes the envelope from Jill's hand. "I just want to take another look while you're in Allure." Brooklin gets in her car holding the card and key, scrutinizing both. "Another red envelope," she says in a low tone. "And again, there is no return address, just my name." She inspects the key slowly turning it from front to back, "Are the red hearts some type of clue? What do they symbolize?" She wonders who placed this on her car and what is the intention behind this harassment. She knows she's being watched, otherwise how would they know about her haircut. She returns the card and key to the envelope and lays her head on the headrest to wait for Jill. She is glad to have friends like Jill and Levy.

Several minutes later, Jill knocks on the car window startling Brooklin. She looks in Jill's hand and asks, "Where is your red bag filled with massage products?"

"As I was about to purchase them the receptionist told me that Levy was here earlier and left with a bag full of their products. So, I guess we were thinking along the same lines."

"Oh wow, sounds like Levy has a hot night planned."

"Yes, I guess so. Listen, Brooklin, are you okay?"

"I'm fine. It's just something I have to deal with."

"Well, I'm glad you have security at your house. All right, give me the envelope and let's go. I'll follow you home."

Brooklin arrives home thinking how glad she will be to just stretch out on the couch and watch television with Blake. Then she realizes, Colin has Blake tonight. Well, she will just have to wait until tomorrow for a night of television with Blake. He is such a big part of the family now. The entire family loves him. After a few moments, Brooklin's thoughts drift back to the envelope left on her car. "Okay, it might just be time to have the police investigate this matter. However," she says becoming indecisive, "I do have to question getting the police involved at this point." She remembers her unnerving conversation with Walt about the bodyguard. "Maybe, I should have Walt arrange a meeting with Brent." She's contemplates, "I'm not certain I want the police involved until I know more about this secret. Yes, I think for now, Brent is my best choice." She calls Walt and tells him she would like to meet with this Brent.

Sunday Brooklin walks into her kitchen wearing a housedress with no undergarments. She decided to just let her body breathe today. Brooklin looks at the wall clock and realizes it's almost noon. She hasn't heard from Greg and wonders what has transpired. Has he found Erica or Kim? She knows she must be patient. He will contact her as soon as he is able. She transfers her thoughts to preparing dinner. Sunday dinners have become customary for their family. She is glad the tradition has continued. It's their day to come together, laugh, talk and discuss their week. Today, Brooklin is looking forward to her brother Jim and his girlfriend Amber joining them.

Laila and Luke enter the kitchen. They are their usual joyful selves, laughing and giving each other a hard time. She is pleased they get along so well.

"Mom, you cut your hair," Laila announces.

Luke turns to look at his mother. "Mom, you cut your beautiful hair?"

"I love it, Mom," Laila says. "It's very chic and stylish. You're looking a little sexy there, Mom. Dad better keep an eye on you."

Luke looks at his mother again. "It's nice. But I liked your hair better long."

"Well, I'm getting use to it. It's a change. However, my hair does grow fast, so I may be looking like my old self soon."

"Or mother, you just may decide to keep this style for awhile."

Brooklin smiles, "Maybe."

"And, you got highlights! Well, all right! Look at Mom becoming fashionable," Laila says laughing.

Brooklin turns to Luke. "So, Luke, how are you?" Brooklin asks thinking of Luke and Taylor holding hands walking into the restaurant yesterday.

"I'm fine. Can't complain."

"So when are we going to meet this girl you are dating?"

Luke looks awkwardly, "Soon, Mom, soon."

"Well, Laila is bringing her friend Randy for dinner next week. Why don't you bring your friend as well?"

"Mom, I'm not ready to introduce her to the family yet. I want to be certain about us as a couple first."

"What's the hesitation, Luke?"

"Mom, can we please not talk about this? I'll introduce her if we begin to get serious."

"Okay, well we would like to meet the young lady you have been spending so much time with," Brooklin says glancing at him again.

The door opens and Blake comes running in as Colin walks in behind him.

Everyone greets Colin and then turns their attention to Blake. "I see the security is stationed outside," Colin comments.

"Yes, I'm thankful they are there."

"Any news about Erica?"

"No, not yet."

"Well hopefully, she will show up soon."

Brooklin wonders about the wording of Colin's comment. "Hopefully, she will show up soon rather than she will be found soon. Maybe, he is right," she thinks. Brooklin envisions Erica walking into her office and explaining everything. Brooklin abruptly stands up straight and returns to cooking while Laila and Luke concentrate on Blake.

"Mom, Blake is getting so big. He's growing so fast," Laila says as she reaches down and pets Blake, who rolls over for more attention. "He's growing up but he still is so lovable. Look at those adorable eyes."

Brooklin looks down at Laila and Blake and smiles, "Yes, he is growing quickly."

Colin walks over to Brooklin, "Can I help with anything?"

"Sure, wash your hands and I'll put you to work."

He whispers in her ear, "I like your haircut. It's rather sexy. And you have color in your hair. Hmm, yes, very sexy."

Brooklin doesn't turn to look at him, she just simply says, "Thank you, Colin."

A few minutes later, Colin is putting the ingredients together for a fresh vegetable salad when Brooklin walks over and says, "I would like to have a private conversation with you. Can you stay after everyone leaves?"

Colin is surprised, "Yes, I can stay the night if you would allow me to."

Brooklin moves away from him, "A few minutes after dinner will suffice." Colin looks at her and grins.

"Well hello, family," Jim says as he enters the kitchen door with Amber. Brooklin and the family focus their full attention on Jim and Amber. Jim introduces Amber and pauses for a moment when he gets to Brooklin and tells her how very nice her haircut is. "Very appealing," Jim adds.

Amber is about 5'7 and very well spoken. Brooklin is genuinely surprised how well she interacts with the family. It turns out to be a great day, full of laughter, good food and conversation. This Sunday Laila has chosen a movie. And, of course, she chooses the scariest movie on Netflix and all watch the movie except Blake. He covers his face with one of his paws and then runs out of the room. Everyone laughs and then refocuses on the movie.

After the movie, Amber and Brooklin are putting dishes away in the kitchen when Jim walks in.

"Brooklin, I wanted to tell you what I learned about Kim."

Brooklin asks immediately, "Did you learn her whereabouts?"

"No, I didn't. None of the kids heard from Kim until two days ago. Brenda got a call from Kim. She wouldn't tell Brenda where she was or where she's been. Brenda said it was a different cell phone number."

"It probably was a burner phone." Brooklin is quiet for a moment. "I wonder where she got the phone."

"I don't know. Brenda said she didn't recognize the number. She said Kim was asking for money."

"She was asking for money?"

"Yes. Brenda said she told Kim she only had a couple of dollars. Apparently Kim told her that wasn't enough." Jim has Brooklin's undivided attention. "Brenda said Kim just said, that's okay and hung up."

"That's all? She couldn't get any other information from her?"

"No, Brenda said it was a short conversation. Very weird."

"Okay, thanks Jim. I will give this information to Detective Ryan. He probably will want Kim's new telephone number from Brenda. I wonder if she is all right."

"That's all I know, sis. I'm sure Kim will be fine. She is very self-sufficient."

"Thanks for the information, Jim, and thanks to you and Amber for coming to dinner. We enjoyed meeting and getting to know you, Amber," Brooklin says.

"Thank you, Brooklin. Everything was lovely. You have a beautiful home and family," Amber replies.

"Thank you, Amber. We hope to see you again soon." Jim and Amber say their goodbyes to the family and leave.

Laila walks into the kitchen a few minutes later, "Mom, I'll stay and help you clean the kitchen."

"That's okay, honey, there's not that much left to do. Amber was gracious enough to help."

"Okay, well dinner was wonderful. I enjoyed having Uncle Jim and Amber here. Amber is pretty cool."

"I agree. It was great having them here. Hopefully, they'll join us more often." Luke and Colin walk into the kitchen.

"Mom, it's about 8pm, so Luke, Blake and I are going home."

"Oh, it's your night with Blake?"

"Yes, tonight is our night with Blake." They hug their mother and father as they leave.

"Brooklin, everything was great. I really enjoyed the evening. Can I pour you a glass of wine?" Colin asks.

"Sure, Colin," Brooklin says as she begins to put the last of the food in the refrigerator. She quickly organizes the kitchen and joins Colin in the family room. Brooklin sits on the sectional; Colin sits near her and gives her the glass of wine. "Colin, we need to discuss Luke."

"What about Luke?"

"He is seeing Taylor again."

"What do you mean he is seeing Taylor? Are they dating?"

"I think so. I was in the car with Jill and saw Taylor walk up to Luke and kiss him."

"What? Luke said he would never get back with Taylor after the way she treated you and Luke as well."

"Apparently, she has her hooks in him again. After the kiss, I saw them walk hand-in-hand into a restaurant."

"Really? Well, I think it's time to have a conversation with Luke."

"I agree. I just didn't want to have that discussion with him tonight while Jim and Amber were here."

"My schedule is pretty hectic tomorrow. Let's invite him here Tuesday evening after his class."

"All right, hopefully this conversation will go well." Brooklin takes a few sips of wine, "Colin, I want to change the subject and talk about us."

"Us? What about us?" he asks apprehensively.

"Colin, I'm really tired of every conversation with you turning into an argument. I feel enough time has passed," she hesitates a moment and takes a few sips of wine. "I just feel that at this point, we should be able to have civil conversations. This bickering concerns me."

"I know, Brooklin. It's me. I'm sorry. But I'm suffering here. I love you." He moves closer to her on the couch. "What am I supposed to do? Just suffer in silence? Not tell you how I feel? Not try to bring my family back together? You tell me, Brooklin, what am I supposed to do? What can I do?"

Brooklin places her glass of wine on the coffee table, "Colin, you walked out on me."

"I know I did. It was a selfish mistake. I have apologized over and over again. I wish I could turn back the clock. If I could, I would stay here with you and support you. But I can't change the past. Listen, Brooklin, I'm really opening up myself to you here. I don't know what to do without you. Give me the opportunity to prove I have changed. We had a good life – a really good life. Brooklin, I don't want to lose you," he whispers."

"Colin, please." Brooklin stands and moves away. He walks behind her.

"Listen, Brooklin, I will admit it. I'm an idiot. I made a mistake. I won't make it again. Can you find it in your heart to forgive me? We are a family and I'm sorry I lost sight of it. I'm here now 100 percent for you and the family.   I'm asking you once again to forgive me. Brooklin, please don't let my mistake cost us our marriage. "

"Colin, honestly all I want to do right now is to get into bed and relax. That's it."

"That's it?" He grabs her arm, turns her to him and kisses her deeply. Brooklin squirms for a moment and then responds to his kiss. He holds her for a minute after the kiss and looks deeply into her eyes. "You haven't forgotten how good we are together. Have you?"

Surprised at her response to Colin, Brooklin pulls away and quickly walks back to the couch. "Colin, it's time for you to leave now."

"Brooklin, I miss you. Don't you miss me?" He asks her softly. "We can work through this. We can have a new start. Brooklin, I will do everything I can to earn your trust back. We had an incredible life. Just give me one more chance." He walks over to the couch and passionately kisses her again. He breathes in and takes in the scent of her skin and hair. Her pulse is elevated and she can feel the sensation of her blood racing through her body. He presses his body tightly against her.

"Colin, please, wait." He kisses her behind her ear, her neck and then his lips meet hers once again.

"You want me to wait?" He asks again, "Tell me if you want me to wait." Her heart is pounding as he lays her down on the couch. He caresses her breasts and they begin to swell underneath his touch as he caresses and kisses them over and over again. She looks up at him and wraps her arms around him tightly. She is drowning in sensation now and too weak to do anything but succumb to the passion.

Chapter 14

Brooklin Covington unlocks her office door at Logan Courtyard and walks to her large mahogany desk, her face aglow, the morning after. Sitting at her desk, she reminisces about last night. Just the thought makes her weak. She remembers smiling at him reassuringly and, of course, he knew there was no need for more words as he pressed his lips on hers, kissing her deeply and passionately. "How could she have allowed this to happen?" she asks herself. She couldn't blame it on the wine. She only had one glass. Brooklin remembers his hands, his mouth on her body, her moans and her response to his touch undeniable. She fights through the passion-filled haze of last night to hear her telephone ringing.

"Brooklin, Diane, the young lady Walt and I chose for my replacement, is here to meet you. If you approve, we will offer her the job tomorrow," Karla says. "Everything went well with the background screening."

"Karla, give me a couple of minutes." Brooklin walks to her refrigerator for a bottle of water. She takes a couple of sips, breathes in and out slowly, then returns to her desk. Brooklin phones Karla to send the young lady in. After meeting Diane, Brooklin attends some department meetings. Thereafter, as she takes her morning walk around the hotel she decides to stop by maintenance to talk to Andy.

Andy calls out, "Hi, Ms. Brooklin. How are you?"

"I'm good, Andy. How are you today?"

"Good, Ms. Brooklin. Do you need me for something?"

"Yes, Andy, I would like to ask you to provide a service that is a little out of the ordinary."

"Sure, Ms. Brooklin. Whatever you need."

"Andy, would you please provide an initial cleaning of Suite 1107, adhering strictly to the hotel's safety precautions guidelines. The front room of the suite is in turmoil. Blood is splattered on the wall, floor and bed. Would you please organize the room, cleanup the blood and discard any items stained with blood?"

"Sure. I'll go up right now."

"Thank you. Andy, don't forget to use the protective equipment for blood cleanup and," she pauses momentarily "and Andy, *please* do not mention the condition of the room to anyone."

"Of course I will not, Ms. Brooklin."

"Thanks, Andy. I knew I could trust you. There will be a bonus in your paycheck next week."

"Thank you, Ms. Brooklin."

"I will have the maids provide a deep cleaning of the suite after you complete this initial sanitation. Remember, I am trusting in your personal loyalty to me that no other person will learn about this matter."

"You have it," he says looking sincere.

"Thanks again, I really appreciate this."

"You are welcome, Ms. Brooklin."

When Brooklin arrives back at her desk, she calls Meghan in accounting and requests the bonus be placed in Andy's next week's check. A few minutes later, Karla phones Brooklin to remind her of their luncheon date at Talb today. "Yes, Karla, I remember. That will give me about forty-five minutes to finish some paperwork."

Karla appears at Brooklin's door about forty minutes later. "I told Jamie at the front desk we were going to lunch."

"Great," Brooklin says. "Perfect timing, I just completed my paperwork."

"Brooklin, I just love your haircut."

"Thank you, Karla. I am getting used to the new style and it is surprisingly low maintenance."

"Well, it's very flattering." Karla smiles and they walk to the staff parking lot.

About fifteen minutes later, they arrive at Talb and are quickly seated at Brooklin's regular table. "I like this restaurant. It's very nice," Karla says looking around.

"This is your first time at Talb's?" Brooklin asks.

"Yes, it is."

"Well, Karla, I think you will like it." The waitress returns and takes their order.

"So, Brooklin, I'm glad you like Diane."

"Yes, I think she will be a great addition."

"Wonderful! Walt said if you liked her, he would call and offer her the job tomorrow.

"Good. Hopefully, she can start soon to give you some much needed help."

"I'm fine. I really enjoy my work."

"That's good to hear. Karla, I have been meaning to ask you about a young lady I saw you with in the lobby on Friday afternoon. She looked very familiar. Who was she?"

"Friday afternoon?" Karla thinks for a moment. "Oh, it must have been one of the ladies we were interviewing from Jill's employment agency. I gave each a tour before their interview."

"All right, she probably just looks like someone I know." Brooklin takes a sip of her water. "So Karla, how do you like the metropolitan area?"

"I absolutely love it. My daughter and I are enjoying exploring the area."

"How old is your daughter?"

"Miriam is 14 years old."

"I remember my kids at 14."

"Yes, I'm told the teen years are really a challenging time for mother and daughter and I'm beginning to believe them." They both laugh as the waitress brings their salads.

They are quiet for a moment as they begin to eat. "Brooklin, you have a wonderful staff at Logan Courtyard. They are committed to you and take pride in their work."

"Well, I've tried to hire only individuals who will compliment our team."

"It certainly shows."

Brooklin smiles. "Karla, do you have any family in the area?"

"No, my parents are deceased and I'm an only child. It's really just my daughter and I."

"I see." Brooklin says.

"Although I was a young mother, I really have tried to be a good mother to Miriam."

"I'm sure you are a good mother."

"Well, Miriam doesn't think I am. I guess my parenting style doesn't meet her standards. She says I want to ruin her life."

"Sometimes our children can make us feel inadequate. I remember having those exact feelings of inadequacy as a parent." Brooklin is quiet for a moment then asks, "Karla, are you dating anyone? Sometimes it helps to have a partner to lean on and talk to when we're having these types of interactions with our children."

"No. Right now, I'm committed to raising my daughter and to my work at the hotel. I haven't dated much since I had Miriam. It's just pretty much been Miriam and me. However, Miriam thinks I wasn't affectionate enough and didn't provide her with all the things the other kids had."

"What do you think?"

"I did my best. I didn't have any experience with kids until I became a mom."

"What about Miriam's father?"

"He helped for a couple of years. However, as the years passed, the child support stopped."

"What about your parents?"

"My father passed away a few years after Miriam was born."

"Did your mother help?"

"Not really ... monetary help sometimes. My mother wasn't really affectionate. I had to figure out how to be a mother. I don't know. I thought I did a decent job. I'm not naive enough to think I didn't make mistakes and I'm sure I will make more in the future. However, do I have to pay for them for the rest of my life? I love my daughter dearly even if she doesn't think I do."

"Well, it sounds like you did the best you could and I'm sure your daughter knows you love her."

"If I wasn't the best mother, it had nothing to do with her. It just had to do with my circumstances. You know, you always want to be a good mother. You want your child to have a good childhood, so they can grow up having good values and a strong character."

Brooklin briefly thinks about Ron. Would life be different for him if he had better parenting? "Did you explain this to Miriam? I think she is old enough to understand now at 14."

"Yes, many times. However, I think she just wants to dislike me. Sometimes she acts as if she hates me. It doesn't matter what I say or do. It's just never enough. I'm afraid we're never going to have a good relationship. I'm just trying to do the best I can and be the best mother I can at this point."

"I'm sorry, Karla," Brooklin is interrupted as the waitress brings their lunch.

Karla then continues, "I see you with your children. I wish I had as good of a relationship with Miriam."

"Well, I've had my ups and downs with my kids. However, as you said, we just do the best we can."

"Yes, I've apologized to Miriam for whatever she felt I did wrong and that's all I can do. I really don't think I've been a bad mother. She was well taken care of … clean, healthy and we took small vacations. I was just probably too young to be a parent."

"Well, I hope our city will help to bring healing and positivity to you and Miriam's relationship."

"Thank you, Brooklin."

"If I can help in any way, please let me know."

"Thanks. You are very kind."

"So, what do you think of Talb's?'

"I absolutely love it and now consider it one of my favorites. The food is delicious, second, of course, only to Logan Courtyard." They both laugh.

When she returns from her luncheon, Brooklin decides to check on the theater addition. She inputs the code and opens the door. John greets her as she walks in. "John, how is everything going?"

"Everything is going well, I'm happy to report. We are on schedule. Well, I should say, our new schedule." As they walk around the site, John shares information about the different stages of the work.

"Thank you for your hard work and your quick response to this situation."

"Of course, Ms. Covington."

"I appreciate your diligence and your persistence with this project."

"You and your mother have been great customers over the years, Ms. Covington. I will always go beyond for Logan Courtyard." As she closes the door and turns the corner, she literally bumps into Colin.

"Colin?"

"Hey, I stopped by to see how you're doing today?"

"I'm fine."

"Can we go to your office to speak privately?"

"Sure. I was just returning to my office."

"Great, I need to talk to you for a few minutes." They walk to Brooklin's office in silence. Colin closes the door behind them. "I wanted to thank you."

"Thank me for what Colin?"

"For last night." He hesitates a moment. "For forgiving me."

"I don't know if I would go as far as saying, I forgave you."

"Brooklin, thank you for letting your guard down. I am so grateful. There was a time I didn't think you would allow me back into your life." He reaches out to touch her as she walks away and stares out the window.

"Please, Brooklin, let's go forward and not backward."

"Colin, I'm not sure. I don't even know how last night happened. I'm just confused."

"Brooklin, do you think I can possibly let you go after being with you last night?" He walks over and stands behind her, wrapping his arms around her waist. "It was so good. I'm more in love with you now than ever." He pulls her to him closer and buries his face in her hair. "I've missed holding and touching you. Brooklin, you can't tell me you didn't enjoy our night together?"

She moves his arms from around her waist and walks to the front of her desk. "I did enjoy our night. But I'm just not certain where we go from here."

"After I left this morning, I was thinking about us as I drove to the Teen Center. Thoughts of where we are now and how we got here."

"You've forgotten how we got here?"

"Brooklin, I'm here now – trying to make amends."

"Colin, I will think about it. I need time to sort through my feelings."

"Can I see you again?"

"See me?"

"Brooklin, I'm not rushing you. Can I take you to dinner tomorrow?"

"Colin, you are rushing me. I'll be at the Teen Center on Friday. We can talk then."

"Talk? I want to do more than talk." He walks closer to her. "When did you start going commando? Sexy haircut and no undies ... I'm loving it!"

"I don't go commando all the time. I was at home and I wanted to be comfortable." She stops. "Why am I explaining this to you?"

He laughs, reaches over and lightly presses his lips against hers. "Brooklin, remember, you are the love of my life," he says as he leaves her office.

"Hi, Dad, you're visiting Mom?" Brooklin hears Luke's voice and quickly pulls herself together and returns to her desk.

"Yes, son. Tomorrow can you meet me at the house after your classes? I want you to help me with something."

"Sure, Dad. Is around 4 okay?"

"Perfect. See you then."

Brooklin remembers she and Colin need to have the Taylor conversation with Luke.

When entering his mother's office, Luke immediately asks, "Mom, Dad was here visiting you?"

"Yes, Luke, he stopped by."

"Wow, I haven't seen Dad here in months. What's going on?"

"Nothing. He was in the area and stopped by for a few minutes. So, how are you doing?"

"I'm fine. Karen is out-of-town at the conference you scheduled for her and I need a signature on these papers."

"Okay, just leave them on my desk and I'll take a look at them. Karla will call you when they're ready."

"Sounds good. I don't know, Mom, you have your little haircut and Dad is visiting you now. Are you two getting back together?"

"You are reading too much into a little visit. Now, is there anything else you need to discuss with me?"

"No."

"Well, don't you have some work to do? I certainly do."

"Bye, Mom," Luke says as he walks toward the door.

"Bye, Luke."

Luke walks into the lobby and sees Taylor sitting on the couch and staring at her phone. He quickly walks up to her, glancing around the lobby to see if any staff members noticed Taylor. "What are you doing here?"

"Waiting for you," she says putting her phone aside.

"Taylor," he says placing emphasis on her name. "I have something to give you."

"It couldn't wait until we got home?"

"So you are calling my place home now?" She smiles and plays with his tie.

"Come on, Taylor, I'm at your place more than I'm at mine, even though I only keep a toothbrush at your apartment. What did you want to give me?"

"Don't rush me. So, what's going on at Logan Courtyard?"

Luke grabs her arm and takes her outside the hotel. "What if Mom sees you here?"

"I'm not sure how to take that. I can't come to Logan Courtyard?"

"Come on, Taylor, give me a break."

"You weren't asking for a break last night."

"Taylor, why are you here?"

"Come on, Luke. What do you say we work together and put ourselves at the top?"

"Taylor, I have no intention whatsoever of overthrowing my mother. And I can't believe you would come here and start this conversation again." Luke pauses for a moment, "Wait! Taylor, did you come here hoping my mother or someone from the hotel staff will see you and tell my mother? What are you trying to do, Taylor? Divide and conquer? Are you trying to cause problems between my mother and me?"

"No, Luke, of course not.

"I hope not. My mother and I have come to an understanding."

"So, I've noticed."

"Taylor, you need to move on. Don't keep trying to turn back the clock. I thought you liked your new job. And where are you working? You never told me."

"Forget it, Luke. I'll see you at home."

"All right, I'll see you at home." Luke walks back into the hotel thinking, "What a day. Dad and Taylor visit the hotel on the same day?" He shakes his head and walks toward his office. He gazes around the lobby again to see what staff may have witnessed Taylor's presence in the hotel and notices that Taylor's phone is on the couch. "Oh great, Taylor left her phone." He walks to the couch, picks up her phone and hurries to reach Taylor before she leaves Logan Courtyard. As he exits the hotel, he sees her driving out of the parking lot.

Luke sprints to his car in pursuit of Taylor. After a short time, he realizes her car is just too far ahead and decides to follow her to her workplace. He can give her the phone there. Traffic is moving a little slowly so Luke changes lanes in order to keep an eye on Taylor's car.

As he drives, his mind begins to wonder about Taylor and her desire to take control of Logan Courtyard. "What is her problem? Does she really think I would attempt to take control of the hotel from my mother? I understand that Taylor has aspirations but the hotel cannot be one of them. Now months later, Taylor is still troubled by the fact that she was fired from Logan Courtyard. Why can't she just get over it?" A car suddenly speeds by and Luke refocuses his attention on the road and Taylor's car, pushing aside the negative thoughts of why Taylor decided to resume their relationship.

Luke trails Taylor as she exits the highway and drives about a mile before turning into the parking lot of Griffin Development. Luke is confused. "Why is Taylor driving into Griffin Development's staff parking lot?" He watches her get out of her car and walk toward the side entrance. Luke slowly follows her then stops abruptly when he sees her use the electronic card access control system to enter the building.

Luke is stunned and angry. He returns to the front of the building, walks up the stairs, enters the building and asks for Taylor.

"Your name please," the receptionist asks.

Luke hesitates a moment, removes Taylor's phone from his pocket and says, "Tell her that she dropped her phone and a gentlemen is here to personally return it to her."

The receptionist looks a little puzzled but says, "Sure. Please have a seat. She will be out shortly."

Taylor's smile quickly fades and turns to a look of horror when she walks into the lobby and sees Luke.

He walks up to her, places her phone in her hand and says, "Here's your phone. You left it at Logan Courtyard." Luke immediately walks out the door and down the stairs.

Taylor walks behind him. As Luke reaches the bottom of the stairs, she calls out to him, "Luke. Luke, please wait." Luke continues walking. Taylor stumbles and begins to get annoyed. "What did you do, Luke? Follow me?" She asks crossly.

"How dare you try to turn this on me?" Luke says as he continues toward his car.

"Luke, you're right. I'm sorry. Can you please just wait? I'm wearing heels."

He turns to her after he reaches his car and says, "Wait for what, Taylor?"

"Luke, please let me explain."

"Explain what, Taylor? That you are working for a man who is trying to take my mother's hotel from her? That you are working for a man who committed murders, cheated people out of their life savings, had sex with underaged girls? Did I miss any crimes that this man has committed?"

"Luke, it's not what it looks like."

"It looks like you were probably feeding information to this man about my family business. It looks like you were using me. I hope it was worth it. Because I can tell you this, Taylor, you will never have the opportunity to use me again."

Taylor calls after him, "Luke, please don't do this. Can't we just talk about this?"

Luke gets into his car and drives out of the parking lot, "Taylor," he says to himself, "I think you have done more than enough talking."

Chapter 15

Colin walks through the doors of the Teen Center and Levy quickly stands to greet him. Colin shakes Levy's hand and smiles at his friend. "Levy, how you doing?"

"Good, good, Colin. Did you forget I was coming by to drop off the information you requested?"

"Man, I'm sorry. It's been a crazy couple of days," Colin says as they walk towards the receptionist desk. "Do you want a cup of coffee? Did Lorna offer you something to drink?"

"Yes, she did. However, I'm fine. I've drank two cups already today."

Colin smiles again and says, "It's good to see you, Levy."

"It's good to see you too, Colin. I thought I would stop by to see you instead of just emailing you the information. I haven't seen you in a few weeks," Levy says as they reach the reception desk. Lorna hands Colin the envelope given to her by Levy and the two men walk to Colin's office.

"So, are you thinking about buying a house? What's up with you needing a list of the top realtors and lawyers in the area?"

"Well, it's regarding the purchase of some real estate. However right now, I'm just tying up some loose ends."

"Okay, I hear you. But you're being a little mysterious."

"I'm not trying to be."

"During our phone conversation, you mentioned it was something you didn't want me to handle. Is this some type of private or confidential venture? You know you can talk to me, right?"

"I know."

"Well, okay," Levy says, looking a little puzzled. "When you called and asked for the list of realtors and lawyers, I was a little curious being you wouldn't provide me with any specifics and you asked for individuals that would be discreet." Levy pauses a moment and then continues, "So, what's going on, Colin?"

"Look, I bought some property and I just need some questions answered and some paperwork finalized."

"All right, I won't inquire any further. You know I'm here for you if you need me. So, what's been happening with you? You said it's been a crazy couple of days."

"Man, I think, I'm finally getting my wife back."

"Brooklin, really?"

"Yes, man. I think I might finally be getting my family back."

"That's great, man. Did something happen?"

Colin smiles and says, "A gentlemen never tells."

Levy looks at Colin with amazement, "Really? You and Brooklin?"

Colin doesn't answer. He just smiles for a moment and then looks past Levy. "I just hope she doesn't change her mind." Changing the conversation, Colin asks, "So, how is Jill?"

"She's fine. She's house hunting. She wants a new house."

"Well give her what she wants. You have a wonderful wife, man."

"I know. She's a keeper. Listen, I hope you don't screw this up with Brooklin. She definitely deserves the best."

"I know and this time I will not screw it up."

"You're not still seeing Lorna, are you?"

"No, no. I never was seeing her. I was with her just that one time. I only slept with her because I missed Brooklin so much. It meant nothing to me. I regret it to this date."

"Well, I don't know what you were thinking. You're sure it was just the one time? Colin, please tell me this real estate purchase doesn't have anything to do with Lorna."

"No, the real estate purchase has nothing to do with Lorna. And truthfully, I only slept with her once. I wasn't thinking and I'd been drinking that night." He pauses, "I hate myself for betraying Brooklin."

"I still don't really understand why you left home. After you made that mistake with Lorna, you should have done everything possible to make it up to Brooklin. Instead, you walked out on her."

"I felt so guilty. And I was angry because she was still spending the majority of her time at Logan Courtyard. I just needed some time to think, to clear my head. That hotel means so much to her. That hotel cost me my marriage."

"No, the breakdown of your marriage was caused by your cheating on your wife. You messed up

215

big time. Stop being jealous of a hotel. Brooklin is and was always dedicated to her family. If you would have just given her the time she needed to turn the hotel around ... if you could have just put her first."

"I know that now, man. But Levy, Brooklin doesn't have to ever learn I was unfaithful with Lorna and I will never tell her you knew. Now please, can we never speak of this again?" Colin asks, looking for reassurance.

"Colin, I advised you when you confided in me to tell your wife the truth and ask for her forgiveness."

"NO, Brooklin can never know. She would never forgive me. Levy, do you understand? I need your word. You are my lawyer too."

"Understood! But, can I ask you one question?"

"Sure, what?"

"Why is Lorna still working here at the Teen Center if you are truly not sleeping with her?"

"Because she threatened to tell Brooklin if I fired her. That's the only reason she's here. Well," Colin hesitates then murmurs, "she is also a good receptionist."

Levy looks at him questioningly. "That is the reason, Colin, you should tell Brooklin the truth yourself."

"I made a mistake but I can't tell Brooklin and risk losing her forever. However trust me, I would never touch Lorna again. I'm not even attracted to her. It disgusts me that I was with her. It was the alcohol. I love Brooklin and I'm fighting to keep my family. You know that Detective Ryan has never hidden the fact that he wants my wife."

Levy doesn't answer.

"Really, man. He has no respect for the sanctity of marriage."

"And you do, Colin? Listen, my advice to you is to remember what's important. We should make the most of what we have while we have it because it could be gone in an instant."

"Man, you said it all. If I get this second chance with Brooklin, I'm going to be true and never let her go. I love that woman."

"Colin, use this time to rebuild trust. You have to be there for your wife and you need to be honest with her.   Brooklin is carrying a heavy load right now including being absolutely devastated about Erica."

"I know. This situation with Erica is unbelievable."

"It is. Colin, just keep talking to your wife. She needs you to be there for her."

"I intend to. And I'm sorry I dragged you in the middle of my marital problems. I know you are a good friend to Brooklin as well as her trusted lawyer."

Levy shakes his head, "Listen, I have to go. We'll talk soon."

"Okay, take care, man. Thanks for bringing that information and for being a good friend," Colin says, grabbing Levy's hand and giving him a firm handshake."

"I hope I don't regret knowing about your night with Lorna. Because if Brooklin or my wife learns that I knew about your indiscretion, I will pay dearly. All right, man, I have to get back to my office."

Brooklin is working in her office when both her work phone and private cell phone begin to ring simultaneously. She looks at both. She doesn't recognize the caller on her work phone. Greg is calling on her private cell phone. She takes a deep breath, "Hello."

"Hi, Gorgeous. How are you?"

"Hi, Greg. You have returned? You're at the precinct?" She feels a little guilty like she has cheated on Greg with Colin.

"It must be hard?"

"What?"

"That you can't get any work done because you can't stop thinking of me."

"It sounds like you're speaking from experience."

Greg laughs, "I am. I would like to stop by to see you later. Would that be okay?"

"I'm guessing from your tone that you didn't find Erica or Kim?"

"No, I didn't."

"I'm grateful they were not part of that sex trafficking ring," Brooklin says relieved.

"I am too. So can I stop by in a couple of hours?"

Brooklin hesitates before answering, "Sure, Greg. I would like to hear about your undercover assignment."

He laughs, "Undercover assignment? Interesting choice of words," he laughs again. "I'll see you soon."

Brooklin places the phone down thinking, "I'm in love with two men. I have to really think if I can resume my marriage with Colin and if I do, can I truly live without Greg in my life."

"Brooklin, can I come in?"

Brooklin turns to see Walt at the door. "Certainly, Walt, come in.

"Brooklin, I called Brent and asked him to come to the hotel."

"Good. As we discussed, I would like to meet him."

"He's here. I met with him for about fifteen minutes and I checked your calendar. You don't have anything on your calendar at this moment. Would you like to meet with him now?"

"Now?"

"If this is not a good time, I can schedule a different time."

"No, now is good. I'll meet with him now."

"Great," Walt says as he leaves Brooklin's office for a few minutes and returns with this strikingly good-looking, well-dressed man.

Brooklin is stunned by his extraordinarily commanding presence. He is about 6'10 and extremely muscular. "Mrs. Covington," Brent says in a deep voice, greeting her warmly, "it is indeed a pleasure to meet you." He walks to her desk and offers a hand that's about twice the size of hers.

"Mr. ..."

"Please call me Brent."

"Brent, it is a pleasure to meet you as well. Please have a seat," she says as she gestures to the chairs in front of her desk. She admires the strong but delicate way he gripped her hand and his refined manner. After Brent is seated, Walt closes the door as he leaves Brooklin's office. Brooklin returns her gaze to Brent asking him to tell her about himself and the types of jobs he normally performs for his employers.

As Brent begins to discuss his employment, the earlier warmth quickly fades. There is an edge to his voice, an empty look in his eyes and the smile on his face replaced with a blank expression. Brooklin realizes this particularly handsome man can be as cold as ice. Brent does not talk about his previous employers or the actual work he does. Instead he discusses his skills and reassures her that he is a trained professional ensuring the personal safety of his clients. He further explains that he can be visible or invisible whichever his employer prefers. And "Of course," he added, "I will handle *any* request for my client with absolute discretion."

"Any request?" Brooklin asks.

"Any request," he says staring directly into her eyes. "I carry personal weapons at all times because my client's personal security always comes first. My clients have *never* been harmed and have always been 100 percent happy with my work.

"Would you oppose a background check?"

"No, Ms. Covington, I would not be opposed to a background check. Walt provided me your email address earlier and I sent you a few recommendation letters."

"Thank you, Brent. And assuming all goes well with the background check, Walt will phone you next week to schedule a follow-up appointment. Then we will sit down and talk about how we can work together."

Brent stands. "Very good, Ms. Covington. And it would be my pleasure to work with you," Brent says as the smile returns to his face as quickly as it disappeared. Brooklin observes him walking out of her office. She turns to her computer satisfied with her decision to hire Brent. She begins to check her emails, eager to learn who had written recommendation letters for Brent as Walt enters her office.

"So, Brooklin, what did you think of Brent?"

"I liked him. Please contact T.J, Inc. to have them perform a background check," Brooklin says and then pauses thinking to herself. "I have yet to read the investigative report on Martina, the young lady in the black car."

"Brooklin, is there something wrong?" Walt asks.

"No, I just remembered something I need to take care of. And, Walt, if all goes well with Brent's background check, I would like you to schedule a second appointment and add him to our payroll."

"I thought you would like him. My previous employer loved Brent. He is one of the best in his field."

"And exactly what field is that?"

Walt smiles, "Bodyguard, of course."

"Well I'm not really looking for a bodyguard. However, I would feel more comfortable knowing Brent is available if I need him. Thanks for the referral, Walt."

He smiles, "No problem."

Detective Ryan appears in Brooklin's doorway about two hours later. "Brooklin, how are you today?"

"I'm fine, Greg. How are you?"

"I'm okay," he says as he sits in a chair facing Brooklin.

Brooklin tells him of Brenda's conversation with Kim. She gives him all the information that her brother Jim gave her.

"Well, that tells me Kim is probably all right. Just in need of money. Brooklin, I wanted to come by to let you know, I spoke to the girls at the party last night and they all told me they had not seen Erica or Kim. I think they were being truthful. They knew we were there to help them and there would be no repercussions for talking to us. However, sometime these victims hesitate speaking out."

"What exactly did you find?"

"There was a party at a house on Oak Street. We found a few state senators, assemblymen and some others engaging in undesirable behaviors. They were part of the good old boys network."

"Partying with prostitutes and underage girls?"

"Yes. All were arrested except for the underage girls. It wasn't what we thought. However, we were able to return the underage girls to their homes. Therefore, I feel it was worth the effort."

"How does this happen? How are they able to secure these underage girls for their parties?"

"Some of the girls run away from home. And of course, some are lured through the internet. They are vulnerable, susceptible and easily led into these situations. Human trafficking is the third biggest criminal enterprise in the world—a $32 billion-a-year industry. Approximately 300,000 Americans under 18 are lured into sex trade every year. The police and the FBI work aggressively to track down traffickers and rescue victims."

"What kind of people would do this? Lure victims into that lifestyle? Was Griffin involved in any way?"

"I can't say at this point. However, Griffin was not there."

Brooklin reflects back to her own childhood, "When I was growing up," Brooklin stares as an empty space on the wall as she speaks, "my parents were always involved in some type of business dealings. I knew they loved me because I was their child; however, they were not present for me. I felt everything was more important than me. I hoped to gain their attention and approval by doing what was expected of me. And later when I married Colin, I continued to do what was expected of me as his wife. I don't feel like I truly came into being until I inherited Logan Courtyard. Now, my life feels so right. I'm not fearful, I'm more confident ... I'm a survivor. I feel I have found my place in life, room to grow and I'm ready for whatever comes next," she says as she turns to look at Greg.

"And Brooklin, that is the reason Logan Courtyard is flourishing. You have come through a difficult time to find yourself and what energizes you and makes you happy. And I'm proud of you. You are a remarkable woman."

Brooklin smiles, "Thanks, Greg. I think highly of

you as well. You are a brilliant detective and a remarkable man. Now what about your childhood? Tell me about you, Greg as a child."

"My childhood was different. My parents were very present and affectionate. We were taught to act properly in all situations, which led me to my work in the correction field. It troubles me when people act dangerously and in an inappropriate manner. So I bring those individuals to justice."

"Now, Greg, I have a question for you. I think we can pretty much talk about anything, right?"

"Are we returning to our conversation regarding my undercover work? Because I can show you better than I can tell you," he says with a grin on his face.

"Thank you, Greg, for your generous offer, but I will decline. Now, may I ask you the question?"

Greg continues, "The answer is *yes* ... just tell me when and where," he says jokingly but daringly.

Brooklin blushes, "Greg, we are having a serious conversation here."

"Who is not being serious? I'm being very serious."

"Greg," Brooklin says with emphasis on his name.

"All right, go ahead. What is the question?"

"What happens when the people in the correction field do not act properly? When there is corruption among you? What then? I often wonder how the good guys turn the other way when their fellow officers commit crimes. You work with them, so you have to know the few who bend the rules and break the law. They are protected by their police family … The Blue Wall of Silence?"

Greg looks at Brooklin intensely wondering what brought about this conversation, "I would hope that you know that it goes without saying that I believe those who enforce the law should apply the law to themselves as well."

"But, Greg, would you report a colleague's misconduct, crimes or even police brutality?"

"Brooklin, I would first go to that officer or stop the misconduct if it happens in my presence. My fellow officers know that I will not engage or tolerate any misconduct," Greg says firmly.

"But, Greg, is it your responsibility to go further? Do more about the dishonest or prejudiced cops?"

Brooklin, I think some people assume they know everything law enforcement knows. Not everybody can understand what we do and how we do it."

"Okay, but who keeps law enforcement honest? Shouldn't law enforcement have to answer to somebody besides themselves? It's an imperfect system run by imperfect people, right? "

"I understand what you are saying, Brooklin. However, does it count that we are trying?"

"It helps but if law enforcement commit crimes, they need to be held accountable for their actions."

Greg is about to comment as his telephone rings. "Hi, Allen." Greg is quiet for a moment. "Really?" He glances at Brooklin and then stares at the floor listening to the caller. "Is she in custody?" Greg speaks a little louder. "Okay, the police have her? And they think it is her?   She gave a different name? Okay, let me wrap this up and I'll be there shortly." Detective Ryan returns the phone to his belt loop and turns to Brooklin. "Sorry, Brooklin, I have to take off."

"Greg, is it Erica? Have they found Erica?"

"No. Someone fitting Kim's description was picked-up at the outlet mall near the harbor for shoplifting."

"Shoplifting?"

"Brooklin, I will call you later. Until then, can you please focus on hotel business? Brooklin, hotel business only."

"Greg, if it's Kim, please call me. I will come down to the precinct to pay her bail or should I get a lawyer to help her with the charges?"

"No, Brooklin, there will not be a need for a lawyer. Let me handle this. I will make sure no charges are brought against Kim."

Brooklin hesitates and then begins to comment, "Greg ..."

At that moment, Greg receives another call. "Yes, Baker, I just got the call. I heard they have someone fitting Kim's description for shoplifting at the outlet mall." He hesitates a moment. "Yes, I'm on my way to the mall now." He listens for a moment, "Oh, they are bringing her to the precinct now? Okay, I'm on my way. And Baker, do not let anyone talk to her before I get there." Greg looks at Brooklin.

"I'll wait for your call." Brooklin says in a quiet tone. " And, Greg, about our conversation, I know who you are. You are one of the good guys and I trust and respect that you truly enforce and uphold the law."

Greg winks at her and gives her a half-smile. She watches as Greg hurries out of her office, hesitates for a moment, then calls Levy.

"Hi, Brooklin, I was just about to call you. The handwriting specialist looked at both the card and the envelope and came to the conclusion that he believes it's a woman's handwriting. He said females tend to write more legibly and demonstrate greater circularity in their handwriting, more curved and bowed-out letters rather than straight. He also said men tend to write smaller and not fill the allotted space."

"Well, I guess that narrows down the suspects. However, we still don't know who is sending the cards. Maybe I should just let the police investigate."

"Let me know what you decide, Brooklin."

"I will. Levy, the reason I called is because I think Kim got arrested at the outlet mall across from the harbor for shoplifting."

"Shoplifting?"

"Yes. Detective Ryan was here in my office when he received a call that someone fitting Kim's description was arrested for shoplifting."

"Okay, let me make a few calls. If it is her, I will send one of my associates down to the precinct."

"Thanks, Levy. If it is Kim, she will definitely need a lawyer. Detective Ryan will want to question her and I don't want him to learn of our involvement with Griffin's case. We want her to cooperate with the police but not provide any information about our connection to this case."

"I'm with you on that front. Maybe I better go down to the precinct and handle this. Our involvement needs to remain between you, Walt and me. I will call you when I know more."

"Thanks. Levy, there is a real possibility that Kim might have some information that may lead us to Erica. If so, I want her to provide that information to Detective Ryan. I want Erica found."

"I know. We will handle this situation very carefully."

"All right, Levy. I trust you to take care of this," Brooklin says. She stares at her doorway knowing it doesn't matter how she looks at this. Challenges lie ahead and she knows there is no guarantee of a successful outcome. However, she also knows she will definitely work every angle. She will not lose her hotel, Erica must be found, and Jack Griffin *must* go to prison.

Chapter 16

Kim is seated in the interrogation room when Detective Ryan walks in. "Kim, were you read your rights?"

"Yes."

"Do you understand them?"

"Yes," she says.

"Kim, why did you leave the Jefferson Counseling Center?"

She looks down at her feet and says, "I don't know."

"Kim, that's a lie and we both know it."

"I'm only 15. It's illegal for you to question me without my mother being here."

"Kim, you were arrested for shoplifting. I would like to help you. Now tell me, why did you leave the Jefferson Counseling Center?"

"We were forced to leave," she says looking at the detective with tears in her eyes. "My mother and I returned to our apartment after counseling and a man was there. He forced us to leave with him."

"What man?" Detective Ryan pauses for a moment to allow Kim to answer his question. Then he continues, "What was the man's name?"

"I don't know. But my mother said she heard him mention Mr. Griffin's name when he was talking on the phone."

The door opens and Levy enters the interrogation room. He identifies himself as Kim's lawyer and tells Kim not to say anything more. He tells

Detective Ryan he would like to talk to his client in private.

Detective Ryan looks at him and then at Kim and leaves the room. He walks to his desk, sits down and stares morosely at his telephone. Then he picks up his phone and calls Brooklin.

"Hello, Greg. Was it Kim?"

"Yes."

"So Kim was arrested for shoplifting?"

"Yes," he says in a low tone. "Brooklin, did you call a lawyer for Kim?"

Brooklin hesitates a moment then answers, "Yes, Greg. I called Levy and told him that Kim might be at the precinct."

"Why didn't you trust me to handle this, Brooklin?"

"I do trust you, Greg. I trust you implicitly."

"You asked me to try to locate Kim and now," he hesitates. "Brooklin, what was your reasoning for having Levy represent Kim?"

"I thought she might need representation."

"And you didn't trust me to handle this situation with Kim?"

"You keep saying, 'I didn't trust you.'" She takes a deep breath. "Of course, I trust you, Greg. I just thought Kim might need a lawyer."

"Brooklin, is there a reason you do not want me to talk to Kim without an attorney being present? Is there some information you do not want Kim to share with me?" He pauses, "And why didn't Levy send one of his associates? Why is he handling this himself?"

"Greg, you're making more of this than it is."

"What's going on, Brooklin? What information are you withholding from me? Are you keeping secrets, Brooklin?"

"Secrets?" Brooklin briefly remembers the anonymous cards. Then she realizes Greg is still talking.

"Should I not trust you, Brooklin?" There is an awkward moment of silence. "Brooklin, talk to me."

"Greg, please. I just wanted Kim to have a lawyer present."

"Listen, I didn't have to tell you that we suspected Kim was the girl who was arrested for shoplifting." Greg's phone beeps. "Brooklin, can you hold for a minute?"

"Sure," she says.

"Yes," Ryan says, switching over to the other line. After a moment, he returns to his conversation with Brooklin. "Okay, Brooklin, I have to go. However, we'll finish this conversation later. And Brooklin, I will want answers."

Detective Ryan re-enters the interrogation room where Kim and Levy are awaiting his arrival. "Kim, are you ready to tell me the circumstances of your leaving the Jefferson Counseling Center now?"

Kim looks at Levy and says, "Yes." She pauses then continues. "Like I told you before, my mother and I returned to our apartment at the Jefferson Center and a man was there. We didn't know the man and we were afraid. He told us we had to come with him."

"Neither you nor your mother have ever met this man previously?"

"No. We never saw him before."

"What exactly did he say to you and your mother?"

"He told us that we had to come with him right then. My mother asked him why did we need to go with him. He told us if we didn't want to get hurt, we should come with him and not ask any questions. We were afraid, so we left with him. He placed both of us in the back seat of the car and told us if we tried to run, he would shoot us. Then he got in the front seat and as we were driving away, he called Griffin and told him he had us in the car."

"What type of car?"

"It was a black Chrysler 300."

"Did you get the plate number?"

"No."

"Was it a new or older model?"

"I'm not sure. The name Chrysler 300 was on the car."

"Okay. Now back to the man's conversation. How do you know the man was talking to Mr. Griffin?"

"I didn't hear him but my mother said she heard him say, 'Yes sir, Mr. Griffin.'"

"You didn't hear him mention Mr. Griffin's name? Only your mother?"

"No, I didn't. He was talking very low."

"Kim, where is your mother now?"

Kim doesn't answer.

"Kim, give Detective Ryan the address where your mother is now," Levy says.

"She's at a friend's house." Kim gives the detective the friend's address.

Detective Ryan excuses himself for a moment, walking to the side of the room. Kim listens as he calls someone and gives them her mother's location. Ryan returns to the table re-focused on Kim, "Now tell me what happened after the man spoke to someone on the telephone?"

"He drove us to this house."

"What house? Do you know the address of the house?"

"It was on Oak Street. I don't know the address. I was scared and I really wasn't paying attention. But I remember I was there before with Griffin, so I was sure my mother was right about the man talking to him."

"When were you there?" Detective Ryan asks.

"A couple of months ago at a party Griffin gave."

"So, you have been to this house before?"

"Yes, twice."

"Can you describe the house? What color is the house?"

"Gray with a small front porch and white wicker chairs."

"Good description, Kim," Detective Ryan says knowing this was the house where he and the FBI arrested the politicians this weekend. "Now, who was at this party?"

"I don't know the men. They were friends of Griffin."

"How do you know they were friends of Griffin?"

"He was laughing and talking to them and I saw them at the last party Griffin gave."

"How many people were there?"

"There were about five men."

"Anyone else?"

"Yes. About eight other ladies were there."

"Who were the ladies?"

"I don't know them. I just have seen some of them at Griffin's other parties."

"What happens at these parties?"

Kim looks at Levy and he nods for her to continue. "They are parties where men and women get together. Now, do I have to talk about this?"

"Yes, Kim. I need details. I need to have a clear understanding of what happened at the parties."

"Griffin would grab me, touch me and force me to do stuff that men and women do. Sometimes he would get really drunk and then he would get rough."

"Rough?"

She looks down at the floor, "Yes."

Detective Ryan closes his free hand under the table tightly into a clenched fist. "Did any of the other men touch you?"

"No, just Griffin. I have already told Agent Dalton and the FBI all about these parties. Can I please just leave?"

"Kim, I want to put the person away that committed these crimes against you. I can't do that unless you are straight with me. Please just tell me the truth."

"What does all this have to do with me being arrested for shoplifting?"

"We are going to get to the shoplifting in a minute."

"How long am I going to be here? I want to go home."

"Kim, where is home? Where are you living now?"

Kim hesitates and then says, "I don't have a home."

"Kim, where have you been living?"

Kim looks at Levy again and Levy says, "Tell him."

"My mother and I were living with Lorna."

"Lorna?"

"Yes, Lorna from the Teen Center."

"How long have you and your mother been living with Lorna?"

"After we escaped from that man, we saw Erica and told her what happened.   She allowed my mother and me to live with her. A few days later, Erica went missing and we didn't know what to do. My mother called Lorna to see if she knew where Erica was and Lorna invited us to stay at her house until Erica returned."

Detective Ryan is astonished. However, he shows no emotion. "Okay, Kim, let's return to the parties. You said that you don't know any of the men or women who attended these parties?"

"No, I don't."

"Okay, I will have an officer show you some photos before you leave. I would like you to tell the officer if you recognize anyone from the parties."

"I'm going to leave? I'm not going to jail?" asks Kim.

"It depends, Kim. If you answer all my questions truthfully, I will discuss releasing you to your lawyer.

However before you are released, I will need to question your mother."

"Now, Kim, how did you and your mother escape from this man who was supposedly holding you and your mother hostage?"

"When we got to the house and the man was letting us out of the car, my mother knocked the folder he was carrying out of his hand. Lots of paper scattered out of the folder. My mother pretended she was going to pick up some of the papers and the man pushed her and reached down to pick up the papers. A city bus had just stopped ahead of us and my mother grabbed the man's car keys out of his hand and pointed to the bus. We ran and jumped on the bus. The man was not fast enough to catch us and we told the bus driver to go. A kind lady on the bus paid our fare. We rode the bus until we saw Erica taking groceries out of her car at her apartment. We got off the bus and told her what happened. That's when Erica told us we could stay with her until she talked to Ms. Covington. She said Ms. Covington would know what to do."

"How long did you stay at Erica's house before she went missing?"

"Just a few days."

"Did Erica tell Ms. Covington what happened with this man?"

"We don't know. Erica just said she was working on it."

"When was the last time you saw Erica?"

"We all went to Speed Dating."

"You, your mother and Erica went to Speed Dating?"

"Yes."

"How did you get into Speed Dating? You're too young to get into a club."

"They didn't want to leave me at home alone. So I got dressed and they put make-up on me." Detective Ryan looks at her skeptically. Kim pauses for a minute. "What can I say, I don't look like I'm 15."

"What club did the three of you go to?"

"Club 54. Erica seemed like she was eager to meet a man."

"Then what happened?"

"Erica participated in Speed Dating. My mother and I weren't interested so we just watched."

"Did Erica meet a guy?"

"Yes. They talked for a couple of hours. My mom and I just sat at a table until Erica was ready to go."

"Okay, what happened after that?"

"Erica and the guy dated for the next couple of nights. My mother and I watched the door each night to make certain the man didn't come into the club. After about three hours of being there that last night, Erica gave us her key to the apartment. Then she and the guy left the club through the back door. That was the last time we saw Erica. She called later that same night and said she wouldn't be home until the next morning."

"Who was the guy?"

"I don't know."

"Who saw Erica with this guy?"

Kim thinks for a minute, "The bartender saw them. He served them drinks."

"Okay, I'll check out this story. Kim, I would like to know, how did you meet Griffin?"

"He was one of the guest speakers at my school."

"A guest speaker?" Detective Ryan asks.

"We have career day a few times a year. Griffin came twice to speak about real estate careers."

"He did? How did the two of you meet?"

"During his first speech, he kept looking at me. After his last speech some months later, I was walking home and he drove up in his car and asked me if I would like a ride home. I said yes. I had never rode in a Bentley before. He asked me for my phone number when he dropped me off at home. I gave him my number and he called me."

"Kim, how long have you been *seeing* him?"

"About three months."

"I see. You said he sometimes gets rough with you?"

"Yes, if I hesitate when he tells me to do something."

"How often do you see him?"

"A couple times a month."

"When was the last time you were with him?"

"I'm not sure, it's been a while."

"Kim, can you be more specific? A few weeks, a month?"

Kim looks down, thinking for a minute. "The last time is when those pictures came out in the blog. He called and threatened me. He warned me if I told anyone about us that he would hurt my mother and me."

"Kim, why were you stealing from the clothing store at the mall?"

"I was afraid Lorna was going to put my mother and me out of her apartment. Griffin was giving me money. After the photos came out, he stopped seeing me. I had saved up some money and I was giving it to Lorna for letting us stay with her. So I stole the clothes to sell to get money to pay Lorna."

"Did you also pay Erica for living with her?"

Kim smiles, "No, Erica was so nice to us. She would never take money from my mother and me."

"Why didn't you contact Ms. Covington for help?"

"I didn't want to get her involved in this mess, even though Erica said she was going to talk to her about helping us. However my attorney said Ms. Covington is going to pay for an apartment for my mother and me for six months. When I leave here, my mother and me will be moving to Georgia. Ms. Covington has a friend who is going to give my mother a job in Georgia. And she has set up for us to meet with a private counselor. She has always been so nice. I should have called her as soon as we got away from that terrible man."

A man dressed in a police uniform enters the interrogation room with a computer. "Kim, this is Officer Jones, our police sketch artist. Please describe the man who was waiting for you in your apartment at the Jefferson Center. Kim, I need you to provide as many details as you can remember about this man. Officer Jones will create a portrait that will help us during our investigation. Afterwards, an officer will show you some photos. Let the officer know if you recognize any men or women from the parties you attended with Griffin. While you are with the officers, I will question your mother. If the information you gave me checks out, I will release you into the custody of your attorney."

Detective Ryan checks his phone and then exits the room.   After some time, Ryan re-enters the room and sits in a chair near the window. A few minutes later, Officer Jones walks over to Detective Ryan, showing him the portrait. Detective Ryan smiles and says, "Bingo."

Chapter 17

Brooklin is providing Karla some details about the hotel's boutique as her brother Jim's girlfriend comes through the double doors. Brooklin smiles, "Hi, Amber. This is a surprise."

"Hi, Brooklin. I was here in the restaurant with a few of my co-workers and wanted to stop by for a moment to talk to you."

"Sure, Amber, please come in," Brooklin says as she escorts Amber into her office. "I know you said you were coming from the restaurant; however can I offer you anything. Something to drink maybe?"

"No, Brooklin, I'm fine. But thank you."

"Was everything okay in the restaurant?"

"Oh yes, the food was delicious and your staff as usual was superb."

"Good."

"Brooklin, I wanted to speak to you about your brother Jim."

"Jim? Is everything all right with Jim?"

"Well, no. He's beginning to drink quite often."

"Jim is drinking again?"

"Jim told me he had some issues with drinking before we began seeing each other socially. However, he's drinking again and it's beginning to be problematic. When I talk to him about it, he gets angry with me."

"I'm very sorry to hear this."

"Brooklin, I was wondering if you could speak to him? Maybe, talk to him about going to a program? Or counseling?"

"Well yes, I will talk to him, although I'm not sure if Jim will listen to me. How long has Jim been drinking?"

"I think a few weeks. But he's beginning to drink excessively."

"Colin hasn't mentioned anything to me. Is he only drinking in the evenings?"

"Well, I don't know because I'm not with him everyday. However, when I do see him in the evening, I can tell he's had more than a couple of drinks."

"Wow, this saddens me. Jim was doing so well. Do you know why he's drinking again?"

"I really don't know. I tried to talk to him but he's not willing to discuss it with me. He's in denial and I can't get through to him." She hesitates a moment. "It's sad because I really care about Jim. However, I don't think I can continue seeing him if he doesn't get help."

"Well, Amber, I definitely will talk to him. However, you can't force someone to get help. An addict has to get to a point where they choose sobriety and learn to live without alcohol or drugs as their crutch."

Amber stands. "Okay, Brooklin, I appreciate you taking the time to speak with me. Hopefully, Jim will not be too upset that I spoke to you about his situation."

Brooklin stands facing Amber, "I truly appreciate your letting me know that Jim is drinking again. And Amber, we are not going to worry about Jim being upset about your telling me. We just need him to take control and responsibility for his actions. Jim needs to stop drinking and begin managing his life again." Amber hugs Brooklin. "Thank you again Amber for telling me. Now, we have to stay strong in dealing with this situation with Jim."

Amber smiles at Brooklin, as she turns and leaves the office.

Brooklin sits back on the couch, reaches over, grabs a pillow and then throws it back on the couch. "What else am I'm going to have to deal with? What else?"

Detective Ryan walks into Grill 55, an eating spot and dance club on Geer Boulevard. He looks to the left of the large bar toward the tables with worn chairs and sees Big Mel seated at his usual table. As he walks in Big Mel's direction, his muscular sidekick seated at a table across from Big Mel stands. "Sit down and remove your hands from your jacket before I take you downtown," Detective Ryan says.

Big Mel laughs and nods for the man to sit down. "Detective Ryan," Big Mel says, showing perfectly white teeth. "We have to stop meeting like this."

"I will be brief. You are coming downtown with me for questioning."

"Downtown? Why do I need to come downtown with you?" He pauses. "We can have a conversation here."

"You can come downtown with me willingly for questioning or I can arrest you here and now. Either way, you're coming with me. Which will it be?"

"My, you are uptight today, Detective. Listen, I will answer any questions you have. Have a seat and let's talk. Really, my intentions are good."

"I could care less about your intentions. Mel Carter, you are under arrest."

"Hold up, Detective. I'll go with you. I'll go downtown and answer your questions." He stands and calls out to his buddy to call his lawyer.

Brooklin is flabbergasted that her brother is drinking again and she phones Colin.

"Hi, Brooklin."

"Hi, Colin. How are you?"

"Good. Is everything okay?"

"No. Amber was just here at the hotel. She told me Jim is drinking again. Were you aware of this?"

"Yes, I was."

"Colin, why didn't you tell me?"

"I talked to Jim. He told me he would go to counseling. I thought I would give him a couple of weeks monitoring his progress before I told you."

"Colin, you should have told me immediately. Please do not keep information from me regarding my family."

"You are right. I should have told you. I was hoping when I talked to you about Jim, I could include that he was getting better due to his counseling sessions."

"Has Jim been coming to work drunk? Is this what the kids at the Teen Center are observing?"

"No. He's not drunk. More like hung over."

"Okay, Colin. Jim needs to take some time off and get help. We cannot allow the kids to witness this behavior and think it is acceptable."

"I will talk to Jim."

"Yes, I will too. I definitely need to have an intense conversation with Jim."

"Brooklin, Jim is feeling some shame about his relapse. We don't want to drive him deeper into addiction."

"Drive him deeper into addiction?"

"Yes, because he doesn't want to feel or deal with the guilt. You know, typically some people relapse several times before they get sober."

"Colin, please. First, don't make excuses. Jim has to stay strong to fight this disease. He needs to go to his meetings and counseling sessions. And second, I'm not and would not try to shame Jim."

"Okay, Brooklin. I hope you will be calmer when you and Jim talk. Nevertheless after I speak to Jim, I will call and let you know the results of our conversation."

As Brooklin places the phone on her desk, it begins ringing again. She sees that Levy is calling. "Hi, Brooklin. Just want to let you know all went well with Kim at the police station. She answered all the questions and did not provide any information that would connect us to this case."

"Great," Brooklin says "and Kim and her mother are on the plane safely?" Just as Levy is responding,

Brooklin looks up to see Greg standing in her doorway. "Okay good, I'm glad all went well. Listen, Levy, I have to go. Detective Ryan is standing in my doorway. We will talk later."

"Okay, but call me when you can talk. Kim provided some information that you will want to know."

"All right, I'll call you later," Brooklin says looking at Greg as he walks in and has a seat at her desk, never removing his eyes from hers.

"Nice haircut."

"Thank you," she says as she shifts in her chair. Brooklin is feeling a bit uncomfortable under his glare. However, she will not allow it to show knowing Greg would enjoy watching her squirm. She is uncertain what is making her so uneasy. Is it the conversation they are about to have or the fact that there is definitely profound chemistry between the two of them? She thinks to herself, "Brooklin, what is wrong with you? Didn't you just make love to your husband?" She takes a deep breath and suddenly Greg's words bring her back to their conversation.

"Brooklin, I'm thinking you might want to start talking. Tell me what is going on."

"Talking? Talking about what?" she says, running her fingers through her hair.

"Brooklin, give me a little credit here. I have this feeling that you might have an inside track. What information are you withholding? I know you are involved in this situation to some degree. What I don't know is, *how* involved?"

"Greg, let's not overanalyze this. I just helped Kim and her mother, if that is what you are implying by saying I was involved."

"Brooklin, cops have a sixth sense. We go where the evidence leads us and right now, it's leading me straight to you."

"Greg, you are being melodramatic."

"Brooklin, if I have to reinvestigate this entire case, I will. I can just have Kim and her mother pulled off the plane and brought back to the precinct for more questioning." He pauses for a moment. "It's your call."

"No, Greg, please don't do that. Think about their safety."

"It's your call."

"Okay, off the books?"

He doesn't answer.

"Greg, I'll tell you what you want to know. But I don't want to incriminate myself."

"Okay, off the books. However, I want to know everything, Brooklin. Everything. Do not leave out any details."

Brooklin tells him that she and Levy provided the pictures and the information to the Buzz and the FBI.

"How did you and Levy obtain this information?"

"I will take the Fifth on that question."

"So you and Levy provided the information that sent the FBI and me on the human trafficking sting?"

Brooklin says in a low voice, "Yes, but I didn't realize until after you confided in me that you would be involved. And I didn't think that Kim or Erica might be involved. We were just trying to provide the FBI with information against Jack Griffin."

"Why, Brooklin, did you feel the need to get involved? I mean, I thought you had your hands full with Logan Courtyard and your family."

Brooklin doesn't answer and stares back at him.

"Is it because Jack Griffin is trying to coerce you into selling Logan Courtyard?

"And because of what he did to Kim," Brooklin adds.

"Is there more, Brooklin?"

"More?" Brooklin asks looking at him.

"Yes, Brooklin, more. Does the FBI know you provided this information to them?"

"No. We made certain it was done in a discreet manner."

"You made certain it was done in a discreet manner." Greg says, shaking his head. "The fact is you and Levy cannot be certain if the FBI knows the two of you provided this information."

"We were very discreet."

"Brooklin, I'm concerned that you don't seem to see the gravity of these infractions."

"I recognize my role in this. And I'm not going to apologize for wanting Griffin to pay for his crimes and to suffer. He deserves it."

"My job is to get to the truth and Brooklin, you deliberately deceived me."

"Go ahead, Greg. Get it all off your chest."

"Brooklin, I told you I didn't want you to be in the line of fire. And what do you do? You start this vendetta against Griffin."

"I started it?"

"Why? Why would you go down this road? Why couldn't you just talk to me?"

"Previously when there were charges against Griffin, evidence disappeared or the witnesses changed their mind about testifying. The police and the FBI never were able to convict him. So I provided evidence that was not going to unravel." Brooklin is quiet for a moment and then continues, "Greg, I'm well aware of the battle I'm taking on."

"Are you now? You are a tough businesswoman, ambitious and driven. And I respect that."

"I am resourceful."

"This has nothing to do with being resourceful. Brooklin, get off this warpath and see the consequences of your actions before it is too late."

"I'm not going to defend myself to you or anyone else for looking after my business. Yes, finishing Griffin was my ultimate goal. This man walks into my office whenever he feels like it." She pauses. "Just the sight of him repulses me. Can I ask you a question? What would you do?" She says in an elevated tone, "I don't want this man darkening my door ever again."

"Brooklin, I know it's frustrating. But you need to talk to me and leave the police work to the FBI and myself. Don't get caught in the middle of this investigation. It's too dangerous. Jack Griffin is one of the worst types of criminals. He is ruthless. And I don't think you are prepared for the risks. These people play for keeps."

"He has caused havoc in a lot of people's lives and the police and FBI did not have enough evidence to charge him. I just provided them with what they needed."

"Brooklin, this vendetta against Griffin is your desire for personal vengeance. I don't want anything to come back and bite you. We've put a lot of man-hours into bringing this man to justice and I don't want anyone to jeopardize this case. We can indict Griffin."

"And I have helped to provide the FBI with an airtight case against Griffin."

"You are not innocent in this, Brooklin. Now, how did you obtain this information?"

"The opportunity presented itself and I took it. You can only push a person so far. I am just a woman who did what she needed to do to protect her own."

"Now, I need to do some damage control to make certain you and Levy are not sitting in a jail cell next to Griffin."

She looks at him annoyed. "You are so generous with your comments. I apologize for keeping you out of the loop. Now, I apologized. Is that good enough for you, Greg?"

"Brooklin, this was an elaborate deception. Let me give you some advice. I recommend ..."

"Greg, I really didn't ask for your recommendations."

"Well, not yet you haven't. But trust me, you are going to need help with fighting this man. You are playing with fire."

"I can take the heat."

He stops, shakes his head and begins to laugh. "What am I going to do with you? Brooklin, you are one tough woman, one that I will stand by. I just do not want any surprises. In order for me to get a full picture, I have to ask questions. I don't want to be blindsided. You need to be open and honest with me. Did you tell me everything?"

Brooklin stands. "I have to go to a meeting."

Greg grabs her arm as she starts toward the door. "Think about what I said, okay?" She doesn't answer and looks down at his strong grasp on her arm. Greg releases her arm. "Brooklin, you know I care about you. I don't want any harm to come to you. That's what this conversation is about. You know that, right?"

Brooklin relaxes a little. "Yes, I know that."

"Then, we're good?"

She nods, "Yes, Greg, we're good.

"Good. Brooklin, you mean too much to me. I don't know what I'd do if anything happens to you."

"Nothing is going to happen to me."

"You are right because I'm not going to allow it. Even if it means protecting you from yourself."

She looks at him and sees the concern in his eyes. "All right Greg, I have to go to my meeting. This conversation is a little too heavy for me. I do appreciate your concern."

"Brooklin, I love you and the only reason I'm not taking you in my arms right now is because I know you are still confused about your marriage."

Brooklin takes a step back. She is surprised that he said he loved her. Greg moves toward her again. "I'm going to give you the time to sort through your feelings. But know I am here for you, no matter the circumstance. I want to have all the moments with you. And I will always support you and put you first. I will never leave you. I'm going to be right here always." He gently strokes her cheek with his forefinger.

Brooklin glances at Greg and then turns her head to avoid his eyes as her heart pounds. She would like to feel not just his finger on her cheek but also his lips on hers. She definitely wanted to be in his arms at this moment. She moves away from him trying to put as much distance between them as possible, struggling with her own thoughts. She needs to escape this office and the urgent desire for his touch. "Greg, I have to go," she says as she walks quickly away from him and out the door.

Chapter 18

As Big Mel and Detective Ryan enter the precinct, Ryan asks one of the officers in the hallway to escort Big Mel to an interrogation room.

"Ryan," Detective Baker says as he spots Detective Ryan walking down the hall.

"What's up, Baker?"

"Big Mel's lawyer is here waiting to see Big Mel. Where have the two of you been?"

"I'm going to get a cup of coffee. Walk with me." The two of them walk down the hall. Ryan grabs a cup of coffee and leads Baker to the corner of the room. "I took him to a remote location and let him sweat while I went to talk to a friend."

"A remote location?"

"Keep your voice down. Yes, a rare remote location. I've been known to improvise when necessary. Jack Griffin is facing the grand jury tomorrow and I thought it was time for Big Mel and me to have a private conversation. After I left him to, let's say, sweat for a while, I returned and explained how now was a good time for him to talk. I put a deal on the table and told him it was only available here and now, so he needed to take advantage of it while he can."

"Did he talk?"

"With what I had on him--human trafficking and false imprisonment--he sang like a canary. And he gave me his permission on tape to record our conversation."

"What kind of deal did you offer him?"

"You know I can't offer any deals without the Sarg's approval."

"But he thinks he has a deal?" Baker asks smiling.

"Yep and I'm going to continue to let him think he has a deal until after he testifies. Then I'm going to throw the book at him. I have been after this guy for years. We had an undercover officer infiltrate the organization but we still were unable to get a conviction. But this time, I think we finally got him and Griffin."

"His lawyer? He'll tell his lawyer about the deal."

"No, he won't. His lawyer is on Jack Griffin's payroll and it would be a death sentence if his lawyer went back and told Griffin that Big Mel is testifying against him. Besides, it's not going to matter. I have him on tape spilling the beans about everything."

"Everything?"

"Everything. He answered every question. Incriminating himself – even doing some bragging. He was like the gift that keeps on giving. Lucky me."

"What? That's crazy. However, there was no luck. Ryan, you are a great detective and if this works, you would have cracked this case wide open."

"Thats exactly what I'm hoping. We do not want an acquittal for these guys under any circumstances."

Baker laughs, "Ryan, pretending to offer Big Mel a deal so he would talk--that was a nice touch."

"All right, Baker, we'll talk later. I need to call Agent Dalton and tell him to add Mel Carter to the witness list to testify before the grand jury tomorrow."

"With Big Mel and Mr. Reed's testimonies, there is no way Jack Griffin will see the light of day. Word is out on the street that Mr. Reed is dead and that Jack Griffin put out a hit on him. I would love to see Griffin's face when Reed and Big Mel walk into the courthouse to testify."

"You said it. In the meantime, however, I need you to escort Big Mel's lawyer to the interrogation room. We don't want him to become suspicious and think Big Mel talked. I told Big Mel that I would be in to question him after he's had a few minutes with his lawyer."

Detective Baker replies, "And of course, his lawyer will tell him not to answer any of your questions."

"Right. And I will then tell Big Mel he is free to go but not to leave town."

"His lawyer will probably ask Big Mel why it took him so long to get to the station."

"Yes and he will tell him I left him handcuffed in the car sulking. That I made a couple of stops before bringing him to the station."

"Ryan, you are a genius."

"I wouldn't go that far but it's time to nail these crooks," Ryan says. "I also need to call Jim and Lorna from the Teen Center and have them come down to the precinct for questioning tomorrow morning. Now go take Big Mel's lawyer to the interrogation room and I'll make the calls to the FBI and the Teen Center."

Baker laughs, "I'm on my way."

Brooklin places the report regarding Martina from TJ, Inc. in one of her bags and leaves Logan Courtyard early to meet Colin and Luke at the house. She is anxious to discuss and learn more about Luke's current relationship with Taylor. Colin pulls into the driveway as Brooklin is about to close the garage. He walks into the garage smiling, "Hi, Brooklin. I see Luke is not here yet."

"No, not yet."

"Good," he kisses her lips gently. "We have a few minutes alone before Luke arrives."

Brooklin stares at him, "Colin, where are you going with this? As I've said before, I'm not sure about whatever this is between us. So, let's just slow down."

"Whatever this is? It's a husband and wife making their way back to each other."

"Colin, I'm not sure about a reconciliation. And," she hesitates, "the reason we are here today is to talk to Luke about his relationship with Taylor--not ours."

"Brookln, I'm not trying to make you feel uncomfortable," Colin says as they enter the house.

Brooklin places her bags on a chair, "Well, Colin, you *are* making me feel uncomfortable. Now, can we return to the subject of Luke? I can't believe we have to have this conversation with him again. He should be smart enough not to let Taylor back into his life."

"I agree. I think I hear his car now. For once, he's on time."

Luke enters the kitchen looking disheveled, wearing a t-shirt and jeans that look as though he slept in both the night before. "Mom, Dad," Luke says as he grabs a bottle of water from the refrigerator and sits at the kitchen table.

Brooklin looks at Colin and then back at Luke. "Luke, is everything okay?" she says as she looks at the dark circles under his eyes. "Luke, are you all right?" Brooklin asks a second time in a concerned voice.

"No, Mom, I'm not all right. But I will be." Luke says as he leans back in his chair sighing. Brooklin and Colin both take a seat at the kitchen table across from Luke. "I made a terrible mistake. I moved in with Taylor again and got screwed yet again. But what's worse, Mom, is I think you got screwed in the process as well."

"Screwed? Screwed how?"

"Taylor was successful in obtaining employment from the one and only Jack Griffin. And I think her sole motive was to provide him with information about Logan Courtyard. Mom, I'm so sorry."

"Do you know what type of information?" Brooklin asks.

"No, but probably everything she knows about the hotel."

"Luke, it's regretful that you became involved with Taylor again but luckily I have protected our computers from unauthorized access. So whatever other information she feeds to Griffin, we can deal with. What's more important is how are you doing?"

"Mom, you'll have to excuse my skepticism, but you need to know that Taylor and Griffin are undoubtedly plotting a strategy to take the hotel from you. I'm sure that is their plan. I think they've been carefully planning and calculating this for a while.

Taylor probably organized everything down to the last detail. And, sadly, I allowed her to use me. Now that I think about it, Taylor and Griffin probably masterminded the setback with the new construction. Mom, I am so sorry."

"In all probability, they probably did. Nonetheless, I think that my biggest attribute to the success of Logan Courtyard is that I've had to not only work hard but to work smart. It's been a tumultuous few weeks and I'm ready for whatever comes. Therefore, Luke, if that is the battle Griffin and Taylor want, let them bring it on. At this point, what is one more fight?"

Luke rambled on. "Time after time, I deluded myself about Taylor. That I could trust her and we were building a really good relationship. Time after time Taylor showed me that the most important person to Taylor was Taylor. However, I still stayed with her. She told me she loved me but she put her self-interest above everybody and everything else. I see now how this relationship with her has been destructive to our family and to me since the beginning. The relationship had to end. And I feel like such a sucker."

"Don't talk like that, Luke. I understand the ups and the downs we may incur in life. But we have to ride through the peaks and the valleys and move forward. There is no other choice. Now, Luke, tell us how you learned Taylor was working for Griffin," Brooklin asks looking at Colin who has been quiet through this entire conversation.

Realizing Brooklin is looking at him, Colin says, "I hope you have finally learned to stay away from that woman."

Brooklin looks at Colin disapprovingly and says, "Colin, please."

"Okay, okay" Colin exclaims shrugging. "Luke, tell us how you learned that Taylor was working for Griffin."

Luke tells his parents about Taylor's visit to Logan Courtyard, his retrieving her cell phone and then following her to return the phone and ending up at Griffin Development. He also informed them of their many conversations in which Taylor continuously told him of her desire to take control of Logan Courtyard. Brooklin and Colin are speechless and disgusted after listening to Luke. And Brooklin is visibly angry. Colin gazes at her, "Brooklin, please, before you embark on a journey of revenge, give it some thought. Getting revenge will not make this situation better nor will it make you feel better."

"However, Colin, sometimes it's necessary," Brooklin replies sharply.

"Brooklin, before you do anything, consider what lasting effects your actions may have. Revenge is not the answer. It can cause more trouble than good. Believe me, I know."

Brooklin looks at him curiously for a moment. But her thoughts quickly return to Taylor. Colin continues to observe Brooklin and recognizes the intent look on her face.

"Mom, what are your thoughts? I feel like this is my fault. I don't know what Jack Griffin and Taylor will do next. I want to help fix this. I'm willing to do whatever it takes."

"Honey, like your father said, we are only responsible for our own actions. What Taylor and Jack Griffin do is not your fault. Right now, I'm just considering if I have all areas of Logan Courtyard shielded and protected."

"I knew better than to get involved with Taylor again. Yet, I did. I knew Taylor was coming from a place of deep vindictiveness. I should have just pulled away. Why did I let her trap me in her web?" Luke says shaking his head and then putting his face in his hands.

"Stop this, Luke. I know you feel overwhelmed now," Brooklin says. "However, Son, you must work through this. In the future, you'll choose your friends more wisely and be sure that a new relationship is built on honesty and respect. Most importantly, you will value yourself and your own integrity."

"You may struggle with this mistake for a time but use it as one of life's lessons. And Luke, you have taken the first step. So now, learn from this and put one foot in front of the other. You will come out on the other side a much stronger and knowledgeable person," Colin adds.

"Okay, I will try," Luke says somberly.

"We don't try in this family," Brooklin stressed. "We *do*. Now listen, go home, clean yourself up and get some rest. And stop worrying. Taylor and Jack Griffin do not deserve and are not worth any more of your thoughts or time. Tomorrow is a new day and we will continue with our plans for Logan Courtyard. Also, focus instead on completing your curriculum for this school year. We will not allow *any* one to stand in our way of completing our goals. You remember that."

Luke hugs his mother and then his father. "Sorry I kept this from the two of you. Mom, hurting you was the last thing I wanted to do. Thanks for being understanding. I appreciate you guys," Luke says as he walks out the kitchen door.

Brooklin walks toward the island in the kitchen, "Taylor has an insidious way of manipulating men."

Colin refocuses on Brooklin. "Luke is a grown man, he needs to figure it out for himself." Brooklin turns and stares at Colin. "Brooklin, did you mean what you said to Luke? Are you going to follow your own advice?" Brooklin doesn't answer and walks into the family room. "Brooklin, talk to me. What are you thinking?"

"I'm thinking my anger for that woman has turned into rage. I've devoted a great deal of time and energy into preparing my family to one day manage Logan Courtyard. This hotel will remain in this family. It's part of our heritage. My mother entrusted this hotel to me and I take it very seriously. It's in our blood and I will pass it on. That's the way it works. I will not drop the ball. These toxic people will *not* destroy what has been set in place. It will not happen. I will not let my work and my mother's work be for nothing."

Colin struggles to find the right words. "What does that mean?" Brooklin doesn't answer. "Brooklin, you have changed."

"I've changed? Well, what does that mean? I should sit back and play nice while these detestable people try to take my hotel? Well, I will not. Griffin and Taylor made the mistake of underestimating me once before."

"You are different, Brooklin. You are almost a completely different person."

"Well, I'm glad you are finally recognizing it. I'm no longer blindly doing what my husband wants me to do. The difference is I finally respect myself and I will not lie down and let others take advantage of me. Now, good night, Colin."

"Brooklin ..."

"Good night, Colin. I think you know your way out," Brooklin says as she walks out of the family room and up the stairs.

After Brooklin hears Colin leave, she returns downstairs, locks the doors and sets the alarms. She walks back upstairs and into her bedroom, "I can't believe the position I find myself in. Erica's disappearance, criminals, alcoholic brother, people plotting against me, receiving anonymous cards. What did I stumble into while working to build my business?"

Brooklin sits on her bed, "Colin says I'm different. I'm certain this statement wasn't meant to be positive. However, how can I not be different? I'm trying to survive." She walks into her bathroom and stares into the mirror. "I have to find the right balance – feel comfortable with myself in all this turmoil. After I inherited the hotel, I tried to find myself as my own person aside from being a wife and a mother. And I entered into this hideous turmoil while trying to reconstruct Logan Courtyard."

Brooklin returns to her bedroom and stands at the foot of her bed, "I just have to trust my instincts." She takes off her shirt and pants and places them on her bed. "Then again, I can't let these people get away. They are forcing my hand and are purposely trying to cause destruction and, in the process, destroy me. What am I to do? If I don't stop this havoc, my hotel and I will become collateral damage. I have to beat them at their own warped game. I must protect what is mine and defeat those who try to injure me and what I have built." Brooklin removes her bra and panties. She steps into the shower and increases the temperature of the water to as hot as she can stand it. "Griffin, I've done what is needed to send you to prison. However--Taylor, I'm not holding back anymore. You have my undivided attention. No one plots to take my hotel away from me," Brooklin says fiercely as she stands in the shower and lets the water run down her face and body. "No one."

Chapter 19

Thursday morning, Detective Ryan enters the precinct, cup of coffee in hand, to find Brooklin's brother Jim in the lobby. As Detective Ryan approaches, Jim stands. "Good morning, Mr. Logan," Detective Ryan says as he shakes Jim's hand.

"Good morning," Jim replies.

"Mr. Logan, it will be a few minutes before I can meet with you."

"Sure," Jim says and returns to his chair.

Detective Ryan walks in the direction of the receptionist and winks at her. "How you doing this morning, Claire?"

"Ryan, don't talk to me. You didn't bring me coffee."

"Next time, Claire, next time," the detective says smiling.

After about five minutes, Claire tells Jim that Detective Ryan will see him now and gives him directions. As Jim is about halfway down the hall, he sees Detective Ryan walking toward him. They make idle conversation as they walk to an interrogation room. "Detective Ryan, I'm not sure why I'm being questioned," Jim says as he sits in the chair facing the detective.

"Mr. Logan, I would like to ask you a few questions regarding one of the girls at the Teen Center, Kim and a secretary at Logan Courtyard, Erica.

"Sure. Although, I'm not certain what information I can provide."

"Before we get started, Mr. Logan, can I get you a cup of coffee, a bottle of water?"

"No, I'm fine."

Detective Ryan laughs. "I understand, man, I try not to drink the coffee here either," Ryan says pointing to the coffee cup he brought in this morning.

Jim smiles and relaxes a little.

Detective Ryan notices that Jim is loosening up a little and he begins his questioning. "Now, Mr. Logan, how well did you know Erica Harris?"

"Not very well. She was my sister's secretary at Logan Courtyard. If there was a problem in your department or if you needed directives from someone other than your supervisor, then you would talk to Erica. Also, she was a volunteer at the Teen Center."

"What type of relationship did you have with her?"

"We were cordial. She was friendly, professional."

"Did the two of you ever have a personal relationship? Did you two date at anytime?"

"No. It was strictly professional. Very rarely did I come in contact with Erica at the hotel. Only if I needed to see my sister or if she needed to provide some type of information, and the majority of time those instructions would be conveyed directly to the supervisors."

"What about at the Teen Center?"

"I think I only saw her a couple times at the Center and we just spoke as we passed in the hallway."

"Has anyone talked to you about Erica's disappearance?"

"I heard she was missing and no one seems to know where she is. I also spoke to Brooklin about Erica briefly. I know she is worried because they were close. However, Brooklin is baffled just like everyone else."

"Do you know or have you heard of Erica having a personal relationship with anyone at Logan Courtyard or at the Teen Center?"

"No, except I know she and Lorna, our receptionist, were friendly."

"Okay, Mr. Logan, what can you tell me about Kim. What have you heard about her disappearance?"

"Nothing really. Kim seems to disappear from the Teen Center every couple of months. Therefore, it's pretty normal for her to be away from the Center from time to time. Brooklin asked me to talk to the kids about Kim's whereabouts." Jim provides Detective Ryan with the information Brenda told him regarding the call from Kim.

"What was your relationship with Kim?"

"Kim was just one of the kids at the Teen Center. I didn't really have a relationship with her."

"Do you know of any close relationships she had with anyone at the Center?"

"She wasn't very friendly and wasn't close to any of the kids or the staff. She seemed to talk to Lorna a little more than other staff members."

"What about your brother-in-law? Did you ever see him having conversations with Ms. Harris or Kim?"

"No, not that I can recall. Colin stays in his office most of the time, attending meetings or talking to staff members."

"Okay, thank you, Mr. Logan. I appreciate your coming to the precinct to answer my questions. If you remember any details that may help us to solve these cases, please let me know."

"Good luck with the cases. I know my sister will be happy when they are solved. As a matter of fact, I'm actually going to Logan Courtyard now to meet with Brooklin." Jim says. He and Detective Ryan shake hands again as Jim leaves the interrogation room.

"Well, give your sister my regards," Detective Ryan says.

"I will," Jim adds.

Detective Ryan returns to the squad room and every eye is staring intently at the wall mounted flat-screened television. "This morning, the grand jury began hearing testimony in connection with the federal and state criminal investigations against Jack Griffin of Griffin Development. Sources say the grand jury activity appears to be the strongest indication that prosecutors might be moving closer to an indictment against Mr. Griffin. Because federal and state grand jury proceedings are conducted in secret, few details are available about the witnesses or the nature of any evidence that may have been or will be presented. Mr. Griffin has been steadfast in maintaining his innocence. We will keep you updated as the grand jury determines whether or not there is probable cause to indict Jack Griffin for the alleged crimes – one of which is murder." Before the news reporter finishes, the entire squad room explodes into applause.

Detective Ryan smiles and begins to make his exit from the squad room. Baker walks over and says, "Where you going, Ryan? We are celebrating!"

"I have some quick investigation work I need to take care of."

"You need some help?"

"No, I'm fine with this one. I'll be back shortly."

"You know, Griffin is going to be indicted and is going to prison this time."

"Baker, I think you are right. This time, I think we got him," Ryan says as he turns and walks out of the squad room.

Brooklin telephones Levy. "Did you see the news bulletin showing Jack Griffin entering the court house for the grand jury hearing?"

"I did," Levy affirms. "The word is, they think the prosecutors have a good case against him. He's facing felony charges for what prosecutors say was a criminal scheme to obtain property along with the murder charges."

"With all the information the FBI has against Griffin and with Mr. Reed's testimony, the grand jury should indict him."

"And I think thereafter, he will be found guilty of all the charges in court." Levy adds.

"Levy, I need to ask you to provide me with some information regarding Griffin."

"What type of information?"

"I need to know Griffin's schedule and his planned whereabouts for the upcoming weekend."

"His schedule?"

"Yes, what's on his calendar. Maybe, where he is having dinner this weekend?"

"Where he is having dinner?" Levy asks curiously.

"Yes, the Buzz shows him frequently having dinner at various restaurants in the area."

"Brooklin, what are you up to?"

"I just want to be in the same restaurant with him, preferably this weekend."

"Brooklin," Levy says putting emphasis on her name.

"It will be fine. It will be quite harmless."

"Brooklin, we are too close now to having Griffin serve time in prison to make any mistakes. I want us to continue to fly under the radar."

"Trust me, Levy. It will be fine."

"Brooklin, I will try to get his schedule for you. However, I will come with you."

"No, Levy, I will do this alone. I know what I'm doing."

"Okay, Brooklin, I'll call you when I get the information."

"Thanks, Levy."

As Brooklin ends the call, Karla walks in. "Brooklin, I just wanted to remind you that Diane, the new office worker, will start tomorrow. Also a quick reminder of the contractors' meeting. I put them on your calendar. However, for the last couple of weeks, you haven't been paying close attention to your calendar."

Brooklin smiles, "You are definitely right about that, Karla. However, I will do better."

"I'm looking forward to the day that construction is completed and we can begin implementing all of the plans and book the grand opening artist," Karla exclaims. "Brooklin, the blueprints for the VIP Rooftop Lounge are amazing. I love the step-down area where the pool and bar will be located."

"Yes, I'm glad we added that area."

"And it was such a great idea to incorporate a retractable roof with the stunning 360-degree view overlooking the beach, the harbor and the city. It will be incredible and just breathtaking. And your insight about renovating the underground storage to add a tunnel system for discreet entrances – just fabulous!"

"Thanks, Karla, I'm looking forward to the new additions as well. And in the meantime, I will try to remember to check my calendar. Thank you again for your help. You have proven yourself to be invaluable to Logan Courtyard."

"Thank you, Brooklin, and I really appreciate the positive feedback."

After a moment, Brooklin looks a little serious, "Karla, I've noticed you seem a bit preoccupied today. Are you okay?"

"The last couple of days have been a little stressful."

Brooklin closes her office door and tells Karla to have a seat on the couch. "Are you having any problems here at the hotel?"

"No. No, everything here is fine. And Brooklin, I'm fine. I don't want to dump my problems on you."

"Karla, it's all right. Tell me what's going on."

"I'm just frustrated. I love my job. If I could stay here around the clock, I would be very happy. It just seems outside of work, no matter what I do, drama seems to follow me. If it's not my daughter, it's the people surrounding me. If I have to hear one more time what a rotten mother I am ..."

"That's just your daughter being a teenager. Sometimes, you just have to let those comments roll off your back."

"I know. But being called a rotten mother because she wants to go out on a school night. And I'm awful for not allowing her to go out with friends when she has not completed her schoolwork. I'm just tired of the arguments. I don't think I'm too strict. But I have to be careful.   I don't want her to get into any trouble."

"'I'm sorry you're having these problems, Karla."

"It's like the majority of the people around me don't take responsibility for their actions. They want to blame me for the things they do ... and really for any negative outcome."

"Karla, people are going to talk no matter what you do ... whether you are doing well or not. It's just a fact of life. There are going to be detractors. However, we cannot base our day or our happiness on what people say. Or focus on other people's narrative of us. As long as we know in our heart that we are doing the best we can, then we let it go. Remember, we are not perfect. We make mistakes. However, we forgive ourselves and try to do better thereafter."

"That's a tall order."

"In the beginning it is. But you get better with it in time. People who are not doing their best do not want you to shine. They think your light makes them appear lesser. Therefore, they try to dim your light. So, Karla, keep doing your best, honey, that's all any of us can do."

"Brooklin, thanks. You always make me feel better."

"You are welcome and you are a good person. Don't let those negative people transfer their negativity to you. Start distancing yourself from them. Try to surround yourself with positive people who are striving to move forward, who have similar goals. Gossip is a bad habit. Often people with low self-esteem try to make themselves feel better by talking about others. The drama they create is really not about you, it's something within them."

"I know but the last couple of days, it has really started to weigh on me. You know, when people close to you are in the midst of the drama." Karla is quiet for a moment. "I know I am a good person. However, I just want to confront them. Do you think good people do bad things? Because I'm at that point now," Karla says.

"I don't think wanting to confront or confronting individuals is doing anything bad. If it makes you feel better, then tell them how you feel and then move on. However, do you really wish to waste your time and energy on them?"

"You're right because if I confronted them the way I would like to, I would just be playing into their hands."

"Well, Karla, we only have control of ourselves. Just remember, their words cannot have any effect on you unless you allow them to. I believe in a higher power. Which means, I don't have the last word and they don't have the last word. When wrong is done, we may not see or know that it comes back to those individuals, but it does. So, let it be on them and not on you. Nonetheless, sometimes, we do have to go into the self-preservation mode."

Karla hugs Brooklin, "Thank you."

"You are welcome. Now, stop stressing. You are a lovely person and they are probably just jealous of you."

"I don't know about that."

"You would be surprised. Just keep your head up and continue to move forward. Sometimes life will throw us a curve ball. However, we don't have to always act, sometimes we can just dodge." Brooklin says smiling. "I should know. In the last week, I have had to dodge about two or three times a day." They both laugh.

Brooklin stands and tells Karla, "It will work out and remember, drop those haters, one by one." They both laugh again.

"Brooklin, did you ever read that report I left for you on your desk from TJ, Inc?"

"No, as a matter of fact, I will read it now. Thanks for the reminder," Brooklin says.

After Karla returns to her office, Brooklin looks through her bag, finds the report and begins reading. After a few minutes, Brooklin sits straight up in her chair. "What? Laila and Martina are friends? This

Martina is Laila's friend, Tina?" Brooklin becomes tense but continues to read the report. Brooklin places the report on her desk and leans back in her chair. She recalls the young lady in the hotel lobby with Karla. It was Martina. She was interviewing for Karla's previous position. "Well, I'm definitely glad we hired Diane instead." Brooklin considers this situation closely, "Martina or Tina, whatever your name is. What game are you playing? What are your intentions? Why are you so desperate to work for Logan Courtyard? Are you targeting my family, Logan Courtyard, me? Martina was hired by Jill's employment agency and then she became friendly with Laila. What are her motives?" Brooklin remembers the accident. "No, she could not have arranged for me to hit her car. I did that all on my own. However, did she focus on my family before or after I hit her car? Maybe before, since she knew my last name was Covington. Is she somehow connected to the notes and key I received?"

Brooklin reads the report again. "Okay, there is no smoking gun here – nothing really out of the ordinary. Martina works for Allure, where my hair stylist is employed. However, I knew that. Laila told me. The receptionist at Allure told me there is a new owner. Is there a connection there?" Brooklin telephones Laila telling her she had her friend investigated and the information she learned.

"Mom, why would you have her investigated?"

"After the car accident, she continues to pop up unexpectedly. Therefore, I had her checked out."

"Well, you didn't really find anything, Mom. So can you please let it go?"

"Laila, if you can, be a little cautious around this young lady. I'm not sure what she is really looking to gain. And I definitely will not hire her to work at Logan Courtyard."

"Maybe, Mom, she is looking to gain a job?"

"Maybe. I just wanted you to be aware of my findings."

"Mom, I'm so busy right now. I very rarely see or talk to Tina."

"Well, good."

"Okay, Mom, fine. I gotta go."

Brooklin contemplates for a minute then calls Jill. "Hi. Quick question. How well do you know the young lady Martina you sent to interview for Karla's position?"

"Hi, Brooklin. Can you hold for a minute? Let me pull up the information on her." Jill is quiet for a minute. "I just have basic information about her. She has good skills, light secretarial experience but very personable and her references check out. Why? Is there a problem?"

"I am just concerned. She is now friendly with Laila and trying to obtain Laila's help to become employed at Logan Courtyard."

"Well, she could just want to work for the best hotel on the east coast."

"I guess. All right, thanks. We'll talk later."

"All right, how about dinner next weekend?"

"Sounds good," Brooklin says as she places the report back in her bag. Her thoughts return to Laila.

"Should I have told Laila about the notes and the key I received? What if they are from this Martina? Laila could be caught in the middle of some type of conspiracy. I just don't know what to think about this situation. However, I hope Laila will be more mindful around this Tina now. And Laila did say, lately she rarely sees or talks to Tina."

Detective Ryan enters Club 54 on the main level dance floor. The upscale venue has dazzling lights and music videos on high def screens mounted on various walls throughout the club. The detective walks to the bar, identifies himself and shows the bartender a photo of Erica. He asks if the bartender remembers seeing this young lady. The bartender nods, "Yes, I know Erica. No word on her yet?"

"When was the last time you saw Erica?"

"Erica frequents our bar. She loves speed dating. The last time I saw her, she was leaving through the back door with some guy."

"Do you know the guy?"

"No, I've never seen before and I haven't seen him since."

"Can you describe him?"

"He was about 6 feet, medium build, black hair with a beard."

"Have you seen her with any other guys?"

"Yes, talking, but I've never seen her leave with any other guy. Erica was here often but she wasn't the type to leave with guys. She's a sweet girl. I was surprised to see her leave with that guy."

"What's your surveillance situation like here?" Detective Ryan asks.

"State of the art, both front and back doors. However, our back door camera's been out for a few months. Someone cut the wires. We're still waiting on the owner to send a repair guy."

"A few months?"

"A few months. What can I say? The owner clearly doesn't care."

"All right. Well, I'm going out back and take a look."

"Sure, be my guest."

Detective Ryan walks through the club and out the rear door. He takes a moment to put on gloves and examines the back parking lot camera. "Very suspicious," he says to himself. "Wires have clearly been snipped. Hmm ... three months?" He reaches in the inside pocket of his jacket for a fingerprint kit. I guess it wouldn't hurt to dust for fingerprints." After a few minutes he returns to his car, "Talk about counterproductive."

Brooklin returns to her office drinking some green tea. As she places the cup on her desk, she hears, "Hi, Brooklin," and she turns to see her brother Jim. She looks at him carefully ascertaining that he is not drunk, although she thinks he's been drinking.

"Hi, Jim. How are you?"

"I'm good. As a matter of fact, I was just questioned by Detective Ryan at the police station."

"Jim, how did you get here?"

"How did I get here? I drove of course."

"Jim, you shouldn't be driving."

"Why shouldn't I be driving, Brooklin?"

Brooklin ignores Jim's question, "Why was Detective Ryan questioning you?"

"He just wanted to know what I knew about Erica and Kim. He told me to give you his regards."

She wished she didn't have to have this conversation with Jim. They had been getting along so well. However, this talk is a must.

"Jim, how have you really been?"

"Good. Why do you ask?"

Brooklin stares at him.

"Oh, someone told you I've been drinking. Who told you? Colin? Amber?"

"Who told me doesn't matter, Jim. I'm concerned about you."

"Well, there's no need for you to be concerned. See," he stretches his arms out, "I haven't been drinking today."

"Jim, why have you begun to drink again? You were doing so well?"

"Listen, this is my life and I'm tired of discussing this with everyone. I'm a grown man."

"Are you going to AA meetings and counseling?"

"Brooklin, can you worry about yourself and stop treating me like a child?"

"I don't want to argue with you, Jim. I'm just concerned."

"Well, I don't want your concern. I don't want anyone's concern," Jim says as he quickly stands up.

"Jim, why are you getting so argumentative? Can't we just have a peaceful conversation?"

"I want you and everyone to stay out of my business. That's what I want."

"Jim, I want you to be okay and I can clearly see you are not. Jim, please think about returning to rehab."

"Rehab? I'm not going back to any rehab. I don't need rehab. I can handle my drinking."

"Jim, it's clear that you cannot. However, I love you and I'm not going to give up on you and I don't want you to give up on yourself either."

"I don't know what you are talking about. I'm out of here."

"Jim, please sit down and let's talk calmly."

He looks at her and then sits down, "I'll stay for a few more minutes."

"All right good, Jim. Thank you," she says looking at him caringly. Jim turns his head and then looks down. "Jim, I'm not trying to criticize you. I just want you to get better. I want my brother back."

"I haven't gone anywhere. I'm here."

"Jim, you know that alcoholism is a disease and you have to get treatment to manage it. You need to take control and responsibility for your sobriety. Jim, please get help so you can continue to move forward and not backwards in life. You have to do this for yourself. I will support you and I know Colin and Amber will support you as well. But you have to want sobriety. No one can force you."

"You are right, no one can force me," Jim shouts.

Brooklin is beginning to get agitated. "Jim, maybe you just want to yell to prove yourself to be right. But Jim, yelling doesn't deflect what is obviously needed here. You gotta get help or I'm afraid ..."

"Afraid of what? That I won't be like you? Proper and good at everything?"

"Jim, please. This is not about me."

"No, it's not. Because you are just so perfect."

"Jim, that's not true. We all are flawed. And right now, I'm going through a difficult time too. But we have to put our best foot forward."

"The only foot I'm putting forward is the one I will use to get out of your office and this hotel. You know, the hotel mom left to you and only you."

"Jim," Brooklin calls out as he walks toward the door.

Luke enters Brooklin's office, looks at Jim and then at his mother. "What's going on here?"

"Ask your mother," Jim says, "She seems to know everything."

"Mom?" Luke says.

"Luke, get your Uncle Jim's car keys. Don't let him drive."

"Don't let him drive? Why can't he drive?"

"Because I'm pretty certain he's been drinking."

"And, take him where?"

"Preferably to rehab."

"What?" Luke asks confused.

"Drive him home. Hurry, Luke, don't let him drive." Luke looks at her again and walks quickly out the door. Brooklin places her head on her desk, absolutely exhausted.

Chapter 20

"Brooklin, do you need anything else before I leave today?" Karla asks as she stands in Brooklin's doorway.

"No, Karla, I'm fine. Go home and have a nice evening with your daughter."

"I will try. Brooklin, thank you again for our talk."

"You are quite welcome," Brooklin says as Karla disappears. Brooklin turns the volume up on her television for some background noise. She just doesn't want to focus on the noise in her head right now and the pain that is radiating from her neck down to her shoulder. She is mentally fatigued. Brooklin looks at the green tea on her desk . "I guess I will take this opportunity to drink my *cold* green tea," Brooklin says aloud.

She walks to the window, peers out and massages her shoulder. After a few minutes, she suddenly feels something wet on her leg. She looks down to see Blake licking her leg. "Blake. Oh Blake, I'm so happy to see you." She looks around, "How did you get here?"

Luke walks in, "I thought you could use a friend, so I brought Blake to see you."

"Thanks, Luke, Blake is just what I need." She feels a twinge in her shoulder as she picks up Blake. Brooklin walks back to her chair with Blake in her arms. "I do love this dog."

"I think the feeling is mutual," Luke says as Blake sits panting in Brooklin's arms. "Blake enjoyed his play date with his rough collie pal."

"That's great, Luke." Smiling, Brooklin looks down at Blake, "You had fun at your play date?"

"Mom, I also wanted you to know, I took Uncle Jim home. I have his keys. I will chauffeur him around until he gets himself clean."

"Thanks so much, Luke. I appreciate this."

"Hey, he's my uncle. I love him." Luke hesitates for a moment. "Mom, when I was driving Uncle Jim home, he continually talked about you."

"I'm sure. What did he say?"

"He kept saying you think you know everything, but you don't know everyone's secrets."

Brooklin suddenly went cold. "*Secrets?*" She's silent for a moment. "He actually said *secrets?*'

"Yes, he said it a few times. However, as soon as I got him home, he passed out on the couch. He also said, you need to worry about your affairs and stop worrying about his business."

They are quiet for a moment. Brooklin clears her throat. She is unnerved by the thought that Jim could have sent her the notes and the key. "No," she says to herself. "Jim would never do that to me."

"All right, Mom, you have Blake tonight and I'm out of here."

"Thanks again, Luke. By the way, Luke, how are you?"

"Mom, I'm fine. What can I say, you just can't stay down long in this family – there's too much drama going on." Brooklin looks up at Luke. He laughs, "I'm just joking, Mom."

"Bye, Luke," Brooklin says as she rubs Blake's fur. "Okay, Blake, I have to put you down. I'm having some sharp pains in my shoulder."

"Mom, are you okay? You're having shoulder pain? Maybe you should go to the spa for a massage."

"I'm okay. Just a little tired." Brooklin returns to the chair behind her desk as Agent Dalton appears in her doorway, "Ms. Covington, how are you?"

"Agent Dalton. Hi, come in."

Luke stands, and says, "Mom, I'll talk to you later."

"Agent Dalton, this is my son, Luke."

"Nice to meet you, Luke."

"Nice meeting you as well," Luke replies. "Mom, I'll call you later."

"Ms. Covington, I must apologize. It seems I'm always visiting you without calling first for an appointment. However, I was driving by and I thought this might be a good time to have a conversation with you again."

"That's fine, Agent Dalton. Please have a seat."

He walks toward her desk as Blake runs out of the back room staring at him. "Well hello, little one. Brooklin, you have a guard dog."

"Agent Dalton, this is Blake. The newest member of my family."

"Well, he is a good looking addition to your family."

"Thank you. Now, would you like something to drink?"

"Well, I'm off duty. How about a beer?"

Brooklin looked surprised. "Sure, sure." She phones the restaurant and orders the beer. She mutes the television. "So Agent Dalton, what did you want to talk to me about?" They are interrupted as one of the kitchen staff enters with Agent Dalton's beer.

"Thank you, my man. Great service as well as swift service," Agent Dalton says taking the beer. "Just what I needed after a day like today, a cold beer." Brooklin waits until the young waiter has left, closing the door behind him. She then returns her attention to Agent Dalton.

"So Agent Dalton, what is the reason for your visit today?"

"Ms. Covington," Agent Dalton says, "I'll come straight to the point. Did you provide the FBI and the Buzz the anonymous information regarding Jack Griffin?"

Brooklin is stunned. "What? What information would you be referring to?"

"Well let me rephrase my question. Did you provide any information to the FBI and the Buzz regarding Jack Griffin?"

"That's a stretch. What are you actually accusing me of here?" Brooklin hesitates for a moment and then continues, "Griffin stands accused of heinous crimes. I'm not going to apologize for wanting Griffin to suffer. He deserves to go to prison. However, there is a crucial difference between wanting something to happen and participating in making it happen."

"Ms. Covington, with all due respect, you are evading the question. I think the information regarding Griffin came from you. You can be honest with me. Remember, I am your ally."

"Did you say, 'You are my ally?'"

"Listen, I don't condone what you did. However, I do understand."

"What I *did*? I'm not quite certain how you are coming to that conclusion. I think, FBI Agent Dalton," Brooklin accentuates his name "you need to stop assuming. Nevertheless, I have been wrapped up in this case so I'm glad there may be a light at the end of the tunnel."

"It's a complicated case and Griffin has tried to cover his tracks. However with our undercover operations, surveillance, informants," Agent Dalton eyes Brooklin knowingly, "and anonymous tips, I think we have all we need despite Griffin's cover-ups."

"Well, hopefully there is no chance of any type of cover-up. Because we both know if Griffin walks, he will just continue his corrupt ways."

"Why do you assume he may get off?"

"Maybe because he's never been held accountable."

"Griffin will not go free. We have too much evidence. Some that was handed to us on a silver platter," he says looking directly into her eyes.

"Well, at any rate, I am definitely happy his reign may be finally coming to an end. He exemplifies what is wrong in this city and he needs to be stopped," Brooklin says adamantly.

"Yes, political corruption. Griffin is at the heart of the corruption in this city. He is a fraudulent, unethical, dirty real estate developer and I am determined to bring him to justice."

"I hope he gets his due and goes to prison for a long time."

"And you were willing to throw everything into the fire so he can finally pay. Compromise your values?"

"Finishing Griffin is the ultimate goal. It's a worthy cause and for that I am not sorry."

"It appears he has lost the support of the people he normally counts on. It's him against the world. He's alone. That could break him or rouse him to magnum. But I promise, I will get justice for all his victims – justice will be done."

"He probably has made contingency plans."

"Probably. And I'm certain Griffin's lawyer will try to cut a deal soon."

Brooklin looks puzzled and opens her mouth to ask a question as her cell phone rings. "Agent Dalton, if you would excuse me for a moment," Brooklin says as she walks over to her desk to answer her phone and realizes it is Levy calling.

"Hi, Brooklin, I got that information for you regarding Griffin. He will be at LaTorra for dinner tomorrow at 7:00pm."

"Really?" she says glancing at Agent Dalton. "I wonder if there is a connection there. Can you check to see whether a connection exists between the man and the dwelling?"

"All right, will do. And Brooklin, I don't know what you are planning. But please remember, where Griffin is concerned, be careful."

"Absolutely," she says. Brooklin's gaze returns to Agent Dalton as she places her phone on her desk. "Now Agent Dalton, back to our conversation. You think Griffin's attorney will try to cut a deal?"

"Yes, for a reduced sentence."

"Do you think a deal will be made?"

"It will save taxpayers money. But the District Attorney will make certain Griffin serves a lot of time."

"I want him to suffer."

"Griffin in prison? Of course, he will suffer."

Brooklin thinks to herself, "It's now or never," as she begins to lay the foundation for her devious plan. "Agent Dalton, it has come to my attention that one of Griffin's employees will be dining at LaTorra's resort restaurant tomorrow evening. I'm thinking you may be able to obtain additional information that you can use in the case against Griffin."

"And who is this employee?"

"Her name is Taylor Daniels. She's 33 years old with black hair and about 5'6."

"And you think she may have information that can help us with this case?"

"Yes, I definitely do."

"Well, I guess there will be no harm in my talking to Ms. Daniels."

Brooklin smiles, "No. No harm at all."

"All right, I will put Ms. Daniels on my calendar. I should be at LaTorra around 6:45pm."

"Great," Brooklin says with an amused look on her face.

Agent Dalton takes another sip of beer, "My beer has gotten a little warm."

"Would you like another?"

"Only if you will have one with me."

"I think I will join you but I'll have wine."

He grins at her, "Let's drink to you, Ms. Covington, the woman who makes everything happens."

Agent Dalton notices Brooklin's hesitation and proclaims, "Why don't we drink to Griffin spending many years in prison?"

"Sounds like a plan to me," Brooklin says smiling as she picks up the phone to call the restaurant. "I do believe that pain in my shoulder is completely gone," she thinks to herself.

Detective Ryan's telephone rings and the receptionist tells him Lorna Young is here. "Send her back, I'll meet her in the hallway." Detective Ryan leaves the squad room and as he enters the hallway, he sees Lorna walking toward him.

"Ms. Young, how are you today?"

"I'll be better when I'm out of here."

"Well, Ms. Young, you need to tell the truth in order to leave this building."

Lorna looks at him with apprehension, "Do I need an attorney?"

"That is totally your call," Detective Ryan says as he opens the interrogation room door for Lorna.

"Ms. Young, I am investigating the disappearances of Kim, a young lady from the Teen Center, and Erica Harris, an employee at Logan Courtyard. I will be recording our conversation. Now I advise you to think before you speak and only provide truthful answers to my questions. Do you understand, Ms. Young?" Lorna nods her head. "Ms. Young, do you understand? I need a verbal answer. As I mentioned earlier, this conversation is being recorded. Now again, Ms. Young, you are not under arrest; however, you may have a lawyer present during questioning. Do you understand, Ms. Young?"

"Yes, I understand."

"Good. If you would please state your full name and address." Visibly shaken, Lorna states her full name and address. "Ms. Young, how long have you been residing at that address?"

"About three years."

"Do you live alone?"

"Yes."

"And are you employed? If so, where are you employed and how long have you been at that employment?"

"I'm employed at the local Teen Center. I've been working there about a year and a half."

"Can you please provide the address of the Center and who your supervisor is currently?"

Lorna answers all questions, naming Colin Covington as her supervisor. "Now, what is your relationship with Mr. Covington?"

"He is my employer."

"Do you have a personal relationship with Mr. Covington?"

"No and what does this line of questioning have to do with Kim or Erica?"

"I will ask the questions here, Ms. Young. Now have you ever had a personal or intimate relationship with your employer, Mr. Covington? And remember my statement to you earlier. Please give only truthful answers."

Lorna hesitates. "Do I have to answer this? I do not want to lose my job."

"Yes, you do have to answer." Detective Ryan is in disbelief, however he shows no emotion. "Now, I will ask you again. Have you ever had an intimate relationship with Mr. Covington? And if so, when did this take place?"

"Yes, I have. But it only happened once."

"When, Ms. Young?"

"I don't remember the date. It was early March of this year."

"Early March. Was it around the time I was investigating Larry Carter's hit and run case?

"Yes, it was around that time. Please do not mention this to anyone especially not Ms. or Mr. Covington. I need my job."

"Why would you think you would lose your job if the Covingtons learn you provided this information?"

Lorna hesitates again, "Because I would have been fired long ago if I didn't keep this secret."

"Mr. Covington would have fired you?"

"Yes, he tried and I told him if he did, I would tell his wife about our sexual affair."

"Now, was it an affair or just the one time?"

"Just that one time."

"What were the circumstances of this experience?"

"Excuse me?"

"What were the circumstances of this one time sexual encounter?"

"Well, Mr. Covington was drinking if that is what you are asking."

"Okay so, when this encounter happened, was Mr. Covington still living with his wife?"

"Yes, but soon after they separated."

"Let me review what you just told me. You had sexual relations with Mr. Covington once (in March of this year) while he was still living with his wife, Ms. Covington. You threatened to tell Ms. Covington of this one time encounter if Mr. Covington fired you. Is this correct?"

"Yes."

"Does anyone else know about this one time experience of yours and Mr. Covington?"

"No."

"What type of relationship do you and Mr. Covington have presently?"

"Not great. Cordial. I think he just tolerates me now only because of this secret and because I'm a good worker."

"Okay, let's move on to Kim. What was your relationship with Kim?"

"She was just one of the kids at the Center."

"Did the two of you have a close relationship?"

"No, I wouldn't call it close. She didn't bond with any of the kids so she would talk to me sometimes."

"What would the two of you talk about?"

"Fashions, television programs and she sometimes talked about her mother."

"What about her mother?"

"She and her mother had a rocky relationship. She thought her mother was too strict. So they argued a lot. Kim wanted to be out in the street."

"What type of relationship did you and her mother have?"

"We didn't really have a relationship. She would call the Teen Center sometimes looking for Kim."

"Now, you mentioned earlier that you lived alone. Have you had any overnight guests in the last couple of months?"

"No."

"This will be my only warning to you to only provide truthful answers."

"Kim and her mother stayed at my apartment for a little over a month."

"Why were they staying at your apartment?" asks Detective Ryan.

"Kim's mother called me looking for Erica. Apparently, they were staying with Erica and were concerned because Erica had not come home. So, I invited Kim and her mother to stay at my house until Erica returned."

"Are they still staying at your apartment?"

"No, they haven't been at my apartment for the last couple of nights. Kim called me yesterday to say they were relocating out of the area."

"Did she say why or where?"

"No, it was a short conversation. She just said they were leaving town."

"What do you know of Ms. Harris's disappearance?"

"I don't know anything about her disappearance. She told me a couple of months earlier that she would not be volunteering any longer at the Teen Center. Then I learned of her disappearance from Kim and her mother."

"Was Erica close to anyone at the Teen Center?"

"No, she came in, taught her cooking class and left right after."

"What about you? Were you close to Erica?"

"We were not very close. We didn't see each other socially. We were just co-worker buddies."

"In the last month that Erica volunteered, you didn't see her talking to anyone?"

"No. I just remember Kim saying that Erica was going to ask Mr. Covington what to do in regards to Kim and her mother's situation."

"Kim told you that Erica was going to talk to Mr. Covington and not to Ms. Covington?"

"I think Kim said Erica told her that she was going to talk to Mr. Covington. I'm not sure. Maybe it was Ms. Covington."

"Ms. Young, that's all the questions I have for you now. If you remember or hear any information regarding these two cases, please let me know."

"I will. And can I ask you again to not mention my sleeping with Mr. Covington to anyone."

"Ms. Young, at this time, I do not intend to mention that information to anyone. However, I will not promise that this information will not be disclosed at some time in the future."

"All right," Lorna says.

"Is your boss at the Teen Center now?"

"Yes, why?"

"I am going to the Teen Center to question Mr. Covington again. However, I will not relate to him the personal information you disclosed."

"Thank you again, Detective," Lorna says heaving a sigh.

Detective Ryan and Lorna leave the interrogation room together. Ryan stops at his desk to check his messages and then leaves for the Teen Center.

After Agent Dalton leaves, Brooklin sits at her desk trying to determine how to arrange tomorrow's meeting between Taylor, Agent Dalton and Griffin. Her plan needs to be ironclad. Then she remembers, Brent, the bodyguard who will perform *special duties* for his employer—never questioning or complaining of any task. "Perfect, since Brent is now on the payroll." Brooklin telephones Brent, providing him with his assignment for tomorrow evening. "After we arrive at LaTorra, you will telephone a young lady giving her specific instructions to be at LaTorra's restaurant at 6:30pm."

Brent asks if there would be anything else required of him. "Yes," Brooklin says, "Just remember, this will be an anonymous phone call and I don't want the call to be traced back to you or me."

"Yes, of course, Ms. Covington. And I will pick you up at your home around 5:00pm."

"That will be fine, Brent." Brooklin ends the call thinking, "Now if only this works." She smiles, feeling very satisfied with herself.

Detective Ryan walks into the Teen Center and asks the volunteer to tell Mr. Covington that Detective Ryan is here to see him. Before Detective Ryan can sit down, Colin walks toward him and asks briskly, "Detective, what do you want? I'm late for a golf outing."

"Well, I will walk out with you. Just have a quick question for you."

"What question?"

"Did Erica speak to you in reference to Kim?"

Colin stares at him. "Did Erica speak to me in reference to Kim?"

"Yes, did Erica discuss Kim and her mother with you?"

"No. Why would Erica discuss Kim and her mother with me?"

"Are you certain?"

"Yes, I'm certain. Detective, can you go and fight crime and stay away from my family and the Teen Center?"

"I'm sure you would love for me to do just that, wouldn't you, Mr. Covington?" Detective Ryan smirks and says, "You see, in my line of work I've learned that the hidden always seems to finds its way to the surface sooner or later." Colin looks at him questioningly. "All right, Mr. Covington, hope you have a good golf game," Detective Ryan says as he turns to walk to his car. Colin observes him for a moment curiously and then gets in his car and drives away.

Detective Ryan drives out of the Teen Center parking lot thinking, "Colin, you disgusting piece of filth. I can't even begin to understand how anyone could cheat on that gorgeous woman. I really could not have fathomed this betrayal or how this relationship would end. However Colin, sooner or later people expose themselves. You have to face your demons! And when that happens, your days as Brooklin's husband are numbered. So go and enjoy your golf outing. You will be out of Brooklin's life soon. And I will help her get over the hurt and pain you have caused her yet again. The only positive in this scenario is you did it to yourself. Thanks, Colin. You literally made my point: you are not good enough for Brooklin."

Chapter 21

    Karla buzzes Brooklin the next morning, "Brooklin, Diane is here. I have introduced her to the first floor staff. Would you like to talk to her before she begins her training?"

    "Yes, that would be great. I have plans for later this afternoon. So please have her come in." Brooklin greets Diane and asks her to have a seat. A few minutes later, Karla buzzes again about a problem with guests on the 11th floor.

    Apparently, there was a problem regarding their flight reservations. Unable to get a flight until tomorrow morning, they want to remain in their room at the hotel. However, the hotel is booked. They are upset that they regularly stay at Logan Courtyard and feel that they should be accommodated. "Karla, tell Jamie at the front desk to arrange for the new guests that are booked for that same room to be reassigned to one of the emergency rooms."

    "I guess Jamie didn't resolve the problem quickly enough, so now they are asking to speak to the manager or the owner." Brooklin is quiet for a moment. Karla reminds Brooklin that Walt cannot handle this situation because he's attending an off-site meeting.

    "Okay, Karla, I am on my way to the 11th floor." She apologizes to Diane and again welcomes her to Logan Courtyard. Brooklin and one of the security personnel walk to the elevator. Brooklin realizes this will give her an opportunity to check Suite 1107 as well. She has not seen the suite since the maids cleaned after Andy had washed down and sanitized the suite following the attack on Mr. Reed. Suite 1107 is one of the suites Brooklin saves for emergencies.

Brooklin and Max arrive at Room 1103 and identify themselves. The problem is resolved quickly. Brooklin phones Jamie explaining the guests in Room 1103 will remain in that room for an additional night and to reassign the new guests to an emergency room. "Also, Jamie, I would like the guests in Room 1103 to be provided a complimentary meal, a bottle of champagne and a spa appointment for tonight. And in the future, if there is a problem with one of our regular patrons, please phone Walt or me before telling them we cannot accommodate them."

"I will and I'm sorry about the confusion."

As Brooklin takes her daily walk around the hotel, Jim phones her. "Just wanted to let you know I'm in rehab, Brooklin. I placed you on the list so you can call me. I can get calls on Fridays between 6 and 9pm."

"Well, Jim, I'm glad you're getting help."

"All right, I wanted to let you know where I am in case you were trying to reach me. Would you tell Colin for me?"

"Yes, Jim, I will. Now is there anything else you need to tell me?"

Jim is quiet for a moment. "No. I just wanted to tell you I'm in rehab."

"Okay, I appreciate your calling. Please take care and just focus on getting better. And Jim, you can call me at any time. I know this has been a very difficult decision for you and I'm proud of you."

"Thanks, Brooklin. Thanks for everything."

Brooklin uses her passkey to enter Suite 1107 and carefully examines each of the six rooms in this expansive suite. She looks at the impressive view of the tree-lined streets through one of the many oversized picture windows. Brooklin thinks of the harmonious mix this area offers – the beaches, the harbor, festivals, sensational shopping and great food. She turns from the window and again looks at the elegant suite. She is satisfied that Andy and the maids have returned the suite to what is expected from a first class hotel. Brooklin leaves the suite and walks down to meet with the contractor where the theater is being constructed.

After about an hour, she exits the construction area and phones Colin as she returns to her office. "Brooklin, hi. How are you today?"

"I'm fine, Colin. I received a call from Jim. He's in rehab."

"Good. I'm glad he finally decided to go."

"I am too. Hopefully all will go well and he will gain a new perspective. All right, Colin, I'll talk to you later. I'm going to try to get some work done before a late meeting."

"Brooklin, wait. How is everything at the hotel?"

"Everything is fine. I just left the contractor and he told me we're on schedule for the renovation and additions."

"That's fantastic, Brooklin."

"Thanks, Colin. All right I'm going to get off this phone now and get some work done."

"All right, I'll see you tomorrow at the Teen Center."

Brooklin dives into work on her computer. She works until 4pm then lets Karla know she is leaving for the day.

Brooklin arrives home, showers and dresses in a teal dress with spaghetti straps. The doorbell rings just as Brooklin reaches the bottom step. Brooklin smiles to herself, my Enforcer is here. She grabs her purse, turns on the foyer light, sets the house security alarm and locks the front door as she exits. They arrive at LaTorra at exactly 5:20pm. Brooklin chooses a table, somewhat hidden in the back corner of the restaurant where she can view the middle of the restaurant and the entrance. Brooklin knows Griffin normally sits at the center table to be seen by all.

Brent returns to their table after making the call to Taylor. "I made the call using a burner phone which I will dispose of after we leave tonight. Taylor said she would be here at 6:30. As you instructed, I told Taylor I was Griffin lawyer's assistant and that Mr. Griffin would like her to meet him at LaTorra and to be on time. "

"Perfect," Brooklin says. The waiter takes their order, wine for Brooklin and coffee for Brent. He pays the waiter in advance saying after their drinks, they will be leaving. Brooklin settles back in her chair and waits for the main event to unfold. After about thirty minutes, Taylor arrives and is seated near the front of the restaurant. Brooklin thinks, "Great. Jack Griffin will be certain to see her when he enters the restaurant." The waiter approaches Taylor's table and

Brooklin is guessing he takes her order. The waiter returns a few minutes later with a drink. Minutes later, Agent Dalton enters the restaurant. Brooklin realizes her plan is working. Then Agent Dalton talks to the host and is directed to the other side of the restaurant. "Where is he going?" Brooklin says aloud.

Brent turns around and scopes the room, "Where is who going?"

Brooklin doesn't answer thinking to herself, "Okay, this is not working. Does he not see her? What should I do? Should I go look for Agent Dalton?" Brooklin sinks back in her chair trying to plan her next move.

"Ms. Covington, is there something I can do to help?" Brent asks.

"No, Brent. I just need to think for a moment."

After a few minutes, Agent Dalton reappears. Brooklin can clearly see him scouting the room for Taylor. When he sees her sitting quietly at the table, he walks over and says something to her. "Maybe he is introducing himself, " Brooklin says to herself. Dalton sits down at the table across from her and Brooklin immediately sees Taylor's confusion. Taylor looks around the room and then back at Agent Dalton. They are having a conversation but Brooklin cannot hear them nor is she close enough to read their lips. Brooklin is so engrossed in watching the two of them that she doesn't notice that Jack Griffin has arrived. She is surprised when Griffin reaches Taylor's table and so is Taylor, her eyes bulging and her mouth wide open. Taylor seems to be breathing deeply as she stares at Griffin. Agent Dalton is quiet and clearly

Griffin is very angry, shaking his finger at her. Taylor's mouth is still open as if she can't believe what she is seeing or hearing.

Brooklin happily says, "Brent, it's time to go now. Let's ease out the side entrance." They get up slowly and inconspicuously while all eyes are on Jack Griffin. They walk fast to Brent's car and drive out of the restaurant's parking lot while Brooklin checks to make certain they are unnoticed. After exiting LaTorra's, Brooklin sits back thinking, "I think I have addressed that problem."

Having decided to spend the night at the hotel, Brooklin asks Brent to drop her off there. Brooklin barely makes it into the office when her telephone rings. "Hello."

"Ms. Covington, what did you do?"

"Excuse me?"

"Ms. Covington, this is Agent Dalton. You set up Taylor and me tonight."

"Oh, hi Agent Dalton. How *was* your meeting with Taylor?"

"How was my meeting? You knew Jack Griffin would come in and find Taylor and me together and think the worse."

"Agent Dalton, please. I merely was trying to help you obtain additional information for your case against Griffin."

"Ms. Covington, are you sure that's all it is?" he says exasperated.

"All I will admit to," Brooklin says to herself. "By the way, how is Mr. Reed?"

"He is fine. He's waiting for the day when he can testify against Griffin in court."

"I'm glad Mr. Reed is doing well." Brooklin is quiet for a moment reflecting. "Well, Agent Dalton, tell me what transpired between Taylor and Griffin."

"Jack Griffin came into the restaurant and assumed Taylor was providing me information about him. Evidence that he believed could be used against him in court."

"Did she give you any additional details that you could use against him?"

"No, but Griffin doesn't know that. He fired her and told her she would never work in this town again. As a matter of fact, he told her it would be in her best interest to leave town."

"Really? And what was Taylor's response?"

"She was totally shocked, scared and denied she was meeting me to share information regarding him. She insisted that she had been set up. However, Griffin didn't believe her."

"Wow. He didn't believe his trusted employee?"

"Ms. Covington, he could put a hit out on her. The only reason he probably won't is because I told him if anything happens to Taylor, he would be looking at more charges."

"Well, I think you handled that well."

"That was your plan, wasn't it? To get her out of town? You had her meet with *me* because you assumed Griffin would not hurt her if I, an FBI agent, were present at that table. You are one shrewd woman."

"Well, I appreciate your giving me credit for your drama-filled evening. However as I said earlier, I was just trying to help you gather more information to use in your case against Griffin. Besides, how would I know Jack Griffin would be at LaTorra tonight?"

"Remind me, Ms. Covington, never to cross you."

"Good night, Agent Dalton."

From her office closet Brooklin chooses clothes for tomorrow, gets her passkey and walks to the elevator. She enters the suite and locks the door behind her. She slips out of her clothes and within minutes, she is soaking in the tub with soft music playing in the background. She reflects about her evening, "Taylor, you and Griffin had to pay for your lying and scheming. I think you both are quite ill equipped to deal with me and that's just the way it is. You didn't realize I would fight until the bitter end for my family and this hotel." Brooklin adjusts herself in the oversized tub and relaxes to the soothing music.

Saturday morning, Brooklin is awakened by her cell phone ringing. She wonders who is calling so early.

"Brooklin, it's Levy."

"Yes, Levy."

"Sorry if I woke you but I have meetings all day."

"You have meetings all day today?"

"I do. Hey, I have to make a living."

"Levy, please."

He laughs. "I've been so busy, I haven't had the opportunity to bring you up-to-date."

"Okay," Brooklin says.

"First, what happened last night with Jack Griffin at LaTorra's?"

Brooklin fills him in on the evening. "Brooklin, that was brilliant. You made it happen. You always do. Except for Agent Dalton knowing it was your plan, you kept your hands clean."

"I know. However, I don't think Agent Dalton will reveal to anyone that I played a part in Taylor's downfall. He owes me a favor after his witness was beaten in my hotel. And Levy, Logan Courtyard was my mother's dream and now it's mine."

"I understand. Now, Brooklin, I want to let you know that Kim told us during her questioning at the precinct that Big Mel kidnapped her and her mother from the counseling center. However, they were able to get away from him and subsequently stayed a couple of nights with Erica until she went missing. Thereafter, they stayed with Lorna until Kim was brought in for shoplifting. And as you know, after Kim and her mother left the precinct, we put them on a plane to Georgia."

"They stayed with Erica? Do they know where is Erica is?"

"No. They have no idea. They are baffled by Erica's disappearance."

"You said they stayed with Lorna after they left Erica's? I called Lorna and asked her if she knew where Kim was and she told me she did not."

"Well, she lied."

"All right. I will deal with her."

"Brooklin," he exclaims, "can you let Colin handle Lorna?"

"I will talk to him about it."

"Good. Now, the last bit of information is that Jack Griffin owns LaTorra. Apparently, he needs to sell it to pay his lawyers."

"Really? I'm sure his legal fees are quite expensive."

"Yes. And I checked, he doesn't have any offers for LaTorra."

"Great. Well, let's make him an offer. However, let's go well below what he paid for the resort. And Levy, I do not want Jack Griffin to know I am making the offer. Let's keep this quiet for now."

"Will do. I will get back to you with some numbers in the next couple of hours."

"This is quite the epiphany. I may be able to acquire one of Griffin's prime businesses while he is not getting his greedy, grimy hands on Logan Courtyard."

"Well at this point you don't have to worry. Jack Griffin definitely does not have the funds to even think about making any offers for Logan Courtyard."

"Levy, I have always thought Griffin was trying to purchase Logan Courtyard for someone else."

"You might be correct about that. All right, I will be in touch."

Brooklin realizes it's 7:20am. She quickly showers and returns to the bedroom to watch the weekend morning show. Later as Brooklin dresses in jeans, a t-shirt and sneakers, her phone rings again.

"Hi, Mom."

"Luke, hi."

"Mom, Taylor just called me."

"Really? What did she want?"

"I didn't answer. She left me a voice mail saying she was leaving town."

"What else did she say?"

"Just that she was at the airport and wanted to let me know she was relocating back to her parent's home and if I wanted to reach her, I have her phone number."

"Really?"

"That's a little weird, don't you think? I wonder what happened with the job with Jack Griffin?"

"Maybe she realizes Jack Griffin may be going to prison."

"That's true. Well, I'm actually glad she is leaving. I can finally close that chapter of my life."

"Well, that's good to hear."

"All right, Mom, will talk to you later. Just wanted to pass along that bit of information."

"Okay, Luke. What do you have planned for today?"

"School work, pizza and I'm babysitting Blake later."

"Have a good day, Son." After some thought, Brooklin picks up the phone and calls Lorna. "Hello, Lorna."

"Yes?"

"It's Brooklin. Are you working at the Teen Center today?"

"No. However, I'm just leaving the Center. Did you need something?"

"Yes. Can you stop by Logan Courtyard for a few minutes?"

"Sure. Is there a problem?"

"How soon can you meet me in my office?"

"I can be there in about twenty minutes."

"Okay, I'll see you then," Brooklin says. Brooklin gathers her things and catches the elevator downstairs. She places her personal belongings in the closet and sits at her desk awaiting Lorna's arrival.

Brooklin gets a bottle of water and takes a couple of swallows as she walks out on her balcony. She observes the different guests sitting, walking, laughing. She loves owning this hotel. "Mom, I have tried to make you proud," Brooklin says aloud.

Hearing the sound of Lorna's voice and light footsteps, Brooklin turns and asks her to come in and have a seat. Brooklin sits behind her desk watching Lorna's expression. First, there is a smile and then a look of uneasiness.

"Lorna, it has come to my attention that Kim and her mother stayed with you for a period of time."

A look of concern crosses Lorna's face. "Yes, that is true."

"Were they living with you when I telephoned you at the Teen Center to ask about Kim's whereabouts?"

"Um yes. But ..."

"But, you lied to me?"

"I did. I just didn't want to get into any trouble."

"Why did you think you would get into trouble by allowing Kim and her mother to stay with you?"

Lorna hesitates. "I knew they were hiding and they wanted to keep their whereabouts unknown."

"Which is it, Lorna? You were afraid you were going to get into trouble or you wanted to help them by keeping their whereabouts unknown?"

Lorna crosses her legs nervously. "Both."

"Both," Brooklin says.

"Yes."

Brooklin's phone rings, interrupting their conversation. "Excuse me a moment, Lorna. Hi, Levy."

Lorna listens but is only able to hear Brooklin's part of the conversation. "That amount is how much lower than what he paid?" Brooklin looks at Lorna as she listens to Levy's answer. "I'm more than comfortable with that number. However, offer him 20% less than the number you gave me." Brooklin pauses again. "I understand but I would like you to offer 20% less than the amount you quoted."

Brooklin places the phone on her desk and continues her conversation with Lorna. "Now, Lorna, it's very important for me to know that I can trust my employees both here at the hotel and at the Teen Center."

"You can trust me."

"Not if you are willfully lying to me."

"It will not happen again."

"No, Lorna, it will not. Because you are dismissed from your responsibilities at the Teen Center."

"I'm fired? You are firing me?"

"Yes, Lorna, I am."

"Does Colin know about this?"

"No, however I will inform him."

"Maybe you should talk to him before you make this decision."

"And why is that Lorna? I don't need his permission to let go an employee."

"Well maybe, he will have something to say about your firing me."

"Lorna, you are fired. I will have one of our security personnel box up your personal effects at the Teen Center and you may pick it up here at the security office on Monday between 8 and 10am. Otherwise, your personal items will be mailed to you. However, you are not to return to the Teen Center. Do you understand?"

"I do. But maybe you don't understand that Colin will not agree with your firing me."

"And why is that, Lorna?"

"Ask him."

"I'm asking you."

"You know what, Brooklin. I don't want to work for you or the Teen Center anymore."

"Good. We are in agreement."

"However, I expect to get a good severance package."

"Really? Now that's an interesting assumption on your part, Ms. Young!"

"Yes, unless you want the Buzz and everyone in this city to know I slept with your husband."

Brooklin is inwardly shocked, however she displays no outer emotion for Lorna to see. "Colin and I are separated. Therefore, you can tell the Buzz or whomever you wish that you slept with Colin."

"Really? I don't think you want me to do that. Put your dirty laundry in the street? You are way too careful for that."

"Well, I'm up for the challenge. Are you? I had planned to be kind enough to give you an additional month's pay. However now, you will be paid *only* for the hours you worked and your time here today." Brooklin looks at her watch. "It's 9:55am. You will be paid up until 10:00am today. Now, that gives you five minutes to get out of my office and remember, do not set foot back into the Teen Center. And Lorna, now I've decided I do not want you to step foot in my hotel either. Your belongings will be mailed to you. If you choose to ignore this request, I will personally see to it that you are arrested for trespassing."

Brooklin picks up the office phone, "Max, Lorna Young is leaving my office now. Please meet her as she exits my office. She has been fired. Therefore, confiscate her badge, key card, parking permit and make certain she exits the hotel and the parking lot immediately. Then call the Teen Center and have her personal effects boxed up and mailed to her." Brooklin pauses for a moment. "Thanks, Max."

Brooklin looks at Lorna and points to the door, "The door is that way." Lorna glares at Brooklin, snorts and storms out. Brooklin turns to her computer and closes Lorna out as a company employee. Then she calls Jeff in tech and asks him to block Lorna's entrance to the hotel and Teen Center computer systems. And last, she would like him to meet with the Teen Center staff on Monday to change their passwords.

Slowly she turns and studies the family photo on her desk. She stares at the smiling faces – Laila, Luke, herself and Colin. Brooklin gathers her thoughts, allowing the shock and sorrow to sink in. "Colin slept with Lorna. He actually slept with Lorna." She returns her gaze to the family portrait and then places the photo face down on her desk. "If you are in the right place at just the right time, you can take a hell of a hit." Brooklin smiles, "Karla, no dodge ball here today. I have to face the revelation that my husband had an affair." Brooklin reaches for her purse and walks out the hotel's side entrance with an increased heart rate and fire in her eyes.

Chapter 22

Brooklin enters the Teen Center, her mind racing and blood pumping wildly through her veins. She passes several staff members but doesn't utter a word. She is intently looking for Colin. She can feel the mad throbbing of her temples. Colin is not in his office and he's not in the conference room. Brooklin walks into the staff lounge and finds Laila in the arms of some man. "Laila," Brooklin says stunned.

Laila turns at the sound of her mother's voice and Brooklin suddenly realizes the man is Officer Randy Baker. Brooklin looks at them questioningly. "Mom, this is Randy. Randy, this is my mother, Mrs. Covington. Mom, this is the friend I was telling you about."

"Yes, we have met," Brooklin says.

"Ms. Covington, it's nice to see you again," Randy adds.

"You too." Brooklin answers.

Brooklin thinks, "Really? Are there surprises around each corner?" She looks around the room and realizes they are alone. "Officer Baker, when I last met you, you didn't mention you were seeing my daughter."

"I didn't. Laila told me that she wanted to tell you. And she invited me to your house for dinner this weekend."

"Yes, that's right. We look forward to getting to know you better, Officer Baker." Brooklin is quiet for a moment with her thoughts, "A police officer?"

"Laila, I'm looking for your father. Have you seen him?"

"I saw him standing at the door of the weight room about ten minutes ago. He was holding the outside door open for someone. I'm not sure who."

"All right, thanks." Randy is about to say something to Brooklin but she has already turned to walk away.

"I'm sorry, Randy. I'm not sure what is going on with my mother today. She is not usually impolite."

"No problem. I'm sure she has a lot on her mind."

Brooklin's phone rings as she walks toward the weight room. She doesn't answer but continues down the hallway. Her phone buzzes. She checks to see who called and texted. It was Levy. Her offer for LaTorra was accepted and he was able to get the large warehouse next door as part of the deal. He says the warehouse is unlocked if she would like to drive over to take a look. Griffin apparently uses it for storage. Brooklin thinks to herself, "I guess Griffin is desperate for money to pay his lawyers." She texts Levy and tells him to do what is necessary to close the deal and to schedule the property to be inspected. She will contact him later.

As Brooklin reaches the door of the weight room, she hears men's voices. She notices that the door is ajar as Colin says, "Just remember, my wife is a very bright woman. You're not the first to have lost a battle of wits to her. She is a formidable opponent and doesn't take anything from anyone."

"I know your wife is very resilient. She's not the type to quit on anything. She always fires back. That's why I need a favor from you."

"I owe you a favor? I think I've done one too many favors for you in the first place. You were not even looking to acquire Logan Courtyard until I brought it to your attention."

Brooklin is flabbergasted. "Colin, how could you? How could you do this to me?" She tries to look into the room. She knows that voice. Who is it? She moves as close to the door as possible without entering the room. The man talking to Colin turns toward the door just enough for Brooklin to gasp in shock as she recognizes him. "It's Mayor Jenkins."

"Brooklin will move mountains to hang on to that hotel," Colin declares.

"Maybe instead of moving mountains, she will have to hit rock bottom before she realizes selling is in her best interest."

"No," Colin says. "Our deal was no one in my family would get hurt."

"No harm will come to your wife and family. I just need you to run some interference. Talk to your wife. I want that hotel."

"No, I will not talk to Brooklin. I thought this would be easy. You would make Brooklin a good offer for the hotel and I will have my wife back at home."

"You are so predictable, Colin. However, I won't accept *no* for an answer. Apparently, you haven't learned that yet. Now be smart and accept my appeal for help."

"Brooklin can be ruthless and will pull out all the stops when it comes to Logan Courtyard. She is very proud and independent. And, she will not vanish without a fight," warns Colin.

"I'm willing to fight for Logan Courtyard. It's a vital part of my plan."

"Mayor, listen to me, Brooklin will not go away quietly and this has gone too far. I just wanted you to purchase the hotel, not try to terrorize my wife during the process. Therefore, I'm choosing to back out on our deal and ignore your request for help. I think the smart choice for you is to walk away from this as well."

Mayor Jenkins points his finger at Colin. "Just because Griffin is on trial does not mean this game is over yet. What happens when your wife and family finds out you were behind this deal? It could cost you your wife, your family and in the end, I still will get Logan Courtyard. Would that be a problem for you? You get my message?"

"I think it is time for you to leave, Mayor. And remember technically if I go down, you go down."

"Colin, I think you should think about what you have to lose." Brooklin sees movement and quickly ducks into the gym next door. Mayor Jenkins walks by the gym and continues down the hall. Brooklin waits to listen for footsteps and then walks into the weight room.

Colin turns, shocked to see Brooklin. Her demeanor says it all. She had heard his conversation with the mayor.

"Brooklin, what are you doing here?"

"Colin, how could you do this?"

"Brooklin, what are you asking?"

"Colin, I heard your conversation with the mayor."

"What do you think you heard?"

"What do I *think* I heard? Are you going to deny your and the mayor's conversation? Are you going to continue to lie?" Colin doesn't answer. "Colin, I demand a response."

"I told the mayor about the hotel's transformation and that I thought it would be a good investment. I never thought it would go this far. After our initial conversation, I tried to stop the deal but to no avail. It was too late. The mayor has become obsessed and consumed with owning Logan Courtyard."

"How could you sell me out?"

"I did it for us."

"No, you didn't. You did it for you."

"It all happened so quickly."

"It happened so quickly? You still don't see it, do you? You brought organized crime into our lives. You are the reason I received threats from Jack Griffin. The reason Jack Griffin had my office bugged. You caused this drama and absurdity."

"Brooklin, it's not something I did on purpose."

"Is that an apology? When you were trying to sell my hotel, did you think about the consequences of your actions or about me? Did you even think about my wanting to carry on my mother's legacy? How I wanted to honor her and make her proud?"

"Make your mother proud? That again? Brooklin, your mother is deceased. I'm not sure what you are trying to recapture here."

"What? What did you just say, Colin?" Brooklin asks angrily. "How heartless and how offensive. However at this point, Colin, I should not be surprised about anything you say or do."

"Brooklin, listen please. With you, it's all about business. I just wanted our life back, the life we had before Logan Courtyard. I wanted my wife to be home. I was lonely."

"Colin, do you hear yourself? Do you know how that sounds? You always wanted to control me. And now I see how far you were willing to go to have that control. You can tell yourself whatever you need to, but you and I had an agreement. We talked before I took over the management of Logan Courtyard. We agreed on a timeline. When you questioned me about the number of hours I was working, I cut back on my hours at Logan Courtyard and asked you to work with me at the hotel. You chose not to. That was your choice. I was *not* going to give up on my mother's hotel and her dreams. And Colin, as for you saying you were lonely, I don't think so."

"I was lonely. I needed my wife."

"That's not what Lorna told me when I fired her."

"What? You fired Lorna?" Then he realized, "What did Lorna tell you?"

Brooklin looks at him with hatred in her eyes and turns to walk away. Colin grabs her arm. "Brooklin, wait. We need to talk about this. My sleeping with Lorna was a mistake. I was drunk. I was missing you," he stammered, "and I don't know. It just happened. I'm sorry. Please give me the chance to make this right."

She jerks her arm away and walks toward the door, "Don't touch me. You get away from me and you stay away from me." Brooklin repeats his words. "It just happened? Really, Colin?"

"Brooklin, I want to reassure you that there has been nothing between Lorna and me except that one time and it never will be again."

"One question, Colin. Did this happen before we separated?"

Colin looks away from Brooklin. "It happened before the separation. Brooklin, please remember that I love you and I made a profound mistake and it will never happen again."

"You love me? You don't know how to love. How do you claim to love me and sleep with another woman? How can you love me and do this to me?" Brooklin hesitates, "and to our family? What happened with all your talk about the family standing together? That life you spoke of has crumbled and shattered."

"I messed up. But, Brooklin, what I want most in this world is you and my family."

"Colin, why couldn't you have really talked to me and made me understand how this was affecting you? We could have worked it out. Instead, you sent mobsters to do your talking and I was left to clean up your mess." Brooklin is quiet for a moment and then looks at him alarmed, "Oh God, I slept with you after our separation. I allowed you to touch me. It sickens me. If I had only known ... however, I see you now for what you are, a lying coward."

"Brooklin, please. I am sincerely sorry."

"I am so sick of hearing you say, 'I'm sorry.' I'm done hearing your lame apologies and I'm done giving you chances. You can't justify what you did. Colin, you had an affair."

"Brooklin, I didn't have an affair. I was with Lorna one time and I am disgusted by what I did. I'm glad you fired her. I would have fired her but she threatened to tell you. This has been weighing on me. Brooklin, you must believe, I truly love you."

"I detest you. You are such a liar."

"Brooklin, why would I lie?"

"Why does anyone lie? I think you are incapable of telling the truth."

"Brooklin, you have to understand."

"No, Colin, I do not have to understand. And I'm done with this conversation."

"Brooklin, don't leave. We haven't finished talking."

"Yes, there is something that has been left unfinished. I'm filing for divorce."

"Brooklin, no. Please! I know what I have done. But please do not end our marriage. We can survive this. I know it will not happen overnight and I know it will take a long time for me to win back your trust. But please give us another opportunity to rebuild our relationship. I know it's easier said than done, but if we can just take it one step at a time. I can't take back what I did or what I was thinking. Maybe when you have a chance to calm, cool down."

"What, Colin? Forgive you? Forget what you have done? You have been lying to me for months. You completely disregarded my aspirations and me. How many times have I stood by you? Forgiven you? Defended you? And when I ask you to stand by me?" Brooklin pauses. "Colin, how many ways did you betray me? You and your criminal friends schemed and tried to intimidate me into selling my hotel and Colin, you slept with Lorna."

At that moment, Laila bursts into the room. "Daddy, no. Daddy, tell me you didn't do this. You worked with those men to take Mom's hotel from her and you slept with Lorna?"

Brooklin and Colin turn to see Laila standing in the doorway. Brooklin walks to Laila trying to comfort her, "Honey."

"Mom, I came looking for you because I wanted to talk to you about Randy and I heard you and Dad arguing." Laila looks at Colin again, "Daddy, did you do this?"

"Laila," Colin says and drops his head.

Laila turns and runs out the side door. Brooklin looks at Colin, calls Laila's name and then follows her.

Colin slams his fist down on the weight equipment shouting, "Is there no privacy in this building?" Then he mutters sadly, "What have I done? What have I done?"

Chapter 23

Brooklin follows Laila out of the weight room and is terrified as she sees Laila race into the street against the light. "Oh no! Laila, stop! Stop, Laila! A car is coming. Laila," Brooklin screams.

Brooklin watches as a woman rushes out pushing Laila out of the path of the oncoming car. She looks in horror as she observes the woman being struck by the car. "No, no," Brooklin says as she looks at both Laila and the woman lying on the ground. Brooklin's chest is pounding as she runs to Laila who is closest to her. "Laila, are you all right? Laila?"

Disoriented, Laila raises her head. "Mom?"

"Laila, are you all right?" Brooklin asks.

"Yes, I'm all right," Laila says struggling to sit up.

"No, don't move. I'll be right back. I have to go and check on the woman hit by the car."

A Teen Center volunteer rushes over and tells Brooklin, "I'll stay here with Laila. You go to the woman."

Brooklin runs to the woman lying motionless in the street. She notices all the blood then stares down in shock. "Erica? Erica, is that you?" Except for the short brown curly hair and the makeup, the woman on the ground looks identical to Erica. She looks at the woman closely. "Oh my God, it *is* Erica. Erica, can you hear me?"

Erica opens her eyes, "Brooklin."

Brooklin recognizes Erica's voice instantly even though it is very soft and faint. "Erica. Erica, it *is* you."

Brooklin kneels beside her, "Honey, don't try to talk." Brooklin looks toward the Teen Center and screams, "Call 911, someone call 911!"

"They are on their way," a voice calls back.

"Erica, it's going to be okay," Brooklin says kneeling on the ground next to Erica, holding her hand. "The ambulance is on its way," Brooklin repeats checking Erica for visible injuries.

Erica closes her eyes again slipping in and out of consciousness. "Erica, Erica, stay with me. I need you to stay awake. I'm going to be right here with you."

"Laila?" Erica murmurs.

"Laila is all right," Brooklin says as she continues to comfort Erica.

"Brooklin, left letter," Erica whispers through labored breathing, "on your car." She grunts and then makes a gasping noise. "I've been leaving notes."

Brooklin looks at Erica questioningly. "Erica, we'll talk about it later. Please save your strength."

"Secret," Erica says with difficulty fighting to raise her voice above a whisper, is in letter." Erica continues to try to talk, moving her lips.

"Erica please, you need to save your strength. We'll talk later when you are stronger."

Finally, Erica forces out the words, "Colin is," she whispers and then gasps for air, "Colin is my father."

Brooklin looks down at Erica. "Erica, you don't know what you're saying. Please don't try to talk anymore. Erica, I hear the ambulance. It's almost here. Help is almost here," Brooklin says rubbing Erica's hand.

"Read letter," she murmurs through labored breathing. "I love you, Brooklin," Erica says softly and then begins gasping for air.

"I love you too, Erica. Try to be calm. Breathe slowly. That's it. Relax. Good, good, Erica. That's much better," Brooklin says comforting Erica. "Save your strength."

The ambulance arrives and rushes to where Erica is lying. "Erica, the ambulance is here. I'm going to move so the paramedics can examine you." Brooklin thinks she notices Erica looking a little panicky. "Erica, I'm not leaving. I'll ride in the ambulance with you to the hospital."

A paramedic says to Brooklin, "Miss, please move back and let us take care of her."

"Sure, sure," Brooklin says stepping back and immediately looking for her daughter. "Laila, where is Laila?"

Colin comes to Brooklin's side quickly. "Erica, it is Erica," he murmurs.

Brooklin stares at him with animosity. "Where is Laila? Is she all right?" she asks.

"Yes, she's fine, just a few bruises and scratches."

"Can you drive her to the hospital to get examined? I'm going to ride with Erica in the ambulance," Brooklin announces.

"Her friend Randy is driving her now." He looks down, "She wouldn't allow me to take her." Brooklin looks at him with disgust and then returns her gaze to Erica and the paramedics. "Someone needs to call Erica's mother."

"I did."

"You did what?"

"I called Kelly."

Brooklin turns and looks at Colin just as she hears the ambulance door shut. She calls out, "Wait," as she runs toward them, "I will ride in the ambulance with her."

One of the paramedics asks, "Are you a relative?"

Brooklin answers, "Yes," then she pauses, "I am her stepmother."

The paramedic opens the door of the ambulance and helps Brooklin climb into the back. Brooklin sits next to Erica and reaches for her hand, "Erica, thank you. I will never forget how you saved my daughter's life."

Erica's eyes open slowly. Brooklin thinks she even saw Erica smile although it was difficult to tell because a mask connected to an oxygen cylinder was placed over her face.

"We'll take her to Memorial Hospital's emergency room," a paramedic riding in the back of the ambulance says as he continually checks and monitors Erica.

"Yes," Brooklin says still holding Erica's hand, "Memorial is fine."

About ten minutes later, they finally arrive. Nurses and doctors are waiting at the E.R. entrance. Erica is rushed in and doctors immediately start cutting off her clothes to determine the extent of her injuries. A nurse and a staff member begin asking Brooklin questions – Erica's name, age, birthday, if Brooklin knew if Erica was taking any medication. If she had been drinking or using any drugs, if she lost consciousness at the scene of the accident, if so, for how long? They asked if Erica had a history of seizures. Brooklin answers what she could. Then doctors ask Brooklin to leave the room.

Brooklin looks at Erica again and the medical equipment hooked up to her. "Erica, I'll see you soon." Erica mouths something, but Brooklin can't hear or understand because Erica's voice is so faint. "Erica, I love you," Brooklin says as she turns and leaves the room. Brooklin walks directly to the end of the hall to the nurses' station and asks, "Is my daughter, Laila Covington, here in the emergency room?"

The nurse checks the computer, "Yes, she is in Room 9."

"Can you please direct me to the room?" Brooklin enters Room 9 where Laila is sitting up in the bed and Randy is in the chair beside her.

Brooklin speaks to Randy and then walks over to the bed and hugs her daughter. "Laila, are you all right?"

"Mom, don't worry. The doctor told me that I'm fine. I just have some scrapes and bruises. I'm being released as soon as the nurse returns with my discharge papers."

"However, the doctor mentioned that we need to observe her for the next four days," Randy adds.

"Officer Baker, thank you for driving my daughter to the hospital and for being here with her now."

"Of course, Ms. Covington. I care a great deal about your daughter and please call me Randy."

Brooklin glances at him again but says nothing.

"Mom, how is Erica?"

"I don't know, Laila. But I suspect, not good. I know she lost a lot of blood. The doctors would *not* say much about her condition while I was in the room."

"I remember running out of the Teen Center ... trying to get away from Dad and then seeing the car coming toward me." Laila stops talking for a moment, "It all happened so fast. My mind was racing and then, Erica pushing me onto the ground."

Brooklin hugs Laila as she cries in Brooklin's arms. "Mom, Erica saved my life."

"I know, honey. I know."

Laila looks at her mother, "Erica has to be all right. I have to thank her for saving my life."

"She knows, honey. I already thanked her," Brooklin says as she sits in the chair near her.

Colin walks into the room and everyone's attention is on him, "Laila, are you all right?"

The tension in the room is palpable ... the anger ... the adrenaline circulating in the room. Finally, Laila breaks the silence, "I'm fine. Just some scrapes and bruises."

"Well, I'm thankful for that," Colin says coming to stand closer to the bed.

"Randy, can you please excuse us for a few minutes?" Colin asks.

Randy glances at Laila as she nods. "Can I get anyone anything from the hospital's cafeteria?" Randy asks.

"No," they all chime in, "but thanks."

"Okay. Laila, I'll check with the nurse about your discharge papers."

"Thanks, Randy."

"Laila, Randy seems like a nice young man," Brooklin says after Randy leaves the room.

"He really is, Mom," Laila adds then looks at her father. "I was very shocked by what I heard you and Mom discussing in the weight room."

"I know, Laila. However, you shouldn't have run out. You should have stayed so we could discuss it like adults."

"Dad, are you really talking to me about what I should and should not do?"

"Can we not discuss this here at the hospital?" Colin asks.

"How is Erica?" Laila asks her father.

"They are prepping her for surgery. I was able to see her briefly then her mother arrived so I decided to come and check on you."

"Dad, did you really try to steal Logan Courtyard from Mom?"

"No, I did not try to steal the hotel. I made some mistakes."

"Yes, you did. You hurt Mom. You gambled with her life."

"I gambled with her life? Laila, I think you are overreacting."

"Mom has become a real force in the hotel industry and you tried to steal that from her by sending criminals to force her to sell. You tried to tank her success. Luke and I and all of Mom's staff honor and respect her success. The hotel highlights her accomplishments in many areas and I'm so proud of her."

Colin doesn't comment. Laila continues, "As a woman, this is very upsetting to me. When it comes to women, there is a double standard. When a woman takes charge and makes decisions, she is spoken about maliciously or someone tries to intimidate her. If a man takes charge, he is seen as a strong businessman who can make tough decisions. Mom and all women have the right to be respected for their achievements. It should be the common thread to bring us together."

"Young lady, I'm still your father. Therefore, watch your tone with me," Colin says sternly. "And Laila," he says in a calmer voice, "I think we should save this discussion for later. You were just injured and you need to focus on healing."

"Dad, it's a few bruises. And I'm just explaining how I feel. Speaking of feelings, are you at all remorseful? Because Dad, this is a major screw up and Mom deserves better. I expected more from you. I can't believe you actually slept with Lorna."

"Just because I'm not showing any outward display of guilt doesn't mean I'm not remorseful."

"Laila, I think you should not upset yourself. This is between your father and me," Brooklin adds.

"No, Mom, this affects Luke and me as well. Breaking up the family hurts us all. Dad, you didn't just betray Mom. You betrayed us all."

Before Colin can comment, Randy enters the room with the nurse. She explains the discharge paperwork to Laila and the need to schedule a follow-up appointment with her doctor. "Laila, I would like for you to stay at the house for a few days," Brooklin says.

"Mom, I'm fine. I'm going home."

"Laila, please do not argue with me. You will stay at the house. I will drive you home."

"All right, Mom, let's compromise. I will stay at the house. However, Randy will drive me."

"That's fine. Thank you, Randy." Laila is helped into a wheelchair and Randy leaves to bring his car around to the hospital entrance.

Brooklin and Colin walk behind the nurse as she pushes Laila in the wheelchair. As they reach the entrance, Randy pulls up in his car and comes around to help Laila get in.

"Laila, I'm going to check on Erica again and then I will come home."

"If it is okay, Ms. Covington, I will stay with Laila until you arrive home."

"Thanks, Randy, I appreciate your help. I'll see the two of you a little later," Brooklin says. Then she bends down and places a kiss on Laila's forehead.

Brooklin walks back into the hospital and down the hall to the emergency room. When she hears, "Brooklin ..."

Immediately, Brooklin throws her hands up in front of Colin, "Stop! I need some truthful answers. After Erica was hit and lying on the ground, she was able to tell me that *you* are her father. Is this true?"

Colin looks down and says, "Brooklin ..."

"A simple yes or no will suffice."

Colin still doesn't answer, "Brooklin, I ..."

"So you will not answer my question?" Brooklin begins walking down the hallway.

Colin is quickly at her side. "Brooklin, please. My daughter is in there, hooked up to machines."

"Oh, now you admit that she is your daughter."

"Yes, Brooklin, but I just learned this in the last few months and it happened before I met you. I'm still coming to terms with her being my daughter."

"Unbelieveable!" Brooklin turns from him and picks up her pace as she continues down the hall.

"Brooklin, let me explain."

"Can you just please go away? Leave me to my thoughts in peace."

Colin starts to comment and then turns and walks in the other direction.

Brooklin arrives at the door of the emergency room as her telephone rings. It's Luke. Brooklin explains everything to Luke and they agree to meet at the house after Brooklin checks on Erica. "Mom, Uncle Jim left rehab. Apparently, he was at the Teen Center when all this happened."

"He was? I didn't see him."

"He was very upset. He called and asked me to drive him back to rehab. So, I did."

"Okay, good. I'm glad he wasn't driving being that he was upset or maybe even drinking. Thanks, Luke."

"All right, Mom, we'll talk more when you get home." Brooklin walks to the room where she last visited Erica. The room is empty and had been cleaned. Brooklin paces back and forth in front of the nurses' station until a nurse returns. "Excuse me, I'm looking for Erica Harris. She was in Room 5."

"That patient has been taken into surgery. Family members can go to the 5th floor surgical waiting room."

"Thank you," Brooklin says, walking away. She presumes Colin and Erica's mother Kelly would be waiting there and, of course, she does not want to interrupt. Therefore, she phones for a car from Logan Courtyard. Then she calls to check on Laila, telling her that since Randy and Luke are there with her, she'll stop by Logan Courtyard for a few minutes before coming home.

After her conversation with Laila, Brooklin reminds herself, "I need to return to the Teen Center to get my car." Brooklin walks to the hospital lobby and patiently waits for the car from Logan Courtyard. She feels totally drained. Her body is limp, her mind overwhelmed by the horror of the accident, her daughter's brush with death, the revelation about Erica's parentage and her heroism in saving Laila. "I'm so thankful that Laila is all right." She prays Erica will make a full recovery. Then her thoughts revert back to Colin, "What happened to him? He used to be one of the good guys. Or was he? Was I so wrong about him? To believe in him? In our marriage?" Brooklin adjusts herself in her seat. "I need to give myself a break ... take some time ... let go of the anger and anxiety and heartbreak."

Brooklin arrives at the Teen Center and thanks the driver. She walks to her car and reaches for the red envelope that Erica had placed on her windshield. "So Erica, it was *you* who sent the key and the notes." Brooklin questions, "What is the significance of the key and what does it unlock? Could there be more? Will the key reveal another secret?"

Chapter 24

Brooklin enters her car with the letter from Erica in hand, speculating as she looks at the red envelope, "Are there more secrets lurking in this letter? I don't know how much more I can handle." Brooklin hesitates and then opens the letter, written in Erica's handwriting.

Brooklin,

First, I would like you to know how much I love and care for you. You have been more than an employer and a friend. You have been like a mother to me. I know you care about me too. That is the reason I could not keep this secret from you. Not even for my mother. You have been there for me even when my mother wasn't. Therefore, I am writing to inform you that I sent you the cards in the red envelopes and, yes, the key. Why, you may ask? I was afraid to call you because I didn't want the call to be traced back to me but I also wanted to check on you. I knew those criminals, those vultures were circling trying to steal Logan Courtyard from you, disrespecting and disregarding what you have built. I worked so closely with you and know the work and immense energy you poured into the hotel. You made great business decisions, making Logan Courtyard the best Five Star Hotel on the east coast. I'm very proud of you and your accomplishments and I know you will fight to the bitter end to keep your inheritance.

Back to the secret that I learned a few months ago that your husband, Colin, is my father. Apparently he and my mother had an affair before he met you. DNA has confirmed he is my father. My mother didn't tell him that I was his daughter until I got myself into some trouble. She wanted him to help me. When I learned that Colin was my father, I asked him to tell you. He said he was afraid of losing you.

Brooklin, I'm sure you know about the trouble I'm speaking of. Yes, I was in the car with Ron when he hit his father, Larry. I was so angry with Larry that I became involved with his son to get revenge. You see, Larry and I had an affair and I became pregnant. When I told him about the baby, he broke off the relationship and told me to get an abortion. I didn't, however I had a miscarriage. I was so hurt and devastated and scared. I blamed Larry and then kind of lost it after that. I realized that I was just some recreational fun to Larry. After I lost my sweet baby, my son, that's when the vendetta against Larry began and I used his son. I'm not proud of what I did and I wish I could take back how I handled that situation. But unfortunately, I can't. I know you may not understand because you have never been in a situation such as this and, my dear friend, I pray that you never will.

I am leaving the state to begin a new life because I can't face a trial, a conviction and jail. Colin bought Allure Beauty and Health Spa for my mother and me. My guess is to ease his conscience. There is an apartment on the 4th floor where I have been staying. Only my mother and Tina knew I was in the building. I sent Tina to apply for a job at Logan Courtyard. She is a good person and I wanted you to have someone at the hotel that you could fully trust since I was no longer there. I'm glad that she and Laila have become good friends.

As for the key, I had placed this letter in locker #29 at Allure and was going to give you the information regarding the locker in my last note. However, I decided instead to place the letter on your car. Oh, I ended the notes with Tay because that's a nickname for my mother and scarlet represented my mother – a scorned woman.

You have always supported me and I hope you will understand. Please forgive me for any pain I have caused. You always listened to me and comforted me when I needed it. I will miss you, my dear friend, and I wish only the best for you, your family and Logan Courtyard.

You always were truthful with me, so I'm going to be truthful with you. Don't let yourself be dominated by the desire for success. Your mother loved and trusted you with her prized possession, Logan Courtyard. And you have made it better than she could have ever imagined. You have nothing left to prove to yourself or anyone. So stop questioning or trying to prove something. Continue to be strong and powerful in business – just don't let it consume you. Be happy. You always reached for the stars … now, it's time to enjoy them. You are a beautiful human being and you need to have a life outside of Logan Courtyard. I move on now to build a different and better life for myself. I know what success looks like because I had you as a role model.

I will forever be grateful and love you.
Erica

As Brooklin places the letter in her purse, she thinks, "If Erica hadn't decided to place the letter on my car instead of the locker, it would be Laila in the hospital fighting for her life. Erica wouldn't have been there to save Laila. Oh Erica, I will be forever grateful to you. I will stand by you through your recovery and whatever comes after." Brooklin exhales, "Finally, the secret is exposed." Tears pour down her face, "Erica, you were planning to leave and instead you're in surgery. With all my heart, I hope and pray your surgery goes well. We will hire the best lawyers for you." Until now, Brooklin didn't realize how much she truly missed her dear friend and now she learns, her second daughter. "Erica, I will talk to Tina about employment. Both you and Laila trust her. So I will give her an opportunity. We are going to need a new receptionist to replace Lorna at the Teen Center." Brooklin sits for a minute thinking about everything she has strived for, everything she has achieved. "My mother built Logan Courtyard. She entrusted it to me. However, I know it can't dominate my life anymore. It represents me, my mother, my lost life, and my accomplishments. It's become an extension of who I am. Now I must gather the strength from what I have learned from this success and spread my wings." Brooklin wipes away the tears, put on her sunglasses and drives to Logan Courtyard. As she rounds the corner to her office, she sees Greg standing in front of her office door.

"Brooklin, there you are."

Brooklin rushes into his arms. "Greg, you heard about Erica, about the accident."

"I did. Give me your key and I'll unlock the office door for you."

Brooklin hands her key to Greg. He opens the door, allows her to enter first then closes the door behind them. Brooklin drops her purse on the desk and turns to look at Greg. The expression on his face says it all. "Greg," her voice quivering, "What's going on? Is Erica...?"

"Yes, Erica was pronounced dead about twenty minutes ago."

"Oh no," Brooklin cries. "No, no. Please, no! Erica, you are not supposed to die. There is nothing right about this."

Greg rushes over and takes her into his arms again. "Brooklin, I'm so sorry." Her knees buckle as she collapses into tears, finally letting go of all the pain and emotion she has held back all day, all the feelings she had bottled up and pushed down. She wraps her arms around Greg. All her defenses are gone. Greg picks her up and carries her to the couch in her office. He holds her in his arms comforting her. "It's all right, Brooklin, let it all out," Greg whispers as he rubs her back gently. Brooklin is torn by grief and sobs softly. "It's okay," he says and kisses her lightly on the forehead. "I'm here for you." He continues to hold her close as tears stream down her face.

She wants to stay here forever and never ever leave his arms. "Greg," Brooklin says, "Thank you for being here. You are always here for me--just liked you promised."

"That's because my promises mean something."

"I am so grateful for you and your support." Her thoughts return to Erica. "I was able to tell Erica I loved her before her surgery. How could I know that those would be my last words to her or that would be the last time I would see her alive."

"I was unable to talk to her before her surgery. However, the doctor told me Erica was not pregnant. Apparently, she had been pregnant about a year ago. So Erica was not pregnant with Ron's child," Greg says.

Brooklin looks at him sadly. "Wait, Greg. Were you at the hospital to arrest Erica?"

"To talk to her. However, an arrest was certain to come." Greg then tells Brooklin that he had followed some leads and learned that Erica was staying in the fourth floor apartment at Allure and that Colin was the new owner of the building. He's uncertain about Colin's reasons for purchasing the building or if he knew Erica was living on the fourth floor. But he also learned that Colin had an affair with Lorna before their separation. Brooklin shakes her head knowingly.

"You knew this, Brooklin?"

"I fired Lorna and she told me about the affair. Then as Erica lay in the street after being hit by the car, she told me Colin was her father and that she had left a letter on my car."

"Colin is Erica's father?"

"I just can't talk about it right now, Greg. I can share her letter with you if you'd like. I learned all this today."

"Well, I do understand all the tears. You've had a horrific day. Brooklin, I want you to know, I will always be here for you. I love you."

"I plan to file for divorce Monday morning."

"I'm rarely surprised by people's selfishness but Colin--he put you in an impossible situation."

"Yes, he is incredibly selfish and he put my family and me at great risk."

"What? How did he do that?"

"Let's discuss it at another time, not now."

"I understand, Brooklin, that this is a difficult time for you and divorces can be complicated. However, it's best to know when to take your losses and walk away."

"True," Brooklin says.

"Brooklin, there was a time when my work meant everything to me until that day I walked into your office. Now, I can't imagine my life without you. I think I fell in love with you the first time I saw you. If you give me the opportunity, I will devote my life to being the man that you deserve."

"Greg, I think you entered my office and my life at the perfect time. I don't know if I could have really seen you if you had come into my life earlier. And Greg, now I can't imagine my life without you either."

"Are you saying what I think you are saying?"

"I am. We have this connection. I actually did everything I could to fight against it. But you were always there giving me a place to land. I didn't want to be careless with my marriage and my vows. However, now I'm willing to give us a chance, to see what we are like together."

Greg stands and pulls Brooklin to her feet. He moves toward her, so close she feels the heat of his body. He takes her into his arms and kisses her passionately sending shivers down her spine. It is the kiss of a man who had waited for this moment and feared it would never come. She loved the smell, the feel of this man who made her body respond with such desire, sending thrills of excitement to places she never knew existed. Brooklin thinks she may faint. She holds him tightly fearing she may not be able to stand if either of them lets go. As their lips part, he stares intently at her, "Brooklin, I'm going to be right here with you always." He smiles, "It's going to be a wild ride."

"I like wild rides," Brooklin says returning the smile and thinking, "If it's anything like that kiss, I'm going to love the ride." Brooklin braces herself as they sit on the couch. Her legs still feel unsteady from his kiss. Greg holds Brooklin in his arms as they sit on the couch. She thought she knew how it would feel to kiss this man and be in his arms. However, she could not imagine how wonderful it would be. She'd never known such excitement, the shocking awareness of the sensual intensity between them. Her feeling for this man is now undeniable. Brooklin closes her eyes, still feeling and tasting his kiss.

Slowly she begins to reflect on today's events. For a few minutes that kiss had almost made her forget. Brooklin sits up abruptly, "Greg, did you talk to the driver of the car that hit Erica?"

"Brooklin, can we just focus on us? Just for a short time? I've waited so long for this."

"I'm sorry, Greg, but please just answer my question first?"

"No, we're still seeking the identity of the driver. He apparently got out of the car and left the scene."

"He?"

"No one at the Teen Center gave me or the other officers a description of the driver. We just learned it was a man driving. However, I called in the make, model and plates to the station. I'm sure the information will be on my desk when I return. Right now, I just want to focus on you." He reaches down and kisses her gently, igniting the spark once again.

She feels the love. "Greg, I have to get home. Laila is there and I want to check on her."

"When will I see you again?"

"Greg, I would like to take it slow."

"Is dinner tomorrow night slow enough?"

Brooklin remembers what Erica said in her letter and this man does make her happy. "Tomorrow is Sunday and I need to spend the day with Laila and Luke."

"And Colin?"

"No. Colin and my marriage are over. He is no longer the man I fell in love with."

"Can we meet for a late dinner?"

"Well, I will be having dinner with Laila and Luke. How about meeting for a glass of wine?"

"Sounds good. I'll call you tomorrow and you can tell me what time I can pick you up."

Brooklin stands. "Thanks, Greg. Thanks for everything. I've had a lot of disappointments in the last year. But not with you. You were loyal and you were committed. And I don't know what I would have done without your support."

"Well, I would have waited for you forever." Greg stands and kisses her lightly on the lips. "I'll see you tomorrow evening." Before exiting, he again asks, "Brooklin, are you okay?"

"I'm okay."

"Are you sure?"

"I'll see you tomorrow, Greg."

Brooklin watches as he leaves. Then she realizes she forgot to mention that Laila and Officer Baker are dating. "Oh well, we can discuss it tomorrow evening." Brooklin refocuses and calls Brent, telling him that she has an unexpected job for him. They talk for a few minutes then she immediately telephones Colin.

"Brooklin, I'm so glad you called. I wasn't sure when I would have another opportunity to talk to you."

"Well, I'm on my way to the warehouse that's located next to LaTorra's. I was told it was for sale and I want to take a look at it. If you want to meet there, we can talk for a few minutes."

"Okay, Brooklin, I'm on my way."

She smiles, thinking how fortuitous that Brent had joined her staff.

Chapter 25

As she is driving to the warehouse, Agent Dalton phones. He tells her that Jack Griffin and his lawyer have cut a deal with prosecutors. Griffin will spend the next twenty years in prison without parole and his victims will be well compensated. "You helped bring a multi-million dollar corporation to its knees. If the public knew, you would be a local hero."

"No," Brooklin says sharply. Then she takes a deep breath and continues. "Agent Dalton, you are again assuming. I'm not quite sure how you are coming to these conclusions. Nevertheless, I am glad this case is finally over."

"Brooklin, I also want you to know that Big Mel accepted a plea deal of fifteen years without parole."

"Good. Another criminal off the street." Agent Dalton further explains that the witnesses including Mr. Reed and Kim will not have to testify. He thinks it's a good deal. Brooklin agrees and thanks Agent Dalton for the call and for the work of his department. Brooklin sits in her car for a moment and takes another deep breath. "My actions were justified. Jack Griffin is going to prison." Her thoughts return to their conversation in her office, "Let's see how tough and fearful our man of steel really is once he's behind prison walls."

Brooklin walks into the warehouse thinking, "I'll telephone Levy when I return to the house tonight. However right now, I must take care of the business at hand." Brooklin looks around the massive interior of the warehouse. "This is perfect," she says aloud.

"Yes, it's perfect for a second storage area or a backup facility for Logan Courtyard," Colin says as he enters the warehouse. Brooklin turns to face him. "Brooklin, I'm glad you called. We must try to work through this. Our priority must be our family."

Brooklin laughs. "What a preposterous joke! Since when? You claim our priority must be our family? That is laughable. Clearly, your priority has not been your family for a very long time. So, I must ask you. What *are* your priorities, Colin? What did the good old boys' network offer you?"

"Offer me? Nothing. I didn't take anything from them? I was hoping you had calmed down and that we would be able to have a reasonable conversation. So, Brooklin, can we?"

"What can you possibly say to justify everything you have done?"

"That I am devoted to you, Brooklin. That I will make this up to you."

"Who are you devoted to, Colin, considering your despicable behavior? Not me, that's for sure."

"I am devoted to you and our family. That's the reason I wanted you to sell the hotel and return home. Brooklin, I love you."

"When it's convenient, you love me."

"Our marriage managed to survive over the years. We were able to handle everything."

"Because I was the one giving all the time, Colin."

"Brooklin, you were not the only one giving. I gave too."

"Yes, Colin, you are absolutely correct. You gave Mayor Jenkins the concept of trying to manipulate me into selling my hotel. I'm told you gave Erica and her mother Allure." Brooklin looks directly at him, "Colin, you bought Allure Beauty and Health Spa for Erica and her mother?"

"I did buy Allure. However, I have not transferred ownership to Erica and her mother. And now that Erica is..." Colin hesitates and then continues sadly, "Now that Erica is deceased, I will have my real estate agent place Allure back on the market. Kelly will not own Allure. Brooklin, Kelly and I were never in a real relationship. We only dated a few times."

"I don't have the slightest desire to hear the sordid details of your relationship with Kelly after so many years. You should have told me years ago. You knew Kelly was Erica's mother. My mother hired Erica and I later promoted her to be my secretary at Logan Courtyard. Don't you think I should have been told that you had dated her mother? It's not like I would have fired Erica. I'm not that type of person."

"Brooklin, I know I owe you an apology."

"You owe me an apology? What an amazing understatement! You think apologizing will fix this?"

"How can I make this up to you? I know you are upset and feeling betrayed, but we can work through this."

"Work through this? Colin, let me just lay it out for you. I don't trust you anymore. Therefore, there is no working through this."

346

"Brooklin, I know I made mistakes but you know me."

"I *thought* I knew you. How could you be so insecure that you would deceive and betray me?" Brooklin shakes her head in disbelief. "You have lied, withheld information from me including having fathered a daughter and having slept with one of our employees. And Colin, it is incomprehensible to me that you could even consider being in a business venture or working with those criminals against me. You gambled with my life. You tried to steal my hotel from me."

"If I could, I would wipe away this entire situation. But Brooklin, I can't. I can only ask for your forgiveness. I was dying inside. You are my life. Being with you is being alive. I was desperate to get you back."

"Get me back? I didn't go anywhere. I was working, Colin. You left me, remember? You are such a disappointment." She moves toward the door.

"Brooklin, can you at least give us some time and wait before filing for divorce? I'm begging for another chance. Not for me, I don't deserve it. But for our children—our family does." She continues walking toward the door. "Brooklin, please we haven't finished talking. Can you please hear me out?"

"No need. We are done."

"Brooklin, I don't know who you are anymore."

Brooklin turns quickly to face Colin. "Me? You do not know *who I am* anymore? Well, let me properly introduce you. I am a woman who owns and manages a hotel. I have earned what I have by working hard. I deserve respect and I will have it. And neither you nor anyone else has a right to take anything from me. I'm a force to be reckoned with and I'm not going anywhere. You hear me, Colin? I'm here to stay. Logan Courtyard has been my tower of strength. And I will fight to be the last one standing to keep my hotel. Now as for us, you disrespected our marriage and me. I can't erase our life together. However after our divorce, I plan to erase you from my mind." As she walks out the door, she sees Brent walking toward her. She almost didn't recognize him because of his disguise. "Brent, you can take care of that job we discussed. He's inside." Brooklin watches as Brent enters the warehouse, disabling the outside camera as he walks in.

Brooklin looks toward the sky as the day comes to an end. She feels sadness because life as she knew it was also coming to an end. She had lost a dear friend today. And her marriage-she shakes her head. "How did we get here? I loved Colin so much. I gave him everything inside of me. Everything. Unconditionally. My children and Colin were my world. It didn't have to be this way. However," she says looking in the direction of the warehouse, "we all make our choices, don't we?" Her thoughts turn to the second culprit in this malicious operation. Brooklin contemplates, "You are absolutely correct, Mr. Mayor, the game is not over yet. You now have my undivided attention. I have found my voice and my confidence. I will never give up and never give in. Mayor Jenkins, I will stop at nothing to take you down," she says emphasizing each word.

Brooklin looks across the parking lot at the new business she just acquired. She's about to embark upon a fresh new start. She will be cautious as she oversees the completion of the new additions at Logan Courtyard and puts her plans in motion for LaTorra. "You said I have changed, Colin, that you don't know who I am. I'm somebody nobody screws over and gets away with it ... nobody. I will not be intimidated," she says slowly but unwavering. Brooklin reaches in her purse for her lipstick. "You see, Colin, I have learned to play the game and I have learned to play it well. I intend for you and the good old boys' network to pay for your betrayal."

Looking in the rear view mirror, Brooklin re-applies her lipstick. After a moment, she looks back in the mirror, adjusts it and asks, "See me now?" Brooklin turns on the ignition, lowers the rooftop on her convertible and drives out of the warehouse parking lot welcoming the gentle breeze. Brooklin remembers a conversation she'd had with her secretary, "Yes, Karla, sometimes good people do bad things. We all have a monster inside. It's the self-preservation mode." She glances at the warehouse again through her rear view mirror, "No dodge ball tonight."

Afterword

Thank you for reading *Breaking Point.*

The first book in this series *Perception*
Available online:
Amazon
Barnes & Noble

Share your thoughts with other readers ...
If you enjoyed this book, spend just a few minutes
leaving a review on the book's Amazon or Barnes &
Noble page. Brooklin and I thank you.

About The Author

Lue Cleveland retired and later relocated to Georgia
from New York. She believes the key to life after
retirement is to stay active and engaged. Therefore,
Lue pursued her love and passion for writing. Walking
the stepping stones of this dream, she found the
inspiration to open more doors and discover new
opportunities. *Breaking Point* is her second mystery
novel and the sequel to *Perception.* She is currently
writing her third book in this series and plan to
publish her children's books in the near future.

Don't miss the next book in the series!
For news on Lue Cleveland or her upcoming books:
Visit website ... Join mailing list: *luecleveland.com*